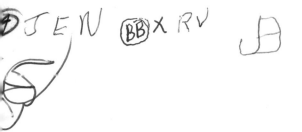

THE DESERT RANGER

THE DESERT RANGER

JAY LUCAS

SAGEBRUSH
Large Print Westerns

First published in Great Britain by ISIS Publishing Ltd.
First published in the United States by Furman

Published in Large Print 2010 by ISIS Publishing Ltd.,
7 Centremead, Osney Mead, Oxford OX2 0ES
United Kingdom
by arrangement with
Golden West Literary Agency

British Library Cataloguing in Publication Data
Lucas, Jay, b. 1894.
Desert Ranger.
1. Western stories.
2. Large type books.
I. Title
813.5'2–dc22

ISBN 978–0–7531–8525–4 (hb)

Printed and bound in Great Britain by
T. J. International Ltd., Padstow, Cornwall

To
"CURLY" ENNIS

May this remind him of the old bar heart
range we knew so well.

CONTENTS

CHAPTER
ONE

Broken

Ten minutes to nine — at last. Clint Yancey got up from the bed where he had been lying fully dressed. He had been dressed and shaved since five, but he had made himself lie there this last hour. That pacing up and down his room, staring out through the window, was enough to drive a fellow crazy. This whole morning felt like a nightmare; but he knew the nightmare to be true. His trial came at nine o'clock, the trial that was to ruin him.

There was another bed besides his in the room, and he stood with his eyes fixed on it a moment. Sergeant Wilson's bed, his pardner's bed. But Wilson had not slept in it the night before — no! he would not sleep in the same room as Lieutenant Yancey, the man whom the whole little force of Arizona Rangers wished dead, the man who had disgraced their name and brought dishonor on them.

How that hurt! Wilson — how often had they stood shoulder to shoulder when it seemed certain that they did not have seconds to live, when they would not have lived if either had weakened for an instant. Big, heavy-set Wilson, with his bulldog jaw and bass voice and red face; he was clumsy, and he was the poorest shot in the rangers, but he would clench that big jaw of his and charge against twenty devils with his pardner Clint Yancey beside him. Pardners; the two of them had been the pride of the force; when the rangers told stories of an evening, it was nearly always about some mad, hopeless trip those two had made into the hills or deserts, and of how they would come back driving before them a little group of horses with wild-eyed men tied in the saddles. Yancey and Wilson.

And — Yancey did not know where Wilson had slept the night before, did not know with whom he had doubled up. Wilson would not have cared who it was, just so he was not breathing air defiled by the pariah Yancey.

Clint crossed the room like a man walking in his sleep, and stared at himself in the mirror. He looked ghastly, with his drawn face and those big rings under his eyes; he was white as paper. That would not do; he had to pretend to keep a stiff upper lip. He went to the washstand and dashed cold water against his face, plunged his face in the enameled basin, and scrubbed the skin harshly with a towel. His appearance seemed improved.

He combed his hair, straightened his clothes — he had his best and cleanest on, and his high-heeled boots shone; he looked very trim and spruce, as an Arizona Ranger should, in his neat cowboy clothes. He buckled on his gun belt, and tied the little string around his leg.

It was as he reached for the little badge on the old dressing table and pinned it to the left side of his unwrinkled shirt that his nerve failed. A little scrap of white metal, intrinsically worth no more than a few cents, but to Clint, as to every other ranger, the thing about which the whole world revolved. For the honor of that little scrap of metal, the last man of them would have laid down his life. It had to be that way, or they could not be rangers; there was too much against them. Clint's eyes went blind, and his hand shook so that he could hardly pin the badge in place. This was the last time he would wear it. There was little doubt of that.

He crossed the room, fumbled for the door knob; his square shoulders hung and his head was bowed. The knob in his hand, he paused an instant, then he walked out onto the dusty street of the little cow town, head and shoulders erect and step firm, almost jaunty. Never had there been a greater example of Ranger nerve or self-control. He looked so calm that but for a slight paleness of his face, one would have thought he was merely going to make some routine report to the Captain. Eyes would be watching him from every window, of course, and — he was still a ranger.

He crossed through the thick dust to the frame hotel where the little dining room had been taken over by the rangers for this trial, and the tables moved out. As he went through the outside door, he saw a girl — a waitress — staring at him with wide eyes. At Clint Yancey, who had been her hero, and who was now — a traitor. He spoke to her:

"Good morning, Kate."

She did not answer; with something like fear in her eyes, she turned and went hurrying down the hall. Even

3

she would not speak to the despised Clint Yancey. Clint pushed the dining room door open and walked in. His step was firm, his head high, his strangely blue eyes level. His voice was quite calm, but low:

"Good morning, Captain. Good morning, men."

Captain Donley looked up at him, and then dropped his eyes back to the papers in his hand; there was not the slightest sign of recognition. None of the others would look at him at all; they sat in two rows, eyes ahead, and never had he seen harder faces. Lean, tanned faces, and hard, cold eyes. And they his old companions, the friends of many a long, weary trail — they would not even glance at him. There was a tense silence but for the clink of spurs as Clint walked up between those two grim lines of seated men. Before the table which served as a desk, he came to a sort of stiff, unaccustomed attention. He said nothing. Presently Donley spoke:

"Are you ready, Lieutenant Yancey?"

"Ready, Captain," he answered in a low voice.

Another silence, but for the crackle of the papers in Captain Donley's hand. Donley was a fine-looking man, with iron-gray hair, and he looked very military. One would never suspect that he was an old cowboy who had won an Army commission with the Rough Riders in Cuba. Now, as head of the Arizona Rangers, he tried to run his men as he would have run a troop of cavalry. The thing puzzled the rangers, but they tried reasonably hard to please him; in his stiff way, he had the courage of a lion, and courage was about all that counted with these men. He spoke:

"Sergeant Wilson, you will come forward and give your evidence."

A heavy tread behind him, and the dull clank of spurs. Wilson! Good God, why had it to be Wilson's evidence that was to ruin him? His pardner's; the man he would have died for, who a week before would have died for him. The man whose former friendship made him now all the more bitter toward Clint.

Clint tried to keep his eyes ahead, but in spite of himself his eyes turned slightly. For once the red face of Wilson was pale; the man seemed to be trembling. Was it purely rage, or had he still some spark of friendship left for this man whom all Arizona despised and hated? A queer daze seemed to fill Clint's head — one would never know it from his face. He heard Sergeant Wilson's words as though they came from a mile off — heard some of them.

". . . sent us out to try to shoot an antelope out of a bunch we'd seen; we needed meat. When we came back, Tex Fletcher was gone."

Captain Donley crackled the papers in his hand; his voice was hard as steel, and as cold.

"How had the prisoner been secured when you left camp?"

"His arms were round a good-sized mesquite tree, and his wrists handcuffed together; he couldn't have got loose by himself, Captain. This fellow was sitting by the camp fire. He said he'd been knocked out, but we didn't see a mark on him, and his clothes weren't messed up."

Captain Donley glanced up at Clint icily.

"Lieutenant, what is your explanation of that?"

"No explanation, Captain. I don't know what happened."

Clint's tone was as cold as that of the Captain.

"Sergeant Wilson, is it true that, the day before, the prisoner had offered you fifteen hundred dollars to assist him in an escape, and that you, of course, refused?"

"Yes, Captain."

"Did you mention this to Lieutenant Yancey?"

"I did, the morning Tex got away, Captain. Of course I'd no notion Cl — Lieutenant Yancey would go to Tex —"

"That will do, Sergeant Wilson; we have, I regret to say, at present no evidence upon which to bring criminal charges against Lieutenant Yancey. Our personal opinions are another thing."

He bent over his papers again, but he was not reading them. Again he looked up.

"Lieutenant Yancey, there are three other rangers whom I can call as witnesses, but I hardly regard that as necessary — unless you insist. Have you anything to say in your own defence?"

"Nothing, Captain."

"Then, Clinton Yancey, you are hereby dishonourably discharged from the Arizona Rangers. You will immediately turn over to Ranger McNeil your commission, your badge, and all other things pertaining to your former service. I need hardly tell you of the blot your treachery has cast upon our organization — a blot that can never be removed. Nor is it necessary for me to tell you of the use that will be made of your act by our enemies, who have been trying to have our new force disbanded, for political reasons. They will undoubtedly succeed now, owing to your conduct. That is all, Yancey."

With a curt nod of dismissal, he picked up his pen and bent over his papers. Still the young man stood there; he started, as though suddenly waking up. McNeil was beside him now, and Wilson gone. Clint was handing McNeil a long envelope with some folded paper in it; he had brought it with him, knowing that it would be needed — his commission. His fingers went up to his badge, but seemed too stiff to unpin it. And suddenly he turned, and spoke in a dry, hurried voice:

"Captain."

Donley looked up coldly, but he said nothing.

"Captain, I know there's no use in saying that — what happened — hurts me a lot more than it does any of you others. I mean — knowing that it'll ruin the rangers, all of you. I — I thought as much of the name of ranger — Captain, would you do me a last favour?"

Donley leaned back in his chair; he turned almost purple; he seemed to swell with anger he was trying hard to hide.

"I am not at all likely to!"

Clint hesitated, but blurted:

"Captain, all I ask is that you let me keep my badge; I have a certain use I want to make of it."

"Yancey, your badge would mean nothing to you, with your name stricken from the rolls."

"I know, Captain, but —"

Suddenly Donley came leaping to his feet. He pointed a shaking finger.

"Yancey, your badge is number eleven. Let me assure you that that discredited number shall never again be given to an honest ranger! What becomes of it is a matter of total indifference to me and —" He caught himself; he had to fight himself to keep from saying things unbecoming to his position, to keep from reverting to the blunt language of his cow-boy youth. He sat down suddenly as though pulled down. Yancey began to turn.

"Good-bye, Captain."

Donley's shaking hand picked up his pen. He dipped it, after jabbing all around the inkwell; he bent over his papers.

Clint was ashy-gray. Slowly, he started down the room. The men were standing now, and he walked between the two stiff lines. He passed between those rows of eyes that were fixed stiffly ahead, not one of them going to meet him, nor even following him, not one recognizing him. In the doorway, he turned.

"Good-bye, men."

Not a muscle in a man's face moved; there was no sound. The Captain did not look up from his desk.

"Men, I — don't blame you for breaking me; I know what you think I am. And I want you to know that I never felt more respect for the ranger force than I do now, when you think that I — I —"

That silence was too much for him — and if only one of them would look at him! If they'd only curse him! He could not finish. Slowly, he turned, walked through the doorway, across the street to his room. He had his horse already saddled, he had only to get his war bag and tie it behind his saddle. Then he would go — where?

He opened the door of his room, and a little gasp of relief rose to his throat — Wilson, his pardner, had stolen over there to bid him good-bye.

"Wilson! You —"

The light died out of Clint's eyes. Wilson — big, stocky, bow-legged — was crossing the room to him, and the fury on his face was terrible to see.

"Yancey! You rat! I came here to say good-bye to you — after all, we've been pardners a long time. And — here's what I found!"

He was holding up some dirty little pieces of paper; there seemed to be some scribbling in pencil on it.

"Wh-what is it?"

Wilson turned purple; he had always had a wild temper.

"Yes! Act like you don't know! You — oh, you dirty skunk!"

And before Clint knew what was happening, a fist crashed into his face. He went over backwards; the washstand upset, and soapy water trickled across the floor. For a second, he lay on one elbow, dazed partly by the blow, more by surprise. He came slowly to his feet, warily.

"Wilson! What's the matter with you? What is it? We've been pardners, Wilson —"

"You skunk! Fight — come on! Damn you, Yancey —"

He struck again. This time the fist caught Clint in his chest and threw him against the wall, hard; Wilson had the strength of a bear. And Clint just stood there, staring with a queer, lost look in his blue eyes.

"I won't fight you, Wilson — I won't! We've been pardners too long. Go ahead and hit me again, Wilson! Go ahead — you won't listen!"

"Get out! Get out, Yancey, for God's sake, before I shoot you! You treacherous — ! Good God, Yancey, what made you do it? If you'd needed the money, I'd have given you my last cent. Now —"

Wilson was panting with rage, and perhaps with something else; his eyes held a wild, hurt look in them — a dangerous look. He shouted again:

"Get out, I tell you! Heaven knows I don't owe you anything; but we been pardners and — I'll give you an hour's start before —" He half raised the piece of paper in his hand.

"Listen, Wilson! You've always been too bull-headed. Let me —"

Wilson was drawing his gun! He would shoot! Clint was beside the door; he opened it and hurried out, without even picking up his war bag — perhaps he forgot it. He knew that the man behind had his gun raised. Was it pointed at his back? Really, he did not much care.

He walked out through the dust of the street; he went to his horse. The fine sorrel turned its head and gave a little welcoming nicker. He did not know of the things that had been going on, and if he knew he would not care. To Reddy, Clint was the greatest man in the world, and always would be. Clint's hand fell gently on the sleek sorrel neck. This horse was now his only friend, his last friend.

Slowly, Clint pivoted up into the saddle. He touched Reddy's neck with a rein and they went down the street in a running walk, thick dust hanging in the air behind them. They went out the rutted road past the last houses, out through the dusty, scrubby cedars, and up the ridge. Now Clint's shoulders were bobbing slowly down behind the ridge, going out of sight of those eyes back in the little town — watching him from every window. Broken! Disgraced!

Out of sight, his hand came up; he unpinned the little badge from his shirt. He held it cupped in his fingers and stared at it as he rode along. His face looked wild, hopeless, and haggard.

Gradually the look changed; a hard set came to his jaw and his lips drew tight. He placed the badge carefully in his pocket, and patted the pocket over it once — it was as though he and that little piece of metal had an understanding.

His strange blue eyes raised to sweep the country ahead. No longer did they hold that lost look; they were the fierce eyes of a hawk, a hawk that has been hurt but is all the more a hawk for that. They swept the road ahead, went on over the barren, burned-looking ridges. Lower and lower those ridges dropped, until they spread out to the desert — bleak, shimmering, deadly, seemingly endless, it stretched away to the very far horizon. Out over the desert went Clint Yancey's eyes, to where that burning sand dipped into the distance, into nothing. He struck a lope. An hour, Wilson had said. He did not understand, but the whole ranger force would be after him in an hour. They must not catch him — and none knew so well as he how hard they were to elude.

Two hours of riding. It was noon now, and the heat out here in the desert was tremendous; his eye-balls seemed about to burst in that heat and white glare. On and on — and still on. Black rivulets of sweat streamed down Reddy's legs, but straight on he was forced, into that blistering nowhere ahead.

After what seemed months, the sun set. Clint looked back. He could not even see the faint line of hills in the distance any more; all around him lay sandy nothing. It was cooler now, suddenly; he touched the horse with a spur. Thirty miles to the first water hole — if he did not miss it, and if it was not dry.

CHAPTER
TWO

Gulch City

Clint Yancey, the ranger, was in Gulch City!

The place had sprung up suddenly when ore was discovered far out in the middle of the desert. It had a brief, wild life. Then the ore pinched out and it was deserted overnight for a newer strike. And so the rustlers had found it, standing there ready for them; even the furniture had not been moved out, for that would cost more than buying new.

It was Tex Fletcher who had thought of making it a rustler stronghold; gradually, finding how safe it was, men who were badly wanted elsewhere had gathered around him. He had run a faro layout here in the days when there were miners with pocketfuls of money; when he got through with them, they did not have so much. In fact, a few who argued with him were dead; he was a holy terror with a gun.

The strong point was that without Tex the oasis — it was called the Silvermine Hills — would have been useless. He alone knew the desert, knew it as nobody else did. He had spent part of his earlier life as a cowboy for Bat Phillips near Cuchilla. When some of Bat's cattle wandered out onto the desert during the brief greenness after a rain, and got trapped there at some drinking puddle, Tex was the only one who could find them. And he had an uncanny knack of working them back safely from water hole to water hole. How he judged which holes were not dry, no one ever knew; perhaps he had learned to watch every passing shower far out there. He kept his secret, because he could make Bat pay him extra wages for it.

Everybody knew what Bat was, but it was said that from the first Tex could give him lessons in rustling, young as he was. That called for another raise, of course. And there were stories about some neighboring cattlemen who had been found shot; young Tex usually seemed a little bit flush of money after a thing like that happened. Then Bat had refused him another raise, and Tex had shot him and skipped out, although no one would have bothered to hang him for it; everybody said that the only unfortunate thing about it was that they hadn't shot each other. He had been gone for years, until he turned up in Gulch City while it was booming. It was two years after the boom burst that he thought of another use for the place. Or perhaps things were getting too hot for him outside.

The fine thing about the Silvermines was the blessed peace it held — as far as freedom from prying officers was concerned; one could pick up a nice shooting scrape on a moment's notice. The place was in an angle of Wayne County that for some reason jutted far out into the desert. Sheriff Dukes was always talking of going there to clean it up, but with only six deputies, and it so far away, nobody blamed him much for putting the thing off. Anyway, Tex stole hardly any cattle in Wayne County, and most of the voters believed in the theory of live and let live, so long as they weren't bothered.

There was an unfortunate yarn that had got out: A man who called on Sheriff Dukes at his home late one night insisted that he had happened to glance under a window shade and seen Dukes and Tex sitting puffing cigars and apparently telling jokes. The thing was very mortifying to "Big Jim" Dukes — of course it was only his brother from Montana, who happened to be about the same size and build as Tex. Big, honest Jim had gone sorrowfully to the man who started the yarn. He had talked to him in a hurt voice, bought him a goodly number of drinks to show that he held no hard feelings, and accepted his woozy apology before everybody in the saloon.

Big Jim was not the man to hold grudges — anybody could make a mistake.

And now, here was a ranger walking around the street any time he felt like it! And he had been here three days; this fourth would be just one too many. If Tex had been in town he could not have flaunted himself in their faces that long; Tex was the brains of the town.

Clint was under no illusions as to how they felt about him. His wearing no badge would mean nothing, since he would have been recognized before he was there ten minutes. Anyhow, an Arizona Ranger seldom wore his badge in sight when out on duty; the organization was almost half way a secret service. If Clint had wanted to explain, nobody would have listened to him. He did not care whether he explained or not; it would be taken for a ranger trick, his story of being dismissed. He had been shunned as a leper on his walks; when he passed a little group or hard-faced men on the street, they would stop talking long before he got to them, and eye him harshly as he passed; he had tried speaking coldly to those he met, but got no answer.

This walk was to be different. He knew it as soon as he turned to go back to where he stayed. The street was as deserted as on the day after the last miner had left, but he knew that eyes were watching him, watching the street, from every window. He gave a sudden deep sigh of relief. So they were not going to shoot him in the back; somebody was going to face him openly to build up a "rep."

Clint was tense as he started back, his boots shuffling through the thick dust. His keen blue eyes might have noticed a lizard moving half a block off. It seemed a brazen thing to do, but he stopped once, took his gun from the holster, and examined it carefully. The more brazen he was the better. For three days he had been trying openly to provoke a gun scrape; it was either provoke one or be shot in the back.

He looked up now, to see a man swing from a doorway a block ahead, and come walking toward him. The man was in the middle of the street, like Clint himself. Quietly, Clint put his gun back and started on again. Somebody was going to be killed within a minute or two; Clint hoped it would not be himself. He had confidence in his own shooting; it never occurred to him to think about his own nerve, or whether he had any or not — Rangers are that way.

There were little measured spurts of dust from swinging boots as the two approached each other. And presently Clint was close enough to make out the man's face. A crafty, evil face, with a nose that had been broken and set crooked; it gave the man a sort of sneering look. Closer now, Clint could see the white weal of an old knife scar across the man's chin.

Red River Shorty! He remembered the face on a Wanted poster. One of the worst gunmen of Texas; his coming to Arizona had not yet been reported to the rangers. So it had got too hot for him in Texas. Naturally, he would try to get well up toward the lead of the biggest rustling ring here — and how better could he prove himself than by shooting it out with Clint Yancey, the ranger who had dared come to Gulch City? He would see no danger in it; he had the name of being one of the best shots in the Southwest, and one of the quickest — which was practically equivalent to saying the best and quickest in the world. Nobody knew how many men he had killed.

Now they had stopped, hardly six feet apart. Shorty spoke in a dry drawl, the brown cigarette wagging up and down in the corner of his wide mouth. In his voice there was a trace of that high-pitched, whining tone often found among Texans — it means nothing, certainly not fear.

"Howdy, stranger. I hear yo're Ranger Yancey."

"My name's Yancey — Clint Yancey."

"I'm Red River Shorty." He said it proudly, as though he thought Clint should tremble. Clint did not; he answered coldly:

"I know it."

There was a pause, each man eying the other, sizing him up. Again the brown cigarette started wagging.

"I hear yo're figurin' on stayin' in Gulch City."

"That's right — as long as I feel like it."

Red River Shorty gave a sudden sidewise flip of his head, somewhat like a bird, and fixed his eyes harder on Clint.

"Yancey, I ain't exactly lookin' for trouble; I got nothin' personal against you. I'll give you five minutes to git out o' town."

Clint nodded. Of course if Shorty could run him out it would bring an even greater reputation than shooting him; trying to bluff an Arizona Ranger was getting the name of being disastrous. Clint's not answering beyond that cold nod seemed to annoy Shorty; he thought his reputation deserved more humility.

"Gettin' out?"

"Why, Shorty," drawled Clint, "I seem to like it here. I think I'll stay."

The wide, loose mouth spread in an ugly grin.

"Might stay too permanent, Ranger!"

"I'll risk it."

"You mean — ?"

"Uh-huh. I'm not looking for trouble; I'm even asking you to mind your own business and let me mind mine. But if you have your heart set on a shooting scrape, I reckon I can accommodate you."

Shorty did something with his tongue that made his cigarette flip up and down once; it seemed to be his way of accepting the words as a challenge. He had probably thought all this out beforehand, for he spoke without a pause:

"Want to draw now — or are you scared to back off a few yards an' have it out?"

Clint gave a dry, mirthless grin; never had his brown face looked so hard, or less afraid.

"You want it to be showy, Shorty — want to build up a big rep out of this thing, don't you? Well, it's your funeral; anything you say."

The word "funeral" did not strike Shorty right; he glared with half-closed eyes. He seemed peeved that this ranger did not seem more scared — the young fellow must be pretty "green" at this sort of thing.

"All right. Stand here."

Standing in dust almost up to his ankles, Clint watched the thick, crooked back retreating. Yes, Red River Shorty had turned his back and walked off. Perhaps he knew that a ranger would be disgraced for life if he shot a man in the back; perhaps it was just bravado.

Clint moved out to the middle of the street, and again he stood still, watching that retreating back.

Unconsciously, his right hand went up to set his wide hat more firmly on his head — it was a cowboy trick, that little tug down on the hat brim in all emergencies.

Red River Shorty whirled suddenly — to see the other man's hand far from his gun butt. His chance!

19

Like a streak, Shorty's gun came out. Too far to fire from the hip; he threw the muzzle up and caught a glimpse of the sights in a split second. A dead bead on Clint's chest. The gun crashed in the stillness of the dusty street.

Clint dropped like a falling post. He heard a shout of "He's got him!" from some window near by. He felt his hat settle back on his boots. Close call! Only that little lag while Shorty's finger pressed the trigger, while the hammer was falling and the bullet coming these few yards — only that had saved him. A fraction of a second.

Clint was lying in the thick dust now, firing. He shot too quickly, before he was settled, and cursed himself for it; he had missed by a foot or more. But the dust flying up against the left side of Shorty's face threw his aim off; he too missed, and more widely than Clint. A revolver must be rock-steady at that distance.

Now, both guns went off seemingly together; it sounded like one shot. But Clint must have shot first by a bare instant; Shorty was hit; he jerked up six inches, and his bullet went wild. Then he was flattened into the dust again, to present the smallest possible target.

Red River Shorty had his elbows on the ground; he was steadying his gun with both hands. That way, he could not miss. Clint had to beat him to it! He knew it. There could be only one more shot fired. No time to bring his left hand up to help hold the gun; had to shoot fast. And a jerked trigger always meant a miss — pull had to be smooth, but quick. Precious instants wasting. The whole fight until now had taken but instants, long though it seemed.

Again the two guns sounded together; two little clouds of black smoke drifted up above the Stetsons. Clint knew first that he himself was not hit; only then did he realize that Red River Shorty was lying peacefully down there in the dust, like a man asleep; he had been dead when his twitching finger pressed the trigger.

Clint stood up slowly. Unhurriedly, he reloaded the empty chambers of his gun. Down the front, he was covered thickly with fine dust; he flapped some of it off with his hat. He glanced at the hat; there were two little holes in the top of the crown, where that first bullet had entered and left; it could not have missed his head by more than an inch or so — he wondered what fraction of a second that had meant, as he pitched himself forward. He had heard of bullets through men's hats before, but this was the first time he had seen the thing happen — and it was his own hat.

Doors were flying open now, and men were coming running out onto the street, gathering in a little knot down there; they were hiding that still figure but for glimpses between their moving legs. Quietly, his gun back in the holster, Clint walked down to them. Now or never he had to make his play to remain in Gulch City, and he had to make it coolly. Would they listen to him, or would friends of Shorty's riddle him with bullets? The fortunate thing was that Shorty would not have been here long enough to have made many friends who might want to avenge him. Clint walked slowly, casually; he seemed the least excited man in the street.

Faces were turning to him as he came close. There was open hostility and hate in them, but a sort of grudging respect. He had done the one thing that might get him listened to or respected in Gulch City. Might! A thin-lipped, thin man spoke dryly:

"Deader'n a stuffed owl! Yancey, you got another mark chalked up for the rangers."

"Rangers?" asked Clint.

"Huh! We all know who you are — Lieutenant Yancey."

"You mean, Yavapai Slim, you know who I was. I've been kicked out of the rangers."

Men glanced at each other sneeringly. One or two sniffed. Only one man there seemed not entirely hostile; he was a red-faced, thick-set man whom Clint did not know; he looked "tough," but at the same time sort of good natured. He spoke:

"Fine yarn! Expect us to believe that?"

The thin man cut in harshly — Clint knew this Yavapai Slim to be Tex Fletcher's right-hand man.

"Another dirty, low-down ranger trick! In here spyin', with a tall story like that!"

Clint spoke first to the red-faced one; he spoke very quietly:

"Word about it will drift in any day now — Tex will know when he gets back."

He whirled suddenly on Yavapai Slim, and bored into him with those icy-cold blue eyes; there was no mistaking the hardness in them. He spoke still more quietly:

"Pardner, I don't like to be made out a liar. If you happen to notice, I still have my gun on me. Savvy?"

The sallow cheeks of Yavapai Slim flushed quickly, and his yellow eyes snapped. But he too spoke quietly:

"Huntin' more trouble, pardner?"

"No — nor dodging it."

His eyes held Slim's, until at last he saw them shift a trifle. That was the sign he was waiting for. He went on coldly, calmly:

"What I want to know is this; did you call me a liar?"

Slim hesitated.

"I didn't. But if yo're huntin' trouble —"

Everybody there could see that Slim did not want a shooting scrape with the grim, brown-faced young man who had just won the street battle. They could see too that Slim would fight if he had to, rather than lose his reputation — that would ruin him forever. And they could see also that Clint was no more afraid of Yavapai Slim than he would be of a rabbit. Clint had been leading up to this point, but did not want things to go further; he did not want to make an enemy of Yavapai Slim if he could help it. He suddenly relaxed. He gave a short laugh; not, to be sure, a very merry laugh, but it got by.

"Well, then, what are you growling about? Come on and have a drink!"

"Shore, pardner — shore! No hard feelings; jest a little misunderstandin' was all."

Slim said it a little more quickly than he had meant to, and he knew it. At the back of the crowd, one man winked at another — he didn't blame Yavapai Slim; looked like a man had come to town who was "tough" enough to show any of them up. If that crazy yarn about him being kicked out of the rangers was right — and if Tex wanted him, of course — he might prove useful. Clint jerked his head.

"Come on, all of you! The drinks are on me for taking Slim wrong that way."

At least it wouldn't hurt to let him buy them a drink or two. They trooped across the street to a low adobe doorway. Clint paused courteously to let his guests enter first, and before he followed them, he glanced back over his shoulder. Red River Shorty still lay out there in the middle of the street, alone; drinks were more important than carrying him off. Yes, this was Gulch City, all right!

CHAPTER
THREE

Clint Meets Tex

Clint's first week after his shooting scrape passed calmly enough. Gulch, City seemed to be an almost stupidly quiet place, but Clint knew why; there could be no such thing as quarreling; one cranky word would mean a killing on the spot among men of this sort. At night, as little groups drifted from the saloons and home, they thought it necessary to let out a few shrill yells and fire a few shots in the air. But this was nothing; most cow towns outside permitted that sort of harmless exuberance.

Very slowly, Clint was coming to be accepted, after a fashion. He was naturally reserved, and he had sense enough not to try to be otherwise now. He was coolly polite to everybody, and no more to anybody. Once in a while, he "set them up" to the crowd in the saloon, but not too often. He did not seem to care a hang whether anybody spoke to him or not; he seemed only to want to be allowed to live in Gulch City in peace from the law. The result of all this reserve was that the first to begin to nod to him distantly were the old heads, men who were among the leaders. It was beginning to dawn on them that perhaps Gulch City had acquired a most desirable citizen, a true gunman.

Things had reached this stage when — Tex Fletcher came to town.

This was the crucial point for Clint, and he knew it. If Tex ordered him put out of the way, put out of the way he would be. And there would be no lone brave shooting it out with him openly on the street to show how tough he was. Clint could not even guess what Tex's attitude toward him might be. One thing he had figured out: the most savage dog is not likely to bite if one can pass him casually enough the first time, pretending not to know that he is ready to bite, and only too willing. On the second meeting, if it is handled right, one may be more or less taken for granted; at least it is not quite as dangerous as the first.

This meant that Clint had to know exactly when Tex was returning, so that the meeting could be of his own arranging. He knew better than to ask questions, but he kept his eyes and ears open. When he saw a little group of men ride hurriedly out of town with their chaps on, but with no pack animals, he knew that the time had come; a big stolen herd was coming in, and these men going to relieve those driving it.

It was almost sundown when a band of weary, dusty riders came dashing into town and, naturally, straight to the saloon; the desert gave a mighty thirst. Clint was in the saloon, waiting. He was standing with both hands in his trouser pockets, staring apparently absently through the small window onto the street. He saw the crowd slide to a dusty stop outside; he saw that one man had a dirty, bloody bandage around one arm, and the arm tied crudely across his chest.

There was Tex! And a very different Tex from the defiant, sneering prisoner; in this town, he was undisputed king. He looked the part; he stood perhaps six feet two, long-legged, lean, with square shoulders. He had a great, curving nose, almost twice normal size; on another man it would have looked ugly, but it was the very thing that gave his dark brown face a look of fierce distinction. From his quick, wiry movements, one would have taken him for a young man, but Clint knew that at close range one could see a good many gray hairs at his temples; it would be hard to guess Tex Fletcher's age; he might be much older than he looked.

Tex turned with a quick swing to give some orders to his men. Their respectful faces told Clint of the fear in which this man was held; it was said that his best friend was the man most in danger from him. In profile this way, one could see the cruelty of his face; he looked entirely merciless.

And then, as Tex turned back, the saloon door swung open, and Clint came dawdling out. He looked sleepy, and slightly bored with life in Gulch City. His eyes seemed to come up a trifle in surprise as he saw Tex. But he did not hesitate; he grinned slightly, waved a hand.

"Hello, Tex."

Tex stood as though frozen, his deep-set eyes fixed on Clint. A look of rage flashed into his face; he was said to have the temper of the very devil himself — and Tex's tempers always meant somebody killed.

Clint did not seem to notice that Tex's right hand was within an inch or two of his gun butt, with the fingers already curved; he did not seem to notice that glare. He himself now had both hands busy rolling a cigarette. As he licked the cigarette, he casually turned his back and went strolling off down the street.

Of course he was straining his ears. There was a dead, frozen silence back there. There was one little slapping sound that might have been a man drawing a gun. Clint saw an open doorway beside him; it took almost superhuman self-control to keep from leaping in there behind the protecting adobe wall.

He did not; he dawdled away, licking the cigarette, striking a match on his trousers to light it.

He slowly turned a corner. Then, he took a deep breath, and blinked. His guess had been right; if he walked slowly enough, seemed casual enough, they were not likely to shoot; if he made one quick motion, he would now be sprawled dead on the sidewalk back there. He had, in a sense, forced Tex to take his presence in the town for granted.

For the rest of the evening, he carefully kept out of sight. Most of those men would get drunk to celebrate their return with the herd. Whether Tex would or not, he did not know, but he did not want to take chances on it; he wanted Tex to be sober when he had his first interview with him.

Clint was on the street next morning when he saw Yavapai Slim come hurrying toward him. Yavapai had never liked him since that first day, but he had only avoided him; he was waiting to see what Tex would have to say when he came back. Now he spoke in a dry, meaning drawl, his eyes half closed:

"Tex wants to see you — right away."

The satisfaction in his tone boded no good for Clint. Clint's heart fell, but he answered quietly:

"O.K. I'll be right up."

"Better be!" And Yavapai hurried on ahead.

Clint went down the street, crossed, and climbed the hotel stairs; Tex's rooms were almost opposite his own, he knew, although he had never seen them opened. They had belonged to old "Cactus" Markham, the discoverer of ore in the Silvermine Hills; when the ore had pinched out, old Cactus had abandoned his rooms as they stood, loading his burro and striking out for the desert once more, to find a better mine. His bones lay out there somewhere; he had not been heard of in five years.

Clint knocked quietly, and heard a voice bid him to come in. He pushed the door open. There, at the other side of the room, stood Tex with his hand poised above the butt of his gun. He was glaring; his great beak of a nose seemed to be pointed at Clint, and all the evil of his face showed. He spoke deliberately:

"Clint, want to draw on me?"

Clint's eyes swept the room; his mind was racing. He saw the faded red plush of the warped chairs, the very bad oil painting; his eyes rested a moment on a big mirror on the wall, in a heavy gilt frame. Then he turned back to the man standing there. He spoke quietly:

"Tex, I didn't come here to shoot it out with you."

"You mean you're scared of me? You don't want to settle things right now?"

"No, I don't want to settle anything right now."

He did not answer the first part of the question, but Tex took it for granted that he was admitting to being afraid; he did not know Clint Yancey very well. He relaxed. With a dry grin, he waved to a chair.

"Sit down, Clint."

His voice was suddenly almost friendly. Clint sat down, and Tex pushed a box of cigars across the table to him.

"Smoke?"

"Thanks, but I'll roll one, if you don't mind. I'm not used to those things."

He noticed that Tex's face took on a self-satisfied air; *he* was used to cigars, and good ones. He bit the end off one, lighted it slowly. He turned.

"Clint, why do you reckon I went to all the trouble of showing you who's boss in this town?"

"Why — just to show me, I suppose."

Tex gave a harsh, amused laugh.

"I know easier ways than that to teach you — easier for me! Well, I'll lay my cards face up: now that you know who's boss, so you're not likely to get too big-headed — well, how about throwing in with me? A man who savvies the rangers' tricks as well as you do would be mighty useful to me."

Clint had not expected this sudden offer. He spoke slowly:

"How do you know I'd play square — that coming here isn't another ranger trick?"

Tex laughed as though he knew of some great joke.

"I'm not worrying about that; the rangers would a sight rather get you than me — and not alive, either."

"Why?" Clint looked hard at him. How could this man know so much about the rangers?

Tex puffed his cigar a moment, eyeing Clint; there was a grin on his evil face. Then, as though absently, his eyes went over Clint's shoulder to the bedroom door, which stood open two or three inches. He wanted to make sure that Yavapai Slim was ready, with his finger on the trigger of the carbine; it held soft-nosed bullets. The sights were squarely on the middle of Clint's back. Tex's eyes drifted back to Clint's, and there was a mocking light in them.

"Well, I scribbled a note in pencil on a scrap of paper, and had it hid in your room — it's been found. It said that I'd raise the ante to two thousand, like you wanted, if you'd turn me loose."

Clint came leaping out of his chair and to his feet. His face flamed, then went white as paper, and his blue eyes blazed. The note Wilson had held in his hand! He, Clint, was now an outlaw, to be shot on sight! Shivering with fury, his hand darted down to his gun butt. He did not know that he was shouting wildly:

"Draw, damn you, Tex! Here is where one of us gets it in the stomach!"

CHAPTER
FOUR

Clint, Gunman

White with rage, Clint stood there, his hand on his gun — the gun was even drawn up an inch or so. And Tex Fletcher, his cigar in his mouth, still sat grinning at him. Tex raised a hand and spoke loudly:

"Wait! Hold it!"

And Clint's hand dropped; both his arms dangled at his side.

"Sit down, Clint — I think you're inclined to be too hot-headed."

Blindly, Clint sank back into his chair; he was still trembling with fury. Tex shoved a bottle and glass across the table.

"Drink, Clint?"

Clint poured one and tossed it down at a gulp — poured a second and swallowed it. A trace of color began to come back to his face, and his trembling was less violent. He spoke bitterly, furiously:

"Tex, that was a dirty trick! It has ruined me for life."

"Then why didn't you shoot?" asked Tex amusedly.

"I — knew I didn't have a chance."

"No, you didn't. Even sitting like I am, I could have plugged you. Glad you know who's boss, Clint."

Tex looked very self-satisfied. Clint's eyes flashed once to the big, gilt-framed mirror on the wall. From where he sat, it showed nothing but the reflection of that cheap oil painting, but as he entered the room he had seen the bedroom door in it. He had seen the carbine pointed at his back, and the evil face of Yavapai Slim behind it. He was helpless — for the present. He had to pretend to agree to whatever Tex Fletcher said, and he had to do it so as not to arouse suspicion. Tex was now suddenly genial; he thought he had Clint completely bluffed. He leaned forward, a look of concern on his face.

"Dang it, Clint, I didn't know you'd take it that hard, or I'd never have done it — not for the world!"

"Well, it's done now, so it can't be helped. But I don't see why you did it."

"That's easy. Them three days you were holding me — I could see that you were the very man I wanted, that you'd be worth a fortune to me. I did it to force you over to us. I had no notion you'd come right here anyway, without that. Why, Clint, if I'd had a notion — !"

He shook his head; never had a man looked more sorry for anything. The dirty hypocrite! thought Clint — he knew Tex's reputation for double dealing.

"But how did you knock me out without leaving any mark?"

Tex laughed.

"Stole up behind you with a bootful of sand; wanted to make it look bad for you."

"And how did you get the handcuffs off?"

"You'd like to know! I can open any handcuffs the rangers put on me, any time I want to — took me three days to find the right chance; I was only waiting to be left alone with you."

Clint was rolling a fresh cigarette. He looked calm now, but it was only by a great effort that he kept his hands from trembling. He spoke:

"Well, what's the proposition?"

Tex took the cigar from his mouth and gave him a friendly grin.

"That's more like it! Another drink? No?"

He tapped the table with his long fingers holding the cigar; he mused a moment.

"Well, here's the layout: I'm not scared of that little bunch of rangers — what the devil can fourteen men do, tell me? But I got to admit they're interfering with business, sort of. You savvy their tricks; you'd know how to get around them. And you've got nerve, and a good head — you're cut out for the rustling business."

"Thanks!"

Tex looked up at him quickly; he could not quite miss the sarcasm in Clint's voice. He only grinned again.

"Well, I'll make it worth your while to play our game."

"Which means doing anything you say?"

"That's it. We can't let every man do what he wants to; there'd be no system in that. Tell you what; I'll give you half again what any of the other men get, if you play ball with us — you'll sure make good money. Well, how about it?"

34

Good money, Clint knew, until this man took a notion to get rid of him. He sat a moment, his eyes on the faded red carpet as though thinking it over. He looked up at last.

"Well, what would you want me to do, to begin?"

He seemed to be giving in. Tex leaned back comfortably in his chair, his cigar in his mouth. He felt pretty well satisfied with himself; he was worried more about that little band of rangers than he would admit. Suddenly he broke out in a short laugh.

"You heard about nesters trying to set up in the cattle business in the Silvermines here?"

Clint nodded:

"Heard something about it. Young fellow called Billy Armour started it, didn't he?"

Tex grinned; he seemed to think the thing very funny.

"That's right. Billy's a young wildcat on wheels; sure pronto with his six-gun. Killed a man outside, and bit off more rustling than he could chew without help. Got so hot for him that he came in here and threw in with our crowd. I figured Billy was all set to be the most useful man I had — and he would have, too, if the young fool hadn't got sore at me about something or other; I don't know what."

Tex shook his head; he could not understand it. Clint had a suspicion that some of Tex's trickery had caused the break, but of course he said nothing. Tex went on:

"So there he is, squatting in an old prospector's shack at the other side of these hills, all set up in the

35

cattle business for himself. He even talked some crazy cowboy friends of his into coming in to try the same game. And," Tex took the cigar from his mouth and laughed suddenly, explosively, "the big joke of it all is this: he began by rustling a bunch of cattle from me, to start his herd!"

Clint sat staring; he had his lips pursed as though to whistle; he seemed inclined to grin. This sounded like the most sublime nerve he had ever heard of — or the greatest piece of foolishness. He wondered what sort of young madman this Billy Armour could be.

"And — you let him get away with it?"

Tex waved his cigar.

"For a while. I figured he'd soon get sense enough to come back; I needed him. Well, he didn't; he's got a fool notion that he can buck me."

Tex seemed to think it was about the funniest thing he had ever heard of. Still grinning, he looked up:

"There's your first job. Go over right away and put a few bullets through him; make sure he's good and dead. Don't bother any of his pals 'less you can't get out of it; I figure they'll throw in with us when Billy's out of the way and can't give 'em notions."

Tex spoke in such a careless, casual way that Clint blinked.

"What! I get him!"

"Sure; why not? You see, it's this way: after you do that, we'll know danged well you can't go back on us; we'll have confidence in you, which we might not otherwise."

Clint nodded slowly. So that was it; get the loop dangling over his head, and Tex had him for life. No wonder he held his gang so intact! Clint sat a long time, looking again at the red carpet; he knew that Tex Fletcher's eyes were on his face all the time. At last he got up slowly, reached for his hat.

"All right. I'll drop over and see what I can do with him. Where does he hang out?"

Tex came bounding from his chair and thrust out a hand.

"Now, you're talking! I was afraid you might balk. Anybody in town can tell you where to find him. Well, watch your step, Clint; don't think that because he's a kid, he's not right sudden on the trigger."

Clint was almost to the doorway when Tex seemed to remember something.

"Oh, say, Clint! Didn't know, did you, that that fast sorrel of yours was stole this morning?"

Clint stopped dead in his tracks. This would be the last blow, his Reddy-horse gone!

"Huh! Stole!"

Tex smiled genially.

"Oh, I wouldn't worry about it, if I was you. Some tin-horn stole him, but I'll see to it that he's back safe in the stable before you get home from Billy's. Trouble is," he added concernedly, "all I could get you to ride is an old skate that will only carry you there and back. If you sort of lost your way and wandered out on the desert — well, you'd be out of luck. Me, I'd rather get shot than die that way."

Clint gave him a sarcastic look.

"I see. I can't get away from here, and if I don't get Billy Armour, something might happen to me. Well, out onto the desert is the last place I'm thinking of going; why should I have come here if I thought the place was a Sunday-school?"

He put on his hat.

"Well, Tex, I'll report to you tonight sometime — unless that kid sees me first. Well, so long."

He straightened his neckerchief, and in doing so glanced casually at the big gilt mirror. He had a glimpse of Yavapai Slim with the carbine half lowered. There was a look of supreme disappointment on the gunman's face; Tex had not given him the prearranged signal to fire that soft-nosed bullet into Clint's back. Not only that; he had been pressing the trigger anyhow, hoping to plead that it was to save his boss's life, when Tex had shouted to him to wait. That was when Clint had stood with his gun half drawn.

Clint could guess all this; in his fury, he had remembered the gunman just in time. And that baffled look on Yavapai's face now did him good. He was grinning harshly when he opened the door — Tex took that grin as a good sign; perhaps Clint was anticipating a gun-scrape that he would enjoy.

"Well, Tex, *hasta la vista*," said Clint gently.

He closed the door behind him. It was just as well that Tex did not see the mocking hardness that suddenly came into his grin; he would have known just to what an extent he had Clint Yancey bluffed — Clint was no more afraid of Tex than he was of Yavapai. He walked across to his own room, to put fresh cartridges in his gun, to see if it needed oil, and to fill the empty loops in his belt.

He went to the stable. Reddy was not there, but that did not worry him; he guessed that he would be less than a block off. With contempt on his face, he saddled the old skate a man pointed out to him — the horse must have been twenty years old, if a day, and almost too stiff to walk. He rode back to the main street, and toward a group of men. These men eyed him as he came up — everybody on the street was eyeing him; the story was out regarding where he was going. Coolly, a cigarette in his mouth, he asked:

"Can any of you fellows tell me the shortest way to Billy Armour's place?"

"Sure, Clint!"

There was, for the first time, friendliness in the tones of these men, and even a companionable respect. He was one of the gang now. They directed him minutely. They asked him to have a drink before he left, but he refused; he told them, truly enough, that he'd already had enough, in Tex's rooms, if he wanted to keep a steady hand.

"That's right, Clint," one of them agreed, "licker an' business don't go together. Well, good luck to you!"

Riding up the street, a red-faced, red-haired man swung off the sidewalk before him. This was Red Barclay, the man who had been first to seem willing to accept him in the town.

"Hey, Clint!"

Clint rode toward him and stopped his horse.

"Hello, Red."

The man came close on his stocky legs, and stopped with one hand resting on the cantle of Clint's saddle in a friendly manner. He spoke in a low voice:

"Pardner, I hear yo're goin' over to get Billy Armour?"

"Didn't say where I'm goin', Red. But it's across the hills, all right."

Red glanced around as if to see that nobody was listening.

"I know. Well, let me give you a tip; that kid's plumb hell — dangerous. Not that he's particular quick with a gun, but he's as full of tricks as a fox, an' he's always ready to shoot. I'm jest warnin' you — he's pretty near sure to get you in the back before you even know where he is."

Clint grinned dryly.

"Well, he wouldn't be the first tried it — an' you'll notice that I'm still alive. I'm pretty good at tricks myself, Red; we'll see who's the best at it. But I sure thank you for warning me; I'll be all the more careful." He paused, and asked: "What sort of fellow is this Billy Armour anyway?"

Red looked around again before answering.

"Well, he's not a bad kid, as rustlers goes — wilder'n a jackrabbit, an' not scared of anything. I wisht he'd sense enough to come back to our crowd, an' not get himself killed."

"But if Tex gave you certain orders?"

Red shrugged:

"Tex is boss here; what he says goes."

"And if I came back without getting Billy — and Tex gave you orders to get me for it?"

Red looked up with concern on his face.

"Clint, you can't come back without bein' able to prove you got him. I think I'm as good a friend as you have in this here town, but I wouldn't be crazy enough to get myself killed by buckin' Tex if he told me — Well, get that kid, an' get him right. An' watch out the thing don't go off backwards; I tell you he's dangerous."

"Thanks, Red; I believe I know where I stand. I'll find that kid all right — I hope. Adios."

"Good luck to you, Clint — you'll need it."

And Clint rode out of town, his brow wrinkled. The trouble was that he himself would be riding through comparatively bare, rolling country, where a horseman could be seen for miles. And Billy Armour undoubtedly was on the lookout; he could cut in ahead, lie in ambush, and put a bullet through anyone looking for him before that man knew there was anybody within miles.

Why, it was just like him and Sergeant Wilson going into the hills after some bad man! They had never known if they would come out again, and sooner or later there would have had to come a time when they did not. But now, he himself was an outlaw, and sent on an outlaw's errand.

CHAPTER
FIVE

Billy Armour

It felt just like old times to Clint, this slipping down among the boulders, stalking a man. And wasn't that young fellow whose back he could see down there another rustler? He had stalked more than one, in his ranger days. The only difference now was that he didn't have his badge on; he might never wear that badge again; he was outlawed.

He had handled this business competently, as an ex-ranger should. He had circled out of sight around two likely looking ambushes, to come on them from the rear and inspect them. All on the chance that Billy Armour might be clever enough to be on the lookout. Clint had a slow, cautious way of going about a thing of this kind; he had found that it paid.

There lay Billy, his carbine resting on a boulder before him, watching the little pass. He had probably seen Clint come riding slowly down the bare side of that distant ridge. That was why he never looked around; he was too intent on watching the trail.

Clint slipped silently from one boulder to another lower down, to pause, surveying the ground for his next move. Then down to the next, always pausing at each to see if the man he stalked showed signs of restlessness. If he did, Clint would stay hidden; Billy might turn. These were the tactics of a mountain lion stalking a deer; Clint used them consciously, judging that there could be no better for this type of country. He had often seen lions hunt.

He had to make only one more little run, and then he would be close enough, and there would be a big boulder for him to hide behind. He darted down quickly, crouched. He did not make a sound that he was aware of.

The young fellow whirled suddenly. He did not wait to turn for his carbine; his hand whipped down to the heavy revolver at his hip and jerked it out. He made a lightning shot.

But Clint had thrown himself flat in the sand. He heard the bullet strike a stone behind him and go zinging off over the hill. He whipped his own gun out as he lay, brought it up before his face.

He was in a bad place; he was twenty feet behind the boulder he had started to. The boulder kept him and Billy from seeing each other, but a slight side-wise movement would bring either man in sight of the other. If one of them could get up close to that boulder, he would be practically safe. Clint knew this, but he could not try to do it now; he had to keep his gun pointed, be ready to shoot fast.

He lay there for what seemed a minute or two, wondering what should be his next move. At last he shouted, his face close to the sand:

"Hey, Billy! You, Billy Armour!"

"That's me. Stick yore head around the rock, an' let me take a shot at it."

"Thanks just the same! I'm waiting to get a sight of yours."

To find out how good a shot the young fellow was, Clint kicked one boot quickly out sidewise, and jerked it back instantly. He found out; the spurt of sand seemed to raise his foot two inches.

"You're handy with that thing, kid!"

"Sorter."

Immediately, the unexpected happened. A big stone came flying over and missed Clint's head by a foot or so; stones would curve over the boulder, as a bullet would not.

"Hey, stop it! I want to talk to you."

"Go ahead; we can talk an' shoot at the same time. I'm better at shootin'."

Another stone, jagged and ugly looking, scooted through the sand and stopped a yard in front of Clint's face. Where he himself lay, there were no stones.

"Billy, have sense! I tell you I want to talk to you!"

"Oh, shore! You sneaked up behind me to whisper a love song in my dainty ear. Here comes another!" Clint stopped this one with his left hand; it cut the palm slightly. He was in a devil of a mess; sooner or later that fool kid would catch him on the head with one of those stones.

That was why Billy was talking to him. To know when he knocked him unconscious. Clever as the devil! It came to Clint that he could suddenly break off short in the middle of a word, when the next stone came over. Then Billy would rush out, and he'd have him. But that wouldn't do.

"Listen, Billy! Stop and think a minute. If I'd been wanting to get you in the back, don't you think I'd have done it before you turned?"

A pause, as Billy meditated on this.

"Sounds pretty reasonable — but why was you sneakin' up behind me?"

"Because if I'd stuck to the trail you'd have perforated me plenty before I got near enough to say anything."

"Shore would! Well?"

"I'll stand up, with my hands in the air, if you'll promise not to shoot. I mean it, about wanting to talk to you."

A shorter pause.

"O. K. Put yore hands in sight first."

Clint did. It was awkward to struggle to his knees, then to his feet, with his hands up thus. Billy had his carbine now; he saw him lower it across his lap, his finger still on the trigger.

"Well, come on."

Clint dropped his arms as he started to walk over. The carbine jerked up; he did not like the looks of it.

"Hold on, kid! I'll lay my gun belt on this rock, if it'll make you feel any easier."

"I think yo're the one that's feelin' none too easy."

The thing was beginning to amuse Clint. With his left hand, he carefully removed his gun belt and laid it down. Then he strolled over, rolling a cigarette.

"Smoke?"

Billy coolly laid down his carbine on the side away from Clint, and took the tobacco and papers.

"Shore."

He grinned up at Clint. Rustler or not, Clint was inclined to like him on sight. He was a thick-set young fellow with a very wide face, and he looked fully as reckless as he was.

"I'm Clint Yancey."

"That's what I reckoned; heard of you. Happy to meet you."

He reached out a hand, and Clint shook it.

"Well, Clint, what can I do for you? I reckon Tex sent you over here to sink a few prospect shafts through me."

"That's right."

"Why didn't you do it; you had the chance?"

"Because I figured you're just the fellow to throw in with me; that's why I came over. We both love Tex's gang like we do a den of rattlesnakes. Maybe we could do something about it if we got together."

Billy bobbed his head twice, slowly, understandingly.

"So *that's* it! You bein' kicked out o' the rangers was only a gag."

"No, Billy — I'm sorry to say. Any ranger seeing me will shoot on sight; they're out to get me, and not alive."

Billy's face puckered up; this was getting pretty deep.

"Then, why in blazes — ?"

"Because I'm going to do the rangers a good turn, or get plugged trying — maybe it'll square me with them, maybe it won't. They all believed they were doing the right thing in kicking me out; I think as much of them now as I ever did, maybe more."

Billy turned deliberately and stared at him.

"Yo're stickin' — After — Clint," he burst out, "I always reckoned I was the biggest dam' fool in the world. Now I know that I'm not — you are."

His look was changing from consternation to something like compassion for such feeble wits. Shaking his head, he got up.

"Where's yore horse? I'll lead him down while yo're puttin' your gun on. Yo're havin' dinner with me."

His shack, a little one-room affair with a pile of torn blankets in a corner, was in a hollow just over the pass. They rode down the trail together. They talked on the way, mostly of Tex Fletcher and his crew. Strangely, Billy held little rancor toward Tex, and he regarded many of the rustlers as his personal friends, even if they were trying to get him. But one thing he made very plain; he was going to fight them to the end. The thing did not seem to be a matter of any great concern to him.

It was not much of a meal that he laid before Clint; nothing but very dry, tasteless jerky and black coffee. Clint did not envy him, sticking out here alone, living on this stuff, and trying to carry on his suicidal fight with Tex and his crew.

Only once did he show anything resembling a care for his life. He set down his cup of coffee.

"Clint, they'll send somebody else over to get me when they find out that you didn't. I wonder if you'd mind gettin' me word, if you hear about it? Then I'd know what to be lookin' for."

"Why, sure. But it would look bad if they found out I was coming over here. How else could we work it?"

"Well, you know Butch Tolleson?"

Clint nodded. Butch was a big, good-natured rustler, not quite smart enough to be among the leaders, but with too much experience in the game to be counted among the riff-raff.

"Uh — ever see his gal, Sally?"

Clint turned, and Billy reddened under his steady stare. A grin crossed Clint's face.

"So that's it! That's why you quit Tex's bunch and want to set up in the cattle business!"

"Aw, shet up! Sally's all right, even if her dad is only a rustler — so'm I, far as that goes. Well, you could leave word with her; I see her every night or two."

"Say, Billy; are you as bad as Tex makes you out — a killer?"

Billy nodded, he looked a little shame-faced.

"That's right."

An embarrassed silence. They finished their scanty meal.

"Clint, here's what's worryin' me; what'll happen to you when you go back an' tell Tex you didn't get me?"

"I figured that out on my way over. You'll do no good sticking away out here; you'll only get shot sooner or later. Why not ride in and make up with Tex? — he wants you to. Then we'll be close together if anything turns up."

"But you — That's right; how could you find me when I was already on my way to town? Sure." He nodded. Suddenly he looked at Clint: "Say, what you figurin' on doin' to Tex and his crowd, all by yourself?"

"I — don't know. I thought if I stuck around I'd see some opening sooner or later, to get at them — I don't know what."

Billy eyed him shrewdly.

"You mean, yo're not goin' to tell me till you know me better. Fair enough, pardner! I'm stickin' with you whatever you try to do. O. K. When do I start?"

Clint looked at his watch.

"Hadn't you better be going? The sooner you get to town, the better it'll look for me. I'll take my time following you there. Blame it, I sure will! That old skate I'm riding will see to that."

A few more words, and Billy rode off. He was whistling merrily; he did not seem to have a care in the world. Clint watched his disappearing back; he nodded approvingly. Two men against a powerful rustling ring was not much, but it was just twice as many as one.

Clint timed his ride so as to reach Gulch City well after dark. He went straight to Tex's rooms, and knocked. He went in with what he hoped was a savage expression on his face.

"Say, Tex! That blamed young rustler kid wasn't at home when I got over there. I —"

Tex held up his hand. He was smiling.

"It's all right, Clint; I know you did your dangdest. It turned out better than I looked for."

"Huh?" Clint tried to look surprised.

"He saw you coming; he had a little spy glass and knew who it was. I didn't think nothing would scare that kid, but Clint Yancey after his scalp sure did — bad. He circled around you and rode here hell-bent-for-election, looking back all the way to see if you were on his trail. Scared plumb stiff! He's back in our bunch; he give up all his fool notions of bucking us."

"Huh!"

Clint's gasp was real this time. Billy Armour seemed to have made up a most wonderful yarn, and made it stick. Tex nodded affably.

"I see now where your name is going to help us a heap; I didn't know you had such a rep, Clint. Well, you sure tried honest; you'll do. But if I was you I'd look out for that kid a few days, till he gets over being sore at you; he might plug you in the back."

"Oh, I'm not scared of him!" Clint sniffed airily.

"Well, be careful anyway; I can't afford to lose you. Say, Clint; you know I was only kidding about your sorrel being stole. Know why?"

"Showing who's boss, I suppose." Clint sounded sour, and Tex realized it.

"Good lord, no — I wouldn't do a thing like that! It was only that I wasn't plumb sure of you, sort of. Clint, I wanted you to save him for tomorrow; a few of us are going on a little job outside. Good money — and you're one of us, of course. You might need a fast horse if anything goes wrong."

"What sort of job?"

"Oh, picking flowers. I never tell the men in advance; some of them might talk. Not," he hastened

50

apologetically, "that you would, but it's a rule we had a long time. Well, get a good night's sleep; you mightn't get much for a few days. Good night, Clint."

" 'Night."

Clint went down the stairs scratching his head. Now what was his move? He could not even guess; he had to wait to see how things turned out.

Directly in front of the old hotel, Billy Armour was lounging against the hitching rail, as though waiting. At sight of Clint, he jerked erect, his broad face glowering. On a sudden impulse, Clint swung over toward Yavapai Slim, who happened to be there too. He whispered quickly:

"Say, Yavapai; the boss said for you to keep an eye on that kid a few days; he's sore at me. Would you kind of get behind him while I walk off?"

Slim nodded dryly. He tried to make his tone friendly:

"Shore, Clint! Go ahead; I'll watch him."

Clint deliberately stood there, rolling a cigarette, while Yavapai lounged around to Billy's back; in spite of his slouching walk, he looked very business-like. Billy saw the move. He threw up his head and gave Clint a glare of rage, then swung furiously on one heel and went stamping down the street in a quick, baffled walk.

Clint turned quickly and started off, so that Yavapai would not see his face; he could not keep it straight to save his life. Billy had put enough melo-dramatics into that glare to serve for a whole tentful of actors. Crazy kid!

But Clint's face soon became serious enough as he walked. That business tomorrow. He was uneasy about it; he had a strong hunch that it was going to get him up to his neck in trouble. Hardly a hunch, at that; common sense told him it would. Still he had to go.

CHAPTER
SIX

The Desert

There was no early, surreptitious start; there was no need for that here. Indeed, there was almost an air of mild celebration in the shabby, bleached little town as the party started off. They had met in front of the saloon, and they rode out of town, horses rearing and chaps flapping, with Tex Fletcher's tall, commanding figure in the lead. It struck Clint that a brass band to see them off would not have been too much out of place.

Clint was disappointed to find that Billy Armour was not there; he had been counting on him. But of course Billy had to be slighted thus to punish him for his one-man revolution. Yavapai Slim was here, naturally; he was Tex's confidential man, the most trusted of the lot, and the most faithful.

There were ten of them, all picked men. This gave Clint reason to believe that something of more than usual importance was on schedule. Trotting along thus, they looked hardly different from a group of cowboys starting out to round stock up honestly, except that instead of the usual wiry pack mules there were very light packs on fast horses, horses not noticeably worse than those they rode, which were of the best. They should have been; they were the pick of half the cattle ranches of Arizona.

For two hours they swung over high, stony, grassy hills, where there were a few stunted cedars. Then they began to drop, the vegetation to grow more scanty. They topped the last high ridge, and the desert lay stretched before them, glittering, glaring, barren, reaching far over the horizon.

By noon they were well out on it. It had been hot in the little town, but here the sun was thrown back at them from the white, sandy ground, until the ground seemed hotter than the sun itself, and more dazzling. Clint looked back, his eyes squinched up to slits against that blinding glare. The Silvermine Hills were a low, indistinct streak behind him on the horizon, blending into the quivering mirage. For the first time, he fully realized how isolated the rustlers' stronghold was from the rest of humanity; it might well be called impregnable, guarded by those wild stretches of desert.

On and on, all day, no yard of their travel seeming different from the yards that had gone before. Clint judged that the temperature was at least a hundred and twenty-five in the shade — if there had been any shade; even the cacti were stunted things. How much hotter it was here in the sun, he could not guess; there was always a difference of perhaps twenty degrees in this dry country. No one seemed to mind; they were all men reared to the saddle, to heat and thirst. There were canteens of water in the packs, but nobody thought of stopping to get one out. Each man had his neckerchief

— black silk, as was invariable among cowboys — pulled up to his eyes; that kept the alkali from eating one's lips raw. Those black masks, away out there, gave the little band of riders a queer, wild look.

Only Tex had his face bare; as leader, it was his privilege to ride in front, out of the dust of hoofs. Now Clint understood why Tex's face was so dark; he was fully as dark-brown as the average Indian. It was still more odd that Tex never wore gloves; he had the almost delicate, undeveloped hands of the real cowboy, but without their whiteness to contrast with his face. Perhaps it was his eternal vigilance, his wariness of treachery among his men — one could not shoot instantly in gloves.

There was a camp that night at an evil little water hole on the side of a barren ridge — who but Tex would have known of it, or found it? And on again at daylight; it would have been cooler to ride by night, but then one would have gone mad trying to sleep, or even to stay in camp during the day, in that terrific, glaring heat.

Tex had been in an evil, taciturn mood during all this ride. Clint knew that this meant nothing; the man varied from this to wild, unreasoning furies over nothing. It was said that sometimes, when drunk, he would go roaring through the streets of Gulch City, and foolish and wise alike stayed inside and barred their doors. Clint had never seen him thus; he had been at his most affable during their two interviews. Now, for the first time since morning, Tex broke his silence. He raised his head, and spoke shortly:

"Clint."

Clint rode to him, and Tex silently swung his horse off at a slight angle from their line of travel, motioning to the others to keep straight on. They went only a little distance to one side when Tex stopped, looking silently at the ground. Clint's eyes followed his.

There, almost hidden in drifting sand, lay the bleached skeleton of a horse. Clint could see some dried, shrunken leather that was the remains of a saddle still encircling the bare ribs. Pity swept over Clint; he spoke in a low voice.

"I wonder where the man is — poor devil!"

No reply. He turned, to see Tex riding silently off through the sand, to join his men. For a moment, Clint sat looking sadly down; then he touched Reddy's neck with a rein and swung back after the others; his head was low.

About five miles further on, Tex turned again. This time he did not even speak, only jerked his head. Again Clint followed him. They swung farther off this time, around a barren, desolate little butte. On the far side of it, Tex pointed ahead as he rode. He laughed harshly, but said nothing.

Clint could see something white there. Bones. He would as soon have kept his eyes from them as he rode up, but he could not. Yes, that was a human skull, and those had been human ribs; they were not so deep in the sand as the skeleton of the horse had been. Clint bowed his head; there was a little catch in his voice.

"The man."

They sat side by side, looking down from their horses at that poor, bleached relic of humanity. A heavy trail led through the sand past what had been a foot; Clint knew the trail to be that of a Gila monster — that foul, bloated lizard of the desert whose bite is death. Suddenly Tex spoke; there was a sort of gloating grimness in his hard voice:

"Ranger Carmody, the man that swore to get me."

Horror crept over Clint; he had been a friend to this man, had slept in the same bed with him in their camps, had ridden many a long day by his side. So this was where Jack Carmody had disappeared — big, determined Irish Jack, with his red face and his roaring laugh. Poor devil! It was hard for Clint to speak; he could only get one word out:

"You — ? You — ?"

Tex rolled a cigarette. He lit it, and flipped the burned match contemptuously at that grinning skull. He spoke shortly:

"You'll find no bullet mark. He lost his way trying to follow me."

And suddenly Tex jerked his head up, stared hard at Clint, straight at him.

"Clint, can you leave a false trail on the desert?"

"Why, it can't be done!"

A queer little burst of a laugh from Tex. Clint looked up; it was well that Tex did not see his face. But Tex was not looking at him; he was staring out across the limitless desert with a little smile that was both cruel and affectionate. From that smile, Clint could see that this man loved the desert, and it alone; he regarded the desert as his friend, his only friend.

Abruptly Tex turned his horse and rode away. Again Clint's eyes went slowly to the thing in the sand. He would have liked to dismount and bury those poor bones, but he knew that that much sympathy shown toward a ranger would be as much as his life was worth; he had no illusions about his companions or their leader. He swung his head, his keen blue eyes taking in every faint little mark between him and the horizon all around; he hoped he could find this place again, but he doubted it.

He turned to join the rest, and as he rode, he realized how easily Tex had found this spot, and the place where the horse lay. And Tex seemed to know every tiniest little water hole, and to know how much water would be in it long before he reached it. No man living had the uncanny knowledge of the desert that Tex Fletcher had, and nobody else ever would. No wonder catching him seemed so hopeless! Even if driven from his oasis, he could lead a chosen band through the desert, striking, raiding where he choose and returning to security. Yes, Tex was a genius in his way — an inhuman, evil genius.

The backs of the others were ahead now, Tex again in the lead, but Clint did not try to come up with them immediately; he rode two hundred yards behind, only slowly closing the distance. A thing that Tex had said was beating through his mind; the grim associations made it stick there. "A false trail on the desert." Well that it did stick in his mind! The remembrance of it was to save his own life before very long.

58

On the third day, they made a very long camp at noon, and when they started, the pack horses were left hobbled by the little water hole. There was no grass here, but oats were poured on the rocks; it seemed to be enough to keep the horses for a day or two. Clint could guess what this meant, and after they had ridden an hour or so he made out a faint line on the horizon ahead; the edge of the desert. Their course had been a long zigzag from water to water; it was difficult for Clint to keep his bearings. Still, he had a hazy notion of where they were. If he was right, there would be no town within a day's ride of where they would leave the desert, and it would be much farther to a railroad. Therefore, it could not be a bank or train holdup. That left only a raid on some stockman — horses or cattle.

If he was anywhere nearly right, he should be able to remember the country ahead pretty well when he got to it. It must be near where, as a boy, he had wrangled horses for the Kite Cross, and where later, as stray man, he had gone to represent that outfit on roundups for many miles around.

But Tex had timed it so that their dust could not be seen from the hills ahead; it was growing dark before they had got close enough for that line to be more than a shimmering blur. Now they swung on faster.

It was dark but for the bright starlight when they rode into a low break where a wash came through from the hilly country beyond. They hurried to get over a high ridge before the moon rose to show them against the skyline. Then they were following the bed of another wash, always climbing higher, slowly.

59

The moon was up now, low in the sky. They were in a country of fairly tall and very dense cedars, almost to the divide where lay the head of the long wash they had been following. Clint seemed to recognize the country very vaguely.

Suddenly from a patch of cedars they were passing came a short, low whistle. Tex instantly threw up his hand to stop his men. He answered with another whistle. Then two short notes, which he answered with three.

A man came riding from the trees and toward them. The first thing Clint noticed was that he had his black neckerchief drawn up to mask his face — of course Clint and the rest had dropped theirs on their chests at sunset. That would mean that no one there but Tex himself was supposed to know who he was. A spy of some sort. Tex spoke shortly to him:

"Everything all right?"

"O. K. They have over a hundred head rounded up and in the pasture. The —"

"Shut up!" snapped Tex. "Where's the water you told me about?"

"First side wash to the left. You'll be all right there tomorrow; they ain't nobody ridin' this part of the range now."

"Good. You get back as quick as you can; we don't want anybody suspecting you."

The spy had ridden in among Tex's men, and Clint had inconspicuously pushed his horse up close to him. His keen eyes were sweeping over the man, trying to find something by which he might remember him if he ever saw him again. There seemed to be nothing; even the brand on his horse had been smeared with mud. But as he lowered his hand to pick up his reins, the moon shone full on it, and Clint noticed a tiny white scar, roughly V shaped, above the root of his thumb. It was a small thing, but it might do.

Five minutes later, they had found the water, Even here, Tex had to permit the men to build a small fire to make coffee and heat their beans, but he kicked it out as soon as possible — the place was well hidden anyhow.

From the first, Clint had had a queer feeling of having seen this spot before. Suddenly it came to him; this was what the cowboys called Secret Tank. Why, it was on the old Kite Cross range, and hardly six miles from headquarters!

The men had only one blanket apiece, which they had tied behind their saddles. Clint lay wrapped in his, staring up at the stars. The Kite Cross — Old Man Judson's range. So the raid was to be on old Henry Judson's stock; he would have nothing else worth stealing. A hundred head, the spy had said. That meant horses; a hundred head of cattle would not be worth all this trouble. Yes, old Henry had been shipping in fine studs, and a few mares, until he had about the best saddle stock in Arizona; it had always been a mania with him, to breed up his horses. Indeed, he had them a little too finely bred for cattle work in this rough country; but a hundred head of them would be worth a lot of money taken on the average, not less than twelve thousand dollars.

For two hours or more Clint lay awake. If this turned out to be a rustling or horse-stealing expedition, he had meant to go through with it as one of the gang — what harm could it do, since the stock would be taken just as well without him? He had had few qualms about it.

But — old "Hank" Judson. The man who had taught him practically all he knew about cowpunching; the man who had been almost a father to him after his own father died. True, old Henry had made him work hard, but he had promoted him to a man's wages and a man's cowboy work long before another would have thought of it. Blazes, he liked that hard-boiled old sinner!

The moon had come around so that Clint's bed was in the shade of a dense cedar. Staring out, wide-eyed, troubled, he caught a movement up in the brush on the skyline. A coyote prowling?

He lay watching the place for a very long time, for so long that he came to believe he had only imagined that little movement. Suddenly he saw it again, indistinctly, through the brush.

No animal, not knowing itself watched, would have kept absolutely still so long. It must be a man. Was the camp surrounded?

CHAPTER
SEVEN

At Secret Tank

Clint slipped out of his blanket silently as a shadow. He was already dressed but for his boots and hat. He did not want the hat; it would show up too plainly. And the high-heeled boots would make too much noise; stones or not, it had to be stocking feet. He buckled on his gun.

Then another thought came to him. If this camp was surrounded, there was no reason why he should stay here and get shot, if he could possibly steal through the cordon around it. He was hardly less anxious to be recognized, and have it known all over Arizona that he had been seen on a horse-stealing expedition with Tex Fletcher's gang. Awkward though it was, he carried his boots and hat in his left hand.

He wound slowly up the side of the wash, mostly on his hands and knees, twisting to follow the shadows of the cedars although it tripled his journey. More and more, the fear of being recognized with this crowd came to him. And Old Man Judson would hear of it, of course, and think he had been trying to rob him of his cherished horses! Clint stopped, and pulled his black neckerchief up over his nose, to the eyes. He went on again, slowly, cautiously.

He came to a long, open place running across the slope before him, the full glare of the moonlight on it. It was so situated that it was most unlikely that anybody either above or below could see him cross it. Still, cautious always, he decided to go around it.

He was just twisting away when he heard a faint sound. Across the opening, from the other side, a man came running. He ran all doubled up, a carbine trailing in his right hand. Crouched as he was, Clint could tell little about the man; he saw mostly the wide brim of his hat. Straight to Clint he came; he was due to bump into him as he knelt on one knee in the black shadow. Clint could do but one thing.

"Up with 'em! Don't make a sound!"

It was a quick whisper from Clint. His gun pointed to the other man's head, and swung up with it. The man was sensible — or timid; he dropped his carbine and his hands rose before his face.

Clint gasped into the black silk. Old Ernie Cox! Still with the Kite Cross — a trifle older, a trifle grayer, but the same rawboned, faithful, old Ernie.

"How many with you?" asked Clint. He tried to disguise his whisper; he would have died if old Ernie recognized him.

"Ugh — ugh — only me."

Just like old Ernie, to turn up at his hour of night, in the last place anybody would have looked for him.

"What are you doing here?"

"I — ugh — was ridin' on the other side of the big wash, goin' home after dark, an' — ugh — I thought I saw a light shinin' up into the cedars. I knew no-body honest — ugh — I mean — ugh —"

Whatever courage had brought old Ernie around here alone to spy, was vanished now. He was not trembling, but he was gulping and swallowing so that he could hardly talk. Clint whispered suddenly:

"Tell old Hank to keep his horses in the home coral tomorrow night, and to watch 'em. Get away from here as quick as you can.

He thought of something else:

"How many men at headquarters now?"

"Th-three, with me. Ugh — who are you, anyways?"

The old man's mouth was opening and closing. He evidently did not know what to make of this; the friendly advice and the ready gun did not seem to go together.

"None of your business. Get going!"

Gingerly, cautiously, old Ernie picked up his carbine; he was very careful to keep his hand away from the hammer and trigger. He turned, and with stiff back walked slowly, sedately, across the patch of moonlight until he was within a short distance of the far shadow. Then he gave a sudden wild leap that took him higher into the air than forwards. Knowing where to look, Clint could see him scurrying up the slope like a great, grizzled badger. Clint had to grin; poor old Ernie had got the scare of his life, and the mystification.

Only three men at headquarters, and nine of the best shots in Arizona lying down there below. But old Hank

was no fool; his memory went back to the
Indian-fighting days. Well, he had sent him warning.
Clint turned, and stole cautiously back down the slope.
He knew that he would be using far better judgment to
crawl away, but that would forever ruin his chances of
getting back to the Silvermines, and back there he had
to go.

He got safely to his blanket. Now that he knew he
had plenty of time, he went down even more cautiously
than he had gone up. Lying there again, he started
suddenly, staring blankly at the sky. He had made a
ghastly blunder — the meeting with old Ernie had been
such a surprise, so sudden.

He had forgotten to warn Ernie to beware of the
man with the scar on his hand.

He was to regret it more next evening. They had
passed the day lounging around there, their horses
picketed but with the saddles on them. Late in the
afternoon, the man with the mask came riding
hurriedly down the little gulch; he seemed excited. He
stopped some distance off and waited for Tex, who was
hurrying afoot to meet him; he seemed too nervous to
take the slightest risk of being identified by the others,
now that it was daylight.

Again Clint could see the smear of mud on the
horse's thigh, hiding the brand. But Clint needed no
brand. Like most cowboys, Clint could more easily
forget a man than a horse which he had once
examined. This horse had been only a long-legged
yearling when he saw it last, but he knew it on sight.

Old Brownie's colt. This spy was a cowboy on the Kite Cross.

There was a long conversation between the two men. Tex would be hearing of old Ernie's strange meeting with one of his own men — a tall young man. As it happened, Clint was the only tall one there besides Tex himself. And the newest man, out on his first raid. And an ex-ranger. Well, something would be happening pretty soon — something not at all pleasant.

And while he was thinking this, Clint was lounging casually with his back to Tex, pretending to listen to the talk of the other men. His eyes were half closed sleepily; his face had not changed a particle.

He thought of getting up and strolling quietly out into the cedars, then trying to run, to hide. No, that would not do. At his first move, Tex would start shooting, would yell to the other men. He'd be riddled before he'd got six feet.

"Clint, that ain't a bad nag that feller's ridin'!" someone remarked.

He heard the voice. He rolled over sleepily on one elbow. Tex was staring straight at him, his brows lowered fiercely. Clint shifted permanently to his new position, as though to look at the horse better. He could keep his eye on Tex now; maybe he could get Tex if he shot quickly, before the others realized what was happening. Yes, he'd get Tex. Then he'd go down, drilled through and through from the back. He yawned.

"That's right. I always did like a solid blood bay."

He slowly rolled a cigarette, lit it.

The man was mounting, turning off. Here came Tex! Straight to him. Glaring.

"Boys, this is a great note! Some old fossil of a cowpuncher saw the light of our camp last night and reported it. They're suspicious; they're leaving the horses in the home corral all night."

A very slight color came to Clint's face, which had been getting pale. So old Ernie — No, it was old Judson who had told Ernie to keep his mouth shut about all he had run into; Old Hank was clever enough to see that anything said about the meeting would put the man who had warned them in danger. Clint blew the ashes from the tip of his cigarette; the hand holding the cigarette was steady as a rock. He spoke:

"Well, that sure is a fine note! What do we do now — go home?"

Tex was in a furious temper. He glared at Clint.

"Like the devil we do! There's only three men at the ranch. We take them horses out of the corral; we can't ride this far for nothing."

And he turned back and stalked off. Only then did Clint draw a very long, deep breath.

He went back to his blanket, a little apart from the others, and lay on his back on it. His eyes were closed, and his hat brim pulled down over them; he appeared to be asleep. But never had he thought so hard, or seemingly to so little purpose. Two things were plain; he had to stay with Tex and his crew, and he wanted to prevent the theft of those horses if possible. A hundred head; it would not hurt old Judson very much financially; the old man was comparatively wealthy. And he had to stay with Tex; once out of the gang, there could be no going back. Looked very much as though he might have to help steal those horses.

At last he rolled over, his back to the men. He slipped a dog-eared little tally book out of his chaps pocket, and a stub of pencil; it was old habit that made him always carry them, a relic of his cowboy days. He wrote a line or two quickly. Then another thought came to him. He rolled the note into a tiny pellet, and pushed it into the ground with his finger, covered it. This time he wrote the same thing in Spanish, carefully:

Watch the man with the little scar like a V on the back of his left hand near the thumb. He rides old Brownie's colt. He is a spy for Tex Fletcher, and told him about the horses.

He closed the book, the page with the note still in it, and put it back in his chaps. They would, of course, think that a Mexican had written it, one who knew no English. He himself would never be suspected. Presently he heard Tex call to him — strangely, now that action was at hand, Tex sounded suddenly jovial; his fit of moroseness had passed.

"Clint — chuck! Hurry up an' let's eat; it's, pretty near dark. We got to be going."

"*Bueno, patrón!*"

Clint said it with a slight, humorous twist to his voice. There was an absent-minded shadow of a grin around his lips; something about the position he had got himself into seemed vaguely funny to him, he

69

himself could not tell why. Perhaps it was this slightly twisted sense of humor that had made him such a good ranger.

Tex looked at him in a friendly way, and clapped him on the back.

"You'll do! I been watching to see how you took it when something like this come up. Never scared once! You're the pick of the bunch!"

Perhaps Tex wondered why Clint threw back his head and laughed so abruptly.

CHAPTER
EIGHT

Rangers!

Tex had had to change his plans. He had expected to find the horses in the pasture, and to begin rounding them up as soon as it was barely dark, so as to have them far out on the desert before moonrise. With the men at the ranch suspicious, that had to be given up.

They had lain for hours among the dense cedars on one ridgeside, peering impatiently across the narrow valley to the next. From the summit of that one, Yavapai Slim was keeping watch on the ranch house below him, waiting until it seemed that everybody on the place had gone to bed. It was well past midnight, and all the men but Tex himself were inclined to nervousness; they did not like this late start. Also, this showed that those at the ranch were undoubtedly very uneasy; staying up until this hour was an unheard of thing.

Suddenly a match flared up on that far hillside; barely flared, to be blown out before the head was well burning.

"Let's go, boys!"

Tex sounded like the soul of good-nature; he seemed to be enjoying this thing. They crossed the valley in a silent trot. Yavapai Slim, afoot, came from behind a cedar.

"Just blew the last light out down there; reckon they figure we wouldn't come so late."

Tex gave a swift order:

"All right, Clint — you offered to go down and open the gate. Rest of you follow a little way behind."

Clint rode silently as a shadow down among the cedars, keeping his horse at a slow walk, sometimes stopping him for an instant, so that anybody who might hear would think that it was a loose horse going down to water. It was not likely that anybody would hear, for Reddy was picking his steps so carefully that there was hardly a sound; he seemed to realize that there was need for caution.

Near the foot of the ridge, Clint slipped silently from the saddle and dropped his reins. He stole forward quietly afoot, crouched behind a thick algerita bush, he peered through the gray starlight.

About the first thing he saw was the faint glow of a cigarette tip near the corral gate. A great guard that was! Clint wondered why he didn't play a tune on a mouth organ while he was watching there by the gate; he might as well.

It struck Clint that, after all, horse stealing was not so very different from rangering; it called for about the same sort of caution, the same tricks. He knew what to do almost without thinking; the fact that the guard was smoking told him that he did not have to try any very subtle plans. He stole quietly around the man, a good distance off, until he was between him and the house.

Then, with a great flapping of chaps, he walked directly toward him. He would be taken for a relief guard, or for somebody with some message.

As he came up, he noticed that the cigarette was gone; the man had probably pinched it out guiltily as soon as he heard somebody coming. A low voice:

"Now what's up? Has the Old Man — ?"

The heavy barrel of Clint's forty-five cracked down on his skull with whole-hearted earnestness; if his skull was not fractured, it was hardly Clint's fault. The guard sagged down limply as an old wet coat. Clint stood over him with a feeling of joy in his heart. He had recognized the voice of the spy.

Now, there was no particular need for silence. Clint walked to the gate post, pulling his little tally book from his chaps pocket. He tore out the note which he had written. He ran his hand up the post until he found a long, loose sliver, and on this he carefully impaled the note. It would be found next morning. One cowboy — if he lived over that crack on the head, as he probably would — would be out of a job in short order, and needing a fast horse.

Clint knew better than to frighten the horses by stealing around. He opened the gate in a quiet, business-like way. He was starting to walk around the corral — a big salt lot — when he heard the first of the horses go through the gateway; they were only too anxious to get out of their confinement. Clint turned and hurried to his horse.

He had not gone fifty feet when a tall figure rose from behind the very same algerita bush behind which he himself had hidden. Tex! He had followed him down afoot, watching him all the time. Tex whispered:

"Clint, I never saw anything done better. You're cut out for a horse thief!"

There was congratulation in his tone, and friendliness.

"Danged if I don't believe you, Tex! Seems to come natural to me — I reckon it's a gift."

Tex chuckled softly.

"Say, I couldn't see very well. Did you stick a knife in that feller, whoever he was?"

Clint whispered with what sounded like regret:

"No; I thought he might yell. But I sure smashed his skull plenty with my gun barrel. Hope I killed him!"

"Say, you sure sound blood-thirsty; didn't think you were that kind, Clint." Tex chuckled again. He seemed to be really enjoying this little game played in the small hours of the morning.

The loose horses had stopped outside the corral gate; now that they were out, they did not seem to know what to do about it, at this hour. Leaning over his saddle horn, peering hard, Clint saw a shadowy figure of a rider drift in a shade closer to them, and stop. The leader of the loose band turned sleepily toward the trail, and started up, the others strung out behind. Tex glanced at the sky, which was light in the east.

"We'll have to shove 'em just a little faster, to get over the ridge before the moon comes. Then we'll have to do some tall drifting. We've rode ours a long ways; we'd better catch fresh mounts out of —"

A sudden pandemonium broke out at the house. Hounds baying! What a din! Clint had forgotten that old Judson always kept a pack of lion hounds, as did most cattlemen in that part of the country; lions were numerous and destructive to stock.

The noise mounted rapidly. Must be a dozen or more of them, and no hundred other animals can make the noise of a dozen long-eared hounds. Baying, wailing, making sounds that could hardly be described. Tex's voice rose sharply:

"Get goin', boys! Light out with 'em!"

Shrill yells sprang up; somebody fired his six-shooter in the air. Tex turned in his saddle and shouted tauntingly:

"Adios, Henry! Thanks for rounding 'em up for me!"

A window flew open. A carbine began to crack rapidly and steadily. Clint wondered why there was only one carbine; both Ernie and old Judson should be there. He heard a reckless laugh from Tex, beside him.

"Too dark to see us; he'll kill some of his own horses."

Probably the grim old-timer would have preferred that to letting them be stolen, but he had other plans. He was not even trying to hit the men; he was throwing bullets at the side of the ridge as fast as he could work the lever of his gun and take hasty aim. If he could stampede the horses badly enough to make them scatter, perhaps by hitting one in the middle of the bunch, it would take a weeks' work in daylight to gather them again. A little horse-stealing like this was old stuff to Hank Judson.

He did not succeed. But one of his bullets struck the earth directly under the nose of a horse well out toward the lead; it went zinging up off a stone. A snort, and the horse whirled off the trail, and the others shied away after him, as horses will. A wild yell from Tex:

"Head 'em, boys!"

Led by the wildest one in the herd, the horses were racing madly diagonally down the side of the ridge, away from the house. The horse is by nature a creature of the steppes; these wanted to strike the level, sandy draw below, where they could run their fastest. Tex knew it.

"Clint, head 'em! Don't let 'em down!"

The two men were riding furiously side by side. Tex was quirting and spurring madly. Clint's quirt was flying too; in the darkness, Tex could not see that it was coming down gently, mostly on Clint's chaps. And Clint's left hand was pulling its hardest on the reins; naturally, Reddy thought his duty was to head these horses, and he could not understand why Clint seemed trying to tear his mouth out. Had Tex known that Clint could head the horses, and wouldn't, there would have been a murder right there.

"Come on, Reddy! Run, boy!"

Clint thought it a dirty trick on a good horse; he had not known how much faster Reddy was than Tex's black. An oath:

"They're down — hell!" Tex shouted to the shadowy, racing men behind: "Stay with 'em, boys! They'll slow up soon!"

76

Still he did not give up trying to head them, and Clint kept only half a length behind him; he judged it good policy not to risk showing Tex that Reddy was the faster of the two mounts. That would hurt Tex's vanity; he would either be angry or insist on buying the horse.

With the yells of the men stopped, they were strangely silent as they swept down the draw in that mad race. The ground was almost pure sand, and the hoofs of the horses made little sound. A mile. The horses showed signs of being ready to slow up. The edge of the moon was just beginning to peep over the cedars.

The band swept around a bend of the draw, with Tex and Clint now creeping slowly up toward the lead; they would soon be able to turn them. And suddenly the leaders of the band swerved to the left across the draw, seemed to take a new start. Tex and Clint raced around the bend, not following. If the band swerved back, they would have taken a short cut and be ahead of it. If it turned up the stony, steep hillside, it would slow down, and very probably stop.

And so the two dashed around the curve, the other men not far behind. There came a sudden wild shout of consternation from Tex:

"Stop! Back, boys!"

A hundred yards or so ahead, a little company of horsemen was riding hard, straight to meet them. A dozen or so, coming on in a dead run.

There was a wild plunging and rearing, horses crashing into each other. Oaths. Shouts. And in an instant order came out of the chaos; they were flying at full speed. A shot came from behind. A shout, in a measured bass voice — a cry that sent a start of remembrance shooting through Clint's mind:

"Stop, for the Arizona Rangers!"

Clint caught his breath. Partly it was from fear; perhaps even more it was from another thing. That shout had once been the pride of his life, as it came from his own throat. It meant that though you dropped every man but one from his saddle, that one would charge grimly on; the name of ranger had to be upheld, even at the cost of one's life.

Wildly, the would-be horse thieves fled up the draw. Sometimes one turned to shoot back. And there were a few shots from behind; not many — the Arizona Rangers were famous for not wasting ammunition at long range; they charged close before they shot much.

A shout from behind in a cracked voice; Clint knew it for old Ernie's:

"Give up, boys! It's the rangers!"

So that was it. Henry Judson had known that, by chance, there was a camp of rangers in the country, and he had sent old Ernie dashing to get them. That was why there had been only one man shooting from the ranch house, why the spy had been the one left on guard.

Few shots from behind. But a man not ten feet from Clint gave a sudden queer grunt, as though struck by a stone, and pitched from his saddle into the sand. He had thrown his hands high before he fell; he was dead before he touched the ground. Those behind saw him fall, or saw his loose horse circling in fright as they passed him. Again that measured cry:

"Stop, for the Arizona Rangers!"

The moon was up now; there was no chance of eluding them in the darkness. Already the Kite Cross ranch houses were before them; they dared not turn up the stony hillside, and thereby slow their horses and let the rangers come within easy shooting distance. Nor could one leave the others and turn up; everybody knew how the rangers shot.

They were sweeping past the buildings, keeping as far as possible to the other side of the draw. A carbine was barking there, not from a window this time but from the old front porch. Clint heard a strangling cry near him:

"They gug — got — !"

Another horse circling off riderless. Another huddled figure left behind on the sand. Tex let out a mighty oath.

"Ride! Ride!"

Quirts cut into horses' sides; spurs raked. Nobody said what they all knew: their horses had been ridden a long way lately; they had been winded by that wild race after the loose band. While the mounts of the rangers were not fresh, they were the fresher, and had started the race unwinded.

They were almost up to the head of the draw now; they would go through that little low pass between the two rounded hills.

That is, if they were not surrounded before they got that far. The rangers, true to their tradition, were trying to take all possible of them alive. They were not even shooting now; they knew that they had already won the race.

Nor were Tex's men shooting back; they would waste too many cartridges shooting backwards from running horses, and besides, twisting around in the saddle threw a horse off his stride, slowed him. Time enough for shooting when it came to that last stand. No, they dared not surrender; they were Tex's picked men, their records well known — the noose was already dangling for them. It was better to be shot than hanged.

A sudden sharp order from Tex. Even now, he sounded more furious than afraid; the man had nerve, when he had to have it.

"Jump off at them rocks ahead, boys — bay up! Fight 'em!"

A cry from somebody —

"They can hold us there till mornin'. There's no chance!"

"We got no chance anyways. Kick loose!"

Clint knew that his face was white, his lips set grimly. So this was to be his end, lying in those rocks ahead until he was riddled with bullets from the rangers' guns. Found there, dead, among that rotten gang. His old companions staring down at what was left of him with contempt and loathing. Old Henry Judson there — and Ernie.

The boulders were just ahead, and the rangers hardly more than a rope-throw behind. Clint whipped his feet from the stirrups, loosened his knees from the saddle. He'd take that tall boulder to the left; not that it made any difference, for there would be rangers all around and every man's back would be exposed.

The rangers were spreading out to encircle them. They knew that they had them. One ranger laughed; they were a grim, tough crowd and not too strong on scruples or sympathies. Again came that measured shout, taunting now, mocking — Sergeant Wilson's voice:

"Stop, for the Arizona Rangers!"

CHAPTER
NINE

Tex's Treachery

Clint had unconsciously let Reddy take the lead from Tex's big black. Now he pulled hard on the reins; he was already loose, preparing to take a flying leap from his saddle. He hoped that he would alight on his feet, but he had never been a trick rider; he was more likely to go rolling over and over. He had picked a sandy spot; even if he did fall, he could soon scramble behind that boulder.

As he slowed, Tex's black went past him. With a quick grunt, Clint grabbed his saddle horn barely in time to keep himself on. Why, Tex was erect in his saddle; he had not loosened. He did not intend to stop with his men! Even with all Clint knew of the man's character, he had not expected such treachery as this.

Neither did any of the others leave their saddles. It is doubtful if any of them noticed what Tex was doing; it was that they were panic stricken and did not obey the leader. Tex may have been glancing back to watch them; he jerked out a sudden new order:

"Stay on! Make the pass!"

As if they had not been staying on already! Tex shouted again:

82

"Ride! Make the pass! Kill your horses!"

And that was about what they were doing. They tore madly up the slope, close packed, quirting and spurring. They drew away from the rangers rapidly now, and the rangers let them do it and saved their own horses. That cruel burst of speed uphill could only be a last gasp; it must end the race.

They heard one of the rangers laugh back behind; those Arizona Rangers were a grimly reckless crowd, and the desperate battle they saw coming would be a thing after their own hearts. A shout came from them; Clint recognized the bass voice of Sergeant Wilson:

"Tex, come back and give me a match!"

And another ranger laughed grimly.

Tex let his men push past him. He was darting quick, measuring glances over their horses as they passed, picking out those most nearly exhausted. Clint could see a crafty look on his face, and wondered what it meant.

Clint refused to pass; he stayed back close to Tex, watching him with hard face. If Tex again tried to desert his men, he would put a bullet through his back before he got twenty feet. He would have no more compunction about it than about killing a rabid coyote; it was the best the man's trickery deserved.

It may be that Tex suspected what was on Clint's mind; he must have seen that Clint was watching him closely. Or possibly it was the still fairly strong condition of Reddy that decided him; it and Tex's black, though panting and staggering, still had some strength left. At any rate, Tex spoke quickly, not loudly enough for the rangers behind to hear:

"Boys! We can get all of 'em! Jump off — Jim, Curly, Dave! Them rocks at the mouth of the pass — hold 'em back — rest of us circle the hill an' come in behind 'em!"

Clint caught his breath — a gasp. It might work!

The pass was so narrow and had such steep sides that it was almost a little canyon. Three men could hold the rangers back a while. The other five coming up from behind could catch them between two fires, and perhaps annihilate them.

It flashed through Clint's mind that if it worked it would be the most desperate deed ever done in Arizona — the destruction of about the whole ranger force in one fight. The country would ring with it. The surviving rustlers would be hunted down like wolves. That did not matter now; all that counted was to get away, to save their lives for the time being.

One horse did not even reach the top of the slope; he fell exhausted fifteen feet from the boulders. His rider went over his head, picked himself up, and ran afoot to the shelter of the rocks. That was Dave Barclay. Curly and Jim were looking from one side to the other jerkily. They saw that Tex had his gun poised in his hand; they knew that he might shoot them if they disobeyed again. Anyhow, their horses were about to go under them. They flung themselves from the saddles and dashed for the boulders.

As they ran, their backs turned, Tex fired twice. Their two horses lurched and fell — that would hold the men here. In the excitement, they would never know that it had been Tex's work.

Tex, thudding heavily by, gave them a last word over his shoulder — encouraging, kindly:

"Hold 'em back, boys! We'll soon be around behind 'em!"

The five left kept steadily on through the pass, in the slow, walloping lope which was the best their horses could do. Clint heard the rattle of guns break out behind. From the sounds, he knew that the rangers had stopped and were shooting back. The five lurched out of the pass and around the hillside, on a level, and the firing behind grew fainter as the hill came between.

In the bright moonlight, Clint's face looked white. He knew what he was going to do, and was planning the details. He had been kicked out in disgrace by those rangers back there, broken; he was sought by them as an outlaw. But at heart he was still one of them, still an Arizona Ranger. He held no rancor; they had only done what they thought he had deserved.

There would be four against him, and all five of them among the best shots in Arizona — it was pretty likely that either he himself or Tex was the very best; the rangers had considered Clint the best. The fight could be only a matter of seconds; they were all men who did not miss at close range.

He had but one chance: he would wait until they were close behind the rangers. Then, if the fight could be drawn out a few moments, some of the rangers would wheel back and take part in it. Of course they would not know what was going on, only that part of the rustler gang had got behind them. They would shoot at everybody they saw there, and shoot to kill. There was little hope in the prospect. But he could not let his old companions be wiped out.

Suddenly Clint's head swung, puzzled. Planning, he had not noticed where he was going; he only knew that he had been keeping beside Tex and slightly behind him. Why, they had swung more than half way around the hill, and now they were turning diagonally away from it. Clint jerked out:

"Why, Tex — ! Why, we — !"

Tex pulled his staggering horse back beside Clint's. He gave an unpleasant little laugh.

"No, we're not. Too bad about them boys back there, but we got to save our own skins."

Clint turned his face to him in dumb disbelief. Such a cold-blooded piece of perfidy as this he had never heard of; he had not thought even the treacherous Tex Fletcher capable of it.

Clint's eyes went slowly to the other men. They were looking at him queerly, at each other. On the faces of two of them was much the same expression as on his own — more disbelief than anything else. Those two men were killers, rustlers, horse thieves — call them what you want to — but this thing seemed to be too much for them. All had stopped their horses. One of the two suddenly picked up his reins.

"I'm goin' back!"

The other hesitated. Yavapai Slim seemed nervous; he was watching Tex anxiously. The man who had spoken was the burly Butch Tolleson, about whose daughter Clint had joked Billy Armour. Butch had been a rustler most of his life, and every-body knew that he was one of those whom Tex always picked for train robberies and such things. But Clint's eyes met his, and from that moment they were friends. After all, there is a certain amount of honor among rustlers.

Tex spoke in his gentlest, friendliest tones — such tones as he had used in that last perfidious assurance to those men whom he had deserted in the pass. He had seen the look on Clint's face, and on Butch's.

"Boys, I sure hate to do it; they was all good men. But would it have helped them if we'd all stayed and got killed with them, like we would have? Can't you see it, boys? Why, there was no chance at all of us all getting away!"

Butch jerked out a short, bitter oath.

"I know it! Come on, Clint!"

He stooped over his saddle horn to strike a lope back. Tex darted out a hand and seized his reins.

"Hold on, Butch! It's all over back there — them poor boys is done for."

It was true. Clint suddenly realized that the shooting back in the pass had stopped.

Yavapai spoke approvingly:

"Tex, yo're right, like you always are!" He turned to the other three accusingly. "We'd all be dead by this time if Tex hadn't used his head — an' a fat lot o' good us goin' with 'em would have done them three boys."

Butch gave him a murderous glance. The man who had been silent so far nodded half heartedly. Without courage to go back with Butch, what vague remnants of a conscience he still possessed were squirming feebly. Butch's big, shaggy head dropped, and he picked up his reins again.

"Let's go home," he muttered; he sounded sick.

Tex spoke quickly:

"Boys, I don't want you sore about this; I knew why I was doing it. The rangers will go straight on through the pass hunting us. All we got to do is go back the other way an' make no noise. That'll let our horses blow, too."

Clint shook his head.

"Our horses! Daylight will catch us back there with worn-out horses. The rangers will be searching the whole country for us, and they can't help finding us. I'd say that we separate, and try to get back singly to the Silvermines the best way we can. With a lot of luck, one or two of us may make it."

Butch Tolleson nodded agreement; he seemed ready to side with Clint and against Tex in almost anything. Tex gave one of his superior little smiles.

"Better leave things to me, Clint; I know a lot more than you do about this sort of thing. Now we're going to get fresh mounts, and good ones."

"Huh!" Butch snorted.

"What you plannin' to do, Tex?" asked Yavapai deferentially.

Tex paused impressively, and spoke:

"Go back and pick up that bunch of horses we had to leave; I saw them turn up on the ridge and stop. We can ride five of the best of them. Then if the rangers do run onto us, we can outrun 'em easy. If they don't —

well, them horses will make a nice little split for five of us."

Clint looked up at Tex, and kept his eyes on him. It seemed to be the most brazen piece of audacity he had ever heard of. Then it came to him that Tex was right; that first part of the plan, at least, was their only chance for safety.

"Yes, Tex, fresh horses are our only chance. But we'll never get away with the rest of them. The rangers will be all around the edge of the desert watching for us."

Tex looked at him patronizingly.

"I know it; knowing where they are that way will help a lot. All we have to do is circle around 'em, without going near the desert, and cut straight for the Mexican line."

Yavapai gave a sneering little laugh, looking out of the corners of his eyes at Clint; he was letting his enmity toward him show again.

"Leave it to Tex Fletcher! Won't everybody in Arizona cuss the rangers when they hear how we made monkeys of 'em!"

"Our pack horses," began Clint, "hobbled out there on the desert, to starve — Of course you'll —"

Tex gave him a venomous glance, but cut in heartily:

"Oh, sure, sure! I was figuring on sending Brad here back to drive 'em home, as soon as we get the bunch going well. Let's get started, boys. Quiet, now!"

They stuck out silently and slowly through the cedars.

Back in the little pass three huddled, distorted figures lay among the boulders. And out toward the desert the rangers plugged grimly along on staggering horses, spread in a wide drag-net, eyes fixed on the country ahead. Surely they should catch up with the rest of the rustlers pretty soon!

At dawn, the cowboys of the Kite Cross were finishing a quick breakfast in the cook shack; old Ernie had gone dashing to bring them from Eagle Springs. They had not stopped to remove their chaps before eating; they would soon be in their saddles again. They had eaten almost in total silence, and now they were quickly rolling cigarettes, in silence. Had Tex Fletcher seen their faces, he might have shivered.

And there they were, standing there, waiting for four who were out to drive in some fresh mounts that they might find on the range; the choice horses of the outfit were gone. Riding anything that could be hastily picked up, they could not hope to overtake the thieves. No wonder that they looked bitter!

Les Bailey came in. He had a bloody bandage around his head, and his clothes were torn. That fight he had had with the four horse thieves the night before had been a desperate thing. They wondered why they had ever been inclined to dislike this new man on the outfit; he had only been there a couple of months. Les had a little piece of paper in his hand, and he was looking puzzled. He spoke:

"Boys, I found this stuck on the gatepost of the corral. Reckon it must be Tex sorter makin' fun of us or somethin'."

Of course Les thought it was that; what else could it be?

"What's it say?" asked somebody, dully.

"I can't read it; it's Spanish. You savvy Spanish, Bud, an' you too, Jerry. What's it say?"

Bud took the paper and glanced over it. He looked at the wall a moment, silently, and handed the thing to Jerry.

"Read it out, Jerry," he said quietly.

He himself stepped back; he happened to get behind Les Bailey. Jerry looked at the note, whitened a trifle. Then, slowly and deliberately, he read:

"Watch the man with a little scar like a V on the back of his left hand near the thumb. He rides old Brownie's colt. He is a spy for Tex Fletcher and told him about the horses."

Les Bailey felt a little tug at his waist, and his hand slapped down on an empty holster. He leaped for the door, but arms seized his elbows from behind. Somebody picked up a rope. Les Bailey screamed horribly, but a hand came over his mouth and he was hustled toward the door. There was a dense clump of tall cedars half way up the ridge —

It is not a pretty story, but the cowboys of the Kite Cross did not pretend to be saints.

Old Henry Judson did not know about it until it was all over. He happened to see the cowboys coming trooping down the ridge, very gravely, with bowed heads. He ran out in horror, and presently went slowly back to the house, his lined old face working.

Later, when his cowboys had ridden out, he sat in his living room talking to Sergeant Wilson. Judson looked old, and tiny, and beaten; his bushy white hair was rumpled. Sergeant Wilson was a great, sturdy man who always stood with his booted legs wide apart. Now he looked haggard, almost wild, his face covered with dust. When he spoke, his bass voice sounded hollow and weary:

"Yes, the same man talked to Ernie and left the note — Ernie said there was something stiff about how he spoke, like he was watching every word. Of course he's a Mexican; lots of 'em speak good English but can't write it."

Old Judson's withered face looked sad, and he shook his head slowly — his thick white hair had a shiny, clean look to it.

"Uh-huh; he must be. I — I was hopin' — kinda — that it might of been Clint Yancey; I hear he's with Tex's gang now."

A swift flush swept up Wilson's cheeks at mention of Yancey's name; he seemed to tremble with sudden fury.

"Yancey! I'm sorry to have to tell you, Mr. Judson, but one of the men in the pass lived long enough to talk a little. Clint Yancey was in the gang stealing your horses. He got to be about Tex's right-hand man; he's the one that stole down and opened the gate to get the horses out; he knew this place."

The old man sagged in his big armchair. He blinked, and there was pain in his eyes, as though he had been struck across the face.

"He — He — Clint used to be a good boy; I thought a heap of Clint. I dunno how — I dunno —"

His voice caught, and his head sank slowly. Sergeant Wilson laid a kindly hand on the thin shoulder.

"Forget the rat! He fooled us as badly as he did you; we thought as much of him as you did."

A pause.

"Mebbe — Mebbe if I didn't press the charge about them horses — ?"

The tiredness left Sergeant Wilson's voice. He spoke slowly, grimly:

"It will make no difference, Mr. Judson. I don't think any of the rangers can take Clint Yancey — alive."

Sadly, slowly, old Judson shook his bowed head. He understood.

There was another pause. Wilson sat down, rolled a cigarette, and looked broodingly at his outstretched boots. After a while, he spoke:

"That Mexican seems to be at outs with the gang — something wrong there. I think you were very wise in telling Ernie to say nothing about that talk at Secret Tank; you say only the three of us know about it. We don't want to get that Mexican killed till we see if he mightn't be useful to us later on. That note on the gatepost — nobody knows where that came from."

The old man nodded absently as though not half hearing the words; he seemed to be thinking, thinking. Wilson stood up, reached for his hat.

"Queer about that spy of Tex's. I wonder how he managed to get away so quickly this morning."

The old man had been looking up. Suddenly his eyes fell and his lips twitched. Sergeant Wilson started, and his keen blue eyes fixed on the old man. A set look came to his face, and he spoke deliberately:

"Mr. Judson, I don't know where Les Bailey could have gone to; I see no reason to make an investigation around the ranch."

He paused in the doorway.

"But Les Bailey was a gentleman compared to Clint Yancey; Bailey's treachery wasn't all practiced on his friends. We let your horses be stolen last night, but one thing we rangers will promise: Clint Yancey is about to the end of his rope; he has not long to live."

With slow, heavy tread, he went out to his horse, mounted, turned up the ridge. His reins lay on his saddle horn, for he had his big revolver in both hands, examining it, spinning the cylinder, seeing that it worked freely. And the set of his heavy jaw was not nice to see.

CHAPTER
TEN

A Rustler's Pledge

Don Luis Cabeza de Vaca sprawled gracefully in a rocking chair in the patio of his ranchería. There were some who said that he had no right to the proud Castilian name of Cabeza de Vaca; but there were more who said that he had been really born to it, and perhaps they were right. At any rate, he looked the Spanish aristocrat.

He was young, and tall, and slender. His skin, only slightly tanned, was very fair, and there was a noticeably brown tinge to his dark hair. He had a graceful little streak of black moustache across his upper lip, and when he smiled, his small, perfect white teeth showed in two even rows. His handsome, gentle eyes were so dark that one could hardly tell where pupil ended and iris began.

There was a very long, chocolate-colored cigarette in his long fingers; he sometimes puffed at it. His immense sombrero alone, with its weighty band of gold and silver, would have been fair trade for the best horse and saddle within many a day's ride; and the rest of his clothes matched, from his little braided jacket to the huge, flaring bell bottoms of his trousers, with their inserts of crimson silk flashing above his small feet. Possibly his spurs were worth more than his sombrero; they weighed very likely a pound apiece; they had rowels as big as saucers; and each had two little bells of pure silver to mingle their sweet tone with the jingle of the rowels when he walked.

Don Luis drew up one graceful knee — the trousers were skin-tight on knees and thighs — and clasped his long fingers around it. He gave his head a slight shake, and smiled sadly, apologetically.

"But Señor Fletcher, not possibly can I pay you fifteen thousand for those horses; I should then have to sell them at a loss."

He spoke almost perfect English; he spoke it rapidly and fluently, without pausing to grope for words.

Tex leaned back in his own chair; as ever, he looked tall and commanding, with his great, impressive beak of a nose. He took his cigar from his mouth and blew a puff of smoke into the air.

"Well, I'm sorry, Don Luis, but I'll have to take them on down to old Alarcón; he'll pay more. I tell you them aren't horses you'll sell in a bunch; it'll be one or two at a time to wealthy *hacendados* or army officers. That's it; some of the showy officers will pay anything for them; you'll be able to clean up a lot on them."

Don Luis looked very sad.

"Ah, how I should love to have the handling of those horses; never have I seen such fine horses. But, my friend, with times as they are in Mexico, I cannot get all those fine horses are worth. Perhaps two hundred dollars for one or two of the best; some to bring me not a hundred. Yes, perhaps Señor Alarcón will pay you more; you must take them there, sadly though I regret that we old friends cannot make the arrangement."

He looked brokenhearted. Tex leaned forward to stand up, his hands on the arms of his chair.

"Well, I'm sorry too, Don Luis."

He paused that way a moment, and suddenly sat back again, his face relaxing; the little game was over.

"All right, *compadre;* seeing as we're old friends, I'll let you have them for the twelve thousand. Anyway, I don't want to make the long drive down to Alarcón's place."

Don Luis did not have to relax; he had been relaxed all the time. He gave a graceful little shrug of assent, and smiled again, took another puff of his long cigarette.

"And now, Señor Fletcher, how do we arrange it for your men?"

Tex looked at the end of his cigar.

"I think some of 'em are getting suspicious. Tell you what we can do: I'll hunt my men up and get them to bunch the horses, saying I have to take 'em down to Alarcón's; and just as we're ready to start, you come strolling out and say that you've decided to come up to my figure and pay nine thousand. I'll play like I'd as soon go on down and try to get more, but you can offer me the money in cash, and I'll take it, right before the men. I'll split with them right there, so they can see how much I'm keeping."

"And now I give you — three thousand, is it not?"

"That's right."

Don Luis reached casually into his pocket and pulled out a big roll of American bills. Carelessly as a bank teller, he thumbed off a few and handed them to Tex. Tex got up and reached for his hat, which lay beside him on the bench. He was going to hold out his hand, but Don Luis was looking absently down at his boot toes.

"Well, thanks, Don. It'll be an hour or two before I can round up my men, I reckon, and get the horses ready to go. You can be on the lookout."

"*Hasta la vista.*"

Don Luis said it sleepily, but with a little smile on his face, and Tex turned and left the patio.

Don Luis sat there with eyes half closed; he had thrown away his cigarette. The little smile was still on his handsome lips — yes, Don Luis was a very handsome man. Presently he raised his head and called:

"Felipe!"

A thick-set, villianous looking Mexican slipped from a doorway and toward him respectfully. Don Luis was king here, and all others his subjects.

"*Sí, patrón.*"

Don Luis mused a moment; he lit a fresh cigarette. Then he nodded, smiled again; he spoke softly without troubling to look up:

"Tonight, Felipe, at Cinco Santos."

"*Sí, patrón.*"

The man hurried off. For a few moments, Don Luis sat relaxed in his chair, that little smile playing gently over his handsome face. Then, with a yawn, he flicked the ashes from his cigarette, stood up, and strolled garcefully through a doorway. He was sleepy; his interview with Tex had made him almost half an hour late for his siesta.

A pace or two from where he had been sitting, there was an open door, and toward it an old Mexican woman came shuffling across the patio. She had the air of one who had wanted to go there sooner but had not dared to disturb the patrón. Inside the room, there came a quick whisper:

"Let's go!"

Clint and Butch Tolleson ran on tiptoe across the room and dived clumsily through a window. Outside, they swept quick, nervous glances all around. There was nothing in sight but a mangy looking dog sleeping in the shadow of the adobe wall, flies thick around him.

"This way!" whispered Clint.

They went hurrying down beside the wall, trying to look unconcerned in case anybody saw them. At the corner, they slowed, and went strolling away. Clint drew a deep breath.

"Thank heavens for the siesta they take! It's all that saved us."

Butch took out a big red handkerchief and mopped his face quietly.

"Well, we *did* get out of there alive! That's the last time I'll let you talk me into getting into a place like that; if we'd been caught in there, we'd have had a dozen knives through our livers by this time."

Clint grinned a little; he seemed to have enjoyed it.

"Oh, I wouldn't say that. But we'd have had to do the fastest shooting of our lives. I'm glad I took to wearing two guns on the way down here; that smooth-looking young Don gives me the creeps — he's dangerous, if anybody ever was."

Out in the open, there was a bench under the shade of a thick chinaberry tree; they had reached it now, and they sat down.

"I wonder," mused Clint, "what that thing was — about Cinco Santos?"

"That — some private business of the Don's, I reckon; his range runs up to about there."

Clint shook his head; he looked slightly uneasy.

"That's where we're staying tonight, on our way home."

Butch was not interested.

"Clint, what I can't figure out is why you took the risk of spyin' on Tex and the Don. Me, I've always had a notion that he might have been holdin' out a little on us, an' likely so had some of the other boys. The point is, a feller that thinks anything that way had better keep it to himself an' say nothin'."

"Why?"

Butch looked at him oddly.

"I see you don't know Gulch City well yet. There's some mighty deep old mine shafts there, with mebbe a hundred feet or more of water at the bottom. I don't know anything for shore — only that it don't pay to make any remarks about Tex Fletcher; you might turn up missin' some mornin'."

Clint sat with his eyebrows close together, looking at the ground. Butch drew a great puff of smoke into his lungs; it came belching slowly out through his mouth as he went on broodingly:

"Tex has about the best snitcher system in the world. Everybody knows Yavapai Slim's the head of it, but they don't know who else is in it. Clint, yo're the only man in the world I'd talk this way to, an' feel sure that I'd be eatin' breakfast tomorrow mornin'."

Clint looked up suddenly, to burst out:

"Then why the devil do you fellows stay in the rustling game? Why — the whole thing's rotten, clean through to the core!"

Butch nodded. The corners of his heavy mouth hung a trifle.

"We know it. But if one of us quits him an' goes outside to try to live, we're danglin' from the end of a rope before you could say scat. Whether Tex has anything to do with that, we don't know, but it happens too regular to look like accident." He shook his grizzled head. "Anyways, I don't know as most of us is so crazy to give up rustlin', or even to quit Tex's bunch. Why, look at this week. Our cut out o' them horses will be about fifteen hundred dollars each. I couldn't make that much clear in two years o' workin' honest, an' I'd do well to make it in a year o' rustlin' without Tex."

Clint sat thinking, and presently he spoke:

"I'm coming to believe that Tex is about the cleverest man in all Arizona. He seems to have a good trick for everything comes up — and a dozen more up his sleeve, to spare."

Butch nodded bitterly.

101

"Sure! A dozen tricks to save Tex Fletcher's neck an' make money for him. When the rest of us is hung, Tex'll be retired an' livin' high in San Francisco or somewhere, smokin' big cigars. He'll fix it for a fake trial for himself, or a pardon or something, when he's ready to quit."

Clint looked up at him suddenly.

"But, what if you could get a pardon?"

Butch slowly shook his head.

"Fine chance I'd have, with my record! Oh, if I could —" He sat looking up into the air a moment, and the cigarette went out in his mouth. "Listen, Clint. I'd do dang near anything to get one; I got a few dollars cached that would start me a little brand. It ain't religion; it's — it's that little gal o' mine." He turned to Clint, his heavy face earnest. "Clint, Gulch City's no place to raise a gal, an' make anything out o' her. An' even if I do keep her decent, when she goes out in the world an' some one asks her what her dad was —"

Butch shook his graying head again, and it sank slowly on his chest. Presently Clint spoke deliberately:

"Old-timer, I think I can talk to you — tell you something I wouldn't dare say to anybody else. What would you think if I told you that I was figuring on trying to take Tex's gang away from him — or at least split it and take all I can of it?"

Butch jerked his head up in astonishment.

"I'd say you was crazy — an' that the bottom o' one o' them old mine shafts is a mighty unpleasant place to end up."

"And if I'd say, just between the two of us, that Tex isn't the only one who can figure out ways to get pardons? Not saying," he added hastily, "that I know it would work."

He saw a slight change in Butch's face.

"No, no, Butch — you got me wrong! I'm not in with the rangers, or with anybody else; they're a lot more anxious to get me than you — or maybe even Tex. And they want me dead; they'll shoot on sight when they see me."

Butch was staring at the ground now, his forehead wrinkled deeply.

"Think — think you can work it, Clint? Any of it?"

"I don't know. I'm honest with you, Butch; I'm taking some long chances, and I know it. If Tex doesn't get me, likely the rangers will; and if not, I'll likely end up with the rope around my neck."

"An' that," muttered Butch to himself, "was why you wanted the straight about Tex crookin' us — to have a story to stir the crowd up against him."

"Yes. It's risky business; I hate to ask you to throw in with me."

Still Butch sat looking at the ground; he was not yet aware that his cigarette had gone out long before. They sat there in silence. Clint's heart was sinking rapidly. If even Butch Tolleson would not go over to him, who would?

They heard a shout, and saw Yavapai Slim waving to them from down near the corrals; that farce of starting to drive the horses away was about to begin. The two stood up slowly. Clint raised a dejected face to find

Butch's faded eyes fixed on his. It struck Clint as odd that this man, a rustler and worse, had about the most honest and straightforward eyes he had ever seen.

Then Butch spoke.

"Clint, I'm stickin' with you!"

There was not even a handshake, but Clint knew that this big rustler was one man upon whom he could depend no matter what happened; he remembered Butch starting stolidly back to the little pass where his friends were, to be killed with them.

"Thanks, Butch."

Side by side, they started walking toward the corrals, where Tex and Yavapai Slim waited impatiently.

CHAPTER
ELEVEN

Cinco Santos

For the twentieth time, Clint got up from his hard, homemade chair and tiptoed to the little window. He yawned, and peered out. He rubbed his chin sleepily; for the life of him, he could not be sure whether it was getting light in the east or not.

He stole back and sat down again, his head resting against the adobe wall a foot from the crack he had left open between door and jamb. Across the corridor was the door of Tex's room. Yavapai had the next one on Tex's side; there had been only three rooms, and Clint and Butch had offered to share one of them. All night they had kept this vigil, in turn; now, Clint could hear the heavy breathing of the sleeping Butch. And that was all Clint could hear — that and the distant yapping of a cur.

Suddenly Clint blinked. He had been dozing, he did not know how long, and something had woke him, he did not know what. He listened intently in the darkness; his ears seemed actually to hurt from straining them so much that night.

There it came again; the crowing of a cock somewhere out among the shabby huddle of flat-roofed adobes that made Cinco Santos. Once more Clint hurried to the window. This time there was no mistake about it; the stars on the eastern horizon were paler than before — but for that, it seemed darker than ever.

He stole across to the homemade wooden bed, and shook Butch's shoulder. Without a sound, with hardly a noticeable change in breathing, Butch sat up, wide awake; a man in his business soon learns to come awake with all his wits about him, or he does not live long.

"Huh? Oh — my turn."

"Daylight, Butch. Say, I've been thinking that we might saddle all our horses and bring them down here; then we can get Tex to make an early start. Wish he'd listened to me last night, and kept on after supper. But of course I could only say I felt uneasy, and not tell him why."

Butch swung his big legs over the side of the bed and stretched.

"Wish you'd tell me! It's morning now, and nothing happened, only that both of us lost half our night's sleep. Why, we prowled all over last night, an' didn't even see that Felipe feller; he wasn't in town at all."

"That's exactly it. If I'd seen him here last night, looking like he was on business, I wouldn't be worried."

Butch was pulling on his boots; but for them, he had slept fully dressed. He grunted disgustedly.

"Clint, I don't sabe you. I still claim that if Tex got a knife stuck in him here it would be the best thing could happen for yore plans."

Clint spoke earnestly:

"It would ruin 'em! I'd have to give up and quit the country. No, I won't tell you why; there's some things you wouldn't like — at first. Come on. Let's slip out the window so nobody can notice us."

"Oh, all right! But this shore is a lot o' fuss, an' all because you didn't like that sorter little smile on Don Luis's face, an' didn't see Felipe here last night!"

Clint went first, and Butch followed slowly, willing to humor him in this nonsense. The *cantina* above which they had found rooms stood all to itself near the middle of the village, a wide space of deep sand around it. It was the only two-story building in the village; they dropped to the flat roof of a shed and from there to the ground.

"No, no — not the main street! Quiet, now!"

There was light enough down there that Clint could see Butch's patient shrug. They had their spurs off, and they slipped down the middle of a narrow street with hardly a sound, two gray shadows. They almost fell over a burro sleeping in the deep, sandy dust. They turned a corner and came to the corral; it was an adobe wall; there was no timber in that barren little valley, and no money to buy timber. Butch glanced over the wall.

"Well, the horses are all right. Can you catch yours without ropin' him?"

"Listen!"

Clint had thrown his hand up warningly. From out on the rutted, narrow road came the clatter of many hoofs moving in a swift trot, the jingle of metal.

"*Soldados!*" grunted Butch in surprise.

"Down! Hide!"

They slipped quickly over the wall and crouched behind it peering over with hats off. The clatter swept close, and with jingle of big spurs the first horsemen rode past, gray and shadowy against the sky. More and more following; Clint made a vague estimate of thirty-five, but there might have been more. Then they were gone, riding swiftly toward the centre of the village, and the fine dust of their passing was settling over Clint and Butch.

"*Soldados*," repeated Butch.

They heard a cautious squeak of a hinge, and they turned to see a sombreroed figure running quickly toward a horse in the corral. The horse dodged off, and in following him the man almost bumped into Clint. Clint had his hand on his gun butt.

"*Zuien es?*" he demanded quickly.

The man jerked back a step, with a gasp, and his hands went up on both sides of the big hat.

"Don't shoot me!" he begged in quick peón dialect. "I am a friend — a good friend of Pedro Durán! All in this poor pueblo are the good friends of Pedro Durán!"

Clint gulped — here was a nice mess! Durán was not the most powerful bandit in Sonora, but he did not come far from being the most dreaded, he and his murderous crew.

"Well, I'm no friend of his. And if you are, why be so anxious to get your horse out of here before they see it?"

The man was trembling.

"But, Señor, Pedro Durán is the *muy fino* —"

"The devil he is! Quick, Butch — the horses."

But long before they had the four saddled, the Mexican was disappearing toward the open country. He was riding furiously bareback; he had not even waited for his saddle.

"Hurry up, Butch! You lead this one."

Butch asked no questions; he swung up and trotted fast but quietly after Clint, whose back was disappearing in the darkness. Straight out of the village Clint led him, and then around it. Down in the main arroyo was a withered looking clump of mesquite which they had passed the evening before as they came to Cinco Santos. Clint, who had a good head for strange country, found it quickly. He rode straight into it, leading the other horse.

"Tie 'em here. Let's hurry back."

"Back!"

There was light enough now to see that Butch was staring at him in disbelief; he had not yet dismounted, and did not seem to be going to.

"Hurry, man! We got to get Tex out of that place, get him home safe!"

"'T' blazes with Tex — the skunk! Come on; let's light out. Would he bother to save our necks?"

Clint did not even stop to answer. He had the two horses tied now, and he was running back toward the village. He was feeling to make sure that both his guns were loose in the holsters. A hundred yards, and he heard a shout behind him:

"Wait for me, Clint!"

Furious at the noise, he stopped and turned. Butch came running up heavily, panting already.

"You —" he puffed, "You blame fool! Clint, yo're the biggest — Aw — gr-r-r — let's go!"

"Slower, Butch! If you get too much out of wind you can't shoot straight."

They could see the *cantina* building looming up taller than the rest; it was easy to find their way to it, in the increasing light. Presently they were crouched at the rear of a house across the street. Clint jerked off his hat and peered cautiously through the window above him. Through a window in the front wall of the room, he could see men hurrying back and forth in the main street outside; he could also see the outline of heads at the window, within, peering out.

He nudged Butch, and they sidled toward the door. He tried it cautiously; it was barred on the inside. He whispered:

"Break it in!"

Butch gave him a furious glare, and backed off a pace or two. He came lunging sidewise, and his huge shoulder smashed into the door like a battering ram. It would have taken only a shove; the whole door collapsed from its hinges, and Butch went sprawling on the floor. But Clint was inside the room before anybody could turn; he had both guns sweeping before him.

"Throw 'em up!"

A woman's voice babbled incoherently:

"Oh, señor! We are the good friends of Señor Pedro! Do not kill us, Señor — !"

"Shut up! Back against that wall, quick."

There was a man and a woman and four children. Now that their first surprise was over, they showed the stolid fatalism of their race; if they were to be killed as they stood lined up there, they were to be killed, and complaining about it would not help. Man and woman stood with their backs to the bare adobe of their little room, and even the children, at a word from their mother, got into line.

Suddenly Clint realized what this must mean to these poor people — to be lined up with their backs against an adobe wall. Poor devils! He whispered quickly, kindly:

"I won't hurt you; we don't belong to that gang."

The man spoke, with that gentle, sad politeness of the peón:

"We thank you, Señor, for not killing us."

A sudden, dull shot across the street; it was in the *cantina* building. Clint whirled. A burst of shots, all in some room.

Holding his breath, Clint kept his eyes glued on the window that he knew belonged to Tex's room. The daylight had grown strong enough now that he could see one pane broken from the small window; it had been intact the night before. And not another sound coming. Clint spoke without turning.

"Butch, I — I reckon they got him."

He heard a heavy grunt of hearty approval from behind, where Butch was guarding the rear door. Nothing could have suited Butch better.

"There he is! There he is!"

Clint dashed his own window open and brought his face up into sight. He was beckoning hastily with his gun barrel. A burst of rifle fire from the street. Clint could see little pieces of the adobe wall opposite come spinning down to the ground. It amazed him that some of them were so far from the window, well though he knew what bad shots most Mexicans were, and how badly they took care of their guns — their rifles would be so eaten with rust in the barrels that nobody knew where they would shoot.

Both Tex's guns were spitting furiously. Men were dropping in the street outside. They were breaking, running; they were not accustomed to such deadly fire as this. There came a crash against the outside door as somebody tried to get in. From back in the room, Butch shot quickly, and Clint heard a sliding sound against the door, a groan.

Clint whirled. He darted a hand into his pocket and jerked out a ten-dollar bill, thrust it into the hand of the Mexican — it would doubly pay him for any damage done to his poor house; it would almost have bought the place and all in it.

"Get out all of you! Quick! Come on, Butch!"

He leaped to the front door, dragged it open. Butch behind him, he sprang into the street, both his guns crashing.

"Tex! Tex! This way!"

Clint had not been seen; the bandits had been watching Tex's room, watching the *cantina*. They whirled; they were caught between two bands of *Americano* devils who killed a man with every bullet. There came the shuffling thud of rawhide *huaraches* as they ran for shelter; one or two of them even dropped their rifles as they ran.

"Tex!"

Tex's long legs came flashing through the window. For an instant he hung from the window sill by his hands, and then he dropped. He stumbled and fell, but as he came up he had both guns in his hands again, and both were barking. And here came Yavapai Slim.

"Hurry, Tex!"

Little need for that! Tex was crossing the street in great strides; to make better speed, he was letting Clint and Butch do the shooting. Yavapai was not far behind; he had not even redrawn his guns after his leap down.

The crackle of rifles was coming again, from doors and windows, from around corners — as yet, it was but desultory; the bandits had not yet all found safe places, nor had time to gather their wits.

Tex's foot slipped in a puddle of blood outside the door, and he sprawled in head first. But Clint sprang and caught him and helped him back to his feet; he had just darted in. An instant, and Yavapai followed.

"This way!"

Clint plunged through the rear door, the other three after him. There was only one man out there, a sallow, long-moustached man on a fine buckskin horse. His mouth was half open; he had not expected any shooting back in this alley, with an adobe house between it and the *cantina*. But he already had his pearl-handled revolver drawn, and it was whipping up. Clint fired. A little black spot appeared on the horseman's forehead, and he sagged and slid queerly to the ground. A gasp from Tex:

"Pedro Durán himself! You got him!"

"Let's go!"

The four had run a block before they were discovered. They stopped at a corner and sent back a fusillade that halted the rush, and then they were running again. Tex spoke quickly, in his most gently assuring tones:

"It's only me they want. You fellers hold 'em while I get —"

Clint darted his eyes across to him, and his teeth showed.

"Come on, you — !"

He called him a name that he had seldom called any man, and his gun muzzle swung sidewise meaningly. The four ran on, paused at the last house to send back another volley, and then sprinted wildly across the open toward that little clump of mesquite.

Clint paused to glance back before he dived into the little grove. Consternation seemed to have stricken the men back there. Some of them were running after him, futilely firing their rifles as they ran, seemingly without aim. An occasional bullet struck fairly close, but he could not even guess where most of them went. And other men were running back toward the village; nobody seemed to know what to do. So word was breaking out that their leader was dead.

Clint turned and ran into the mesquite grove. He saw a curious sight: Yavapai had already disappeared, and Butch was in his saddle, a grim look on his heavy face and his gun in his hand. Tex's big black lay stretched on the ground; a stray bullet had caught him squarely in the back of the neck and broken his spine.

And Tex? He stood holding Reddy's reins, and glaring at Butch. He would have left Clint, who had barely saved his life, there afoot to the slender mercies of the bandits. Out of the corner of his eye, Tex saw Clint come running. He turned; he spoke with a frankness that made Clint almost believe him:

"I was just leading him out to you. Can we ride him double?"

"Got to. Climb on — no, you first!"

He did not want Tex at his back. In a moment they were loping off. It was amazing to see how lightly Reddy could travel even with that double load; one could see why Clint thought so much of him. Tex spoke over his shoulder, spoke with a sincere feeling that almost made a catch in his voice:

"Clint, I'll never forget this for you. But for you I'd have been dead by now."

Clint answered very, very softly:

"I know you won't forget it, Tex — but I know you'd have done the same for me."

"I sure would!"

Butch, riding alongside, heard the words. He turned, his face suddenly purple and his yellow teeth bare. Clint threw him a grin, but it was not at all pleasant to see, and Butch was cautious enough to choke off whatever words he had been about to say.

"Here they come!"

There were only fifteen or so men following them; what the rest were doing in their confusion, they could not guess. During it all, Tex had been cool, with his wits working fast. He spoke:

"Sure badly mounted — but they can catch us riding double."

Badly mounted they were, on all sorts of non-descript, ill-fed horses. All but one; in the lead was the fine buckskin which had been Pedro Durán's, coming with the swift, smooth stride of a racer. On his back was a young man dressed in what might have been a shabby but gaudy version of Don Luis's splendour — or Don Luis's cast-off clothes.

"It's Ramón Costello," grunted Butch.

Of course Clint knew the name well; Ramón was Pedro's second in command — now, he would be the leader, if he could hold the bandits together. A young cutthroat if ever there was one.

"Slow him, Tex! Slow him!"

Tex had been taking the ridgeside a little too fast for the weight Reddy was carrying. Glancing ahead, Clint saw Yavapai waiting for them on top — and incidentally perhaps letting his horse get its wind, so that he could run away from them again if things again looked too hot to suit him.

They leveled out to the summit, and Clint looked back again. Ramón was far in the lead now, but Clint could see that even the slowest was more than holding his own with the three they pursued. In less than half an hour, they would have the double-ridden horse surrounded. Clint spoke suddenly:

"Slow up! I'm getting off!"

Never had Tex obeyed an order so joyfully or so promptly. Reddy slid his hoofs, and before he had stopped Clint was on the ground, running back. He heard the quick rattle of hoofs as Tex put the sorrel down the slope at a dead run; now, the weight halved, Reddy could strike his long stride, and not even that fast buckskin could catch him.

Squarely on top of the ridge, Clint threw himself behind a cactus; he had doubled his legs up close, so that they could not be easily seen by any one facing him. He had his gun cocked in his hand.

He heard the thud of hoofs coming closer, the laboured breathing of a horse approaching swiftly. Sooner than he had expected, a sombrero appeared over the curve of the ridge, and beneath it a pockmarked, evil face.

Ramón Costello had the eyes of a Mexican eagle, and he was an old hand at such games as this. Before his shoulders were well in sight, he had seen Clint in spite of his concealment; probably he had picked that cactus instantly as the only possible hiding place.

They fired almost together. The Mexican threw up both hands, his revolver flying high in the air, and rolled backwards out of the saddle. Sand spurted up and struck Clint's face, drawing blood; the match had almost been a tie, with both losing.

The buckskin came plunging up, hardly knowing what had happened. Before he could collect himself enough to whirl off, Clint had leaped and seized the cheek of the bridle. Now the horse turned quickly, almost raising Clint from his feet; he snorted wildly, and his eyes protruded. A twist, a boot shooting into the air, and Clint was in the saddle.

He turned the horse. From its back, he could see more heads and shoulders appearing up the slope. There were five cartridges left in the gun, and he fired them deliberately, aiming as well as he could from the rearing, plunging buckskin. All the heads disappeared. He did not know, but he hoped that he had hit three — he was fairly sure of two.

No sound down there; all the bandits had stopped. Well, he wouldn't let them hear him running; if they thought he was still there, they would either pause to hold a council or swing far around to get behind him. In a trot, he went down the ridge, swerving quickly from side to side to keep to the softest ground. Only when he was almost to the bottom did he loose his reins and strike a run. On the next ridge, half a mile off, three men were sitting their horses waiting for him. Of course that was perfectly safe; they would have plenty of time to get away, well mounted as they were, after they saw the pursuers come into sight on their panting, rag-tag mounts.

He was within fifteen feet of them when he heard an exclamation from Yavapai:

"There they are!"

He looked around. A little group of horsemen had stopped on the summit of that first ridge, two hundred yards to one side of where Clint had been. Clint took off his wide hat and waved it tauntingly at them. They did not stir; they knew it was no use.

"Let's change horses, Tex."

They slipped out of their saddles. Tex came forward with his hand out.

"Clint, I'll never forget this morning for you, as long as I live!"

It seemed that Clint misunderstood the friendly gesture. He dropped the buckskin's reins into Tex's hand, without even touching it with his fingers. He turned toward Reddy.

"I know you won't, Tex."

He spoke with a solemn gravity even greater than Tex's own. Mounting, he caught Butch's eye, and he saw the little sarcastic twinkle there; his lips tightened in answer. He picked up Reddy's reins, and spoke softly:

"Well, Tex, ready to go?"

Tex nodded, smiled at him benignantly, and turned off, beside Yavapai Slim. Clint and Butch dropped behind, side by side. Clint shook his head.

"There's one man I don't understand! From the things he tried to do, you'd think he was scared stiff back there. He wasn't; he wasn't scared at all. I'm not sure he didn't enjoy all of it."

"No." Butch spoke slowly. "Tex never gets scared; he has nerve enough for six men. But I know him better than you do; the thing is that, with him, nobody counts only Tex. He thinks it's only fair enough that you, or me, or any other man he has, should get killed to save him a little inconvenience — or to make him fifty dollars. Clint, the butt of a cigar he's smokin' means more to Tex Fletcher than the life of any one of us."

Again Clint shook his head. He was farther than ever from understanding Tex; he could not understand how any man living could be so totally devoid of human feeling, of the most rudimentary feeling of friendship or loyalty — surely even a snake crawling the desert must have some sense of fellowship with his kind, some sort of vague, instinctive principle in his dealings.

No, Clint never could understand; his own mind belonged to the opposite pole. Tex Fletcher was a genius in his way, but from his clever, crafty brain something had been left out at his birth — the thing that makes one human.

Butch spoke slowly, hesitantly:

"Clint, do you remember what you called him back there?"

Clint flushed.

"I — I reckon I lost my temper."

"An' you refusin' to shake hands with him — he knew it wasn't a misonderstandin'. Clint, you should have seen the look in his eye when you turned yore back to him; a mad dog couldn't have looked at yore back that way. Clint, he has you marked; if I was you, I wouldn't go back to the Silvermines."

Clint spoke quietly:

"I'm going back."

Butch sighed; his heavy face looked sad.

"I know it."

CHAPTER
TWELVE

The Brown-eyed Woman

With their early and fast start, they crossed the line into Arizona in the early afternoon. Here, Clint knew where he was. He rode up to Tex.

"Tex, I think I'll turn off to Wacker if you don't mind. I want to write a letter, and mail it."

"A letter?" Tex looked at him suspiciously.

Clint had the thing planned. Purposely, he spoke as though slightly confused.

"I — I haven't written her in a long time."

Tex laughed suddenly, patronizingly.

"I might have known! You young fellers! Sure — go ahead. Want us to wait for you somewhere?"

This time Clint's slight confusion was genuine; he had not counted on this courtesy. But he was quick witted.

"Why, I thought I might maybe go to see her. I have a nice little bunch of money in my pocket."

Tex did not seem to like this so well, but he could find no reasonable objection.

"Why, sure, Clint! But get back to Gulch City as soon as you can — I may need you. How long do you expect to be gone?"

"Oh, two, three days."

"That's fine! Well, good luck to you. They all like the jingle of money."

Clint turned off. It was out of his way, and hard on his horse, but he circled a little butte and climbed it from the back. Lying on the summit, he watched the three figures disappearing slowly toward the north; not until they had become a faint, distant dot did he return to his horse and start down.

It was not far to the little hamlet of Wacker; he reached it just before sunset. From far off, he saw that the place had an odd, unaccustomed look; closer, he knew that it was because some of the few houses were missing. Riding into the shabby street, he stared around in astonishment. A fire had swept the little town, but in some strange manner it had picked out scattered houses; little curls of white smoke still came up from some of the ruins.

He had been hoping that nobody there would recognize him; if they did, he hardly expected that the few Americans living there would give him any trouble, and he knew that the Mexicans would not. Those he met on the street seemed not even to notice him as he rode by; their faces looked stupid, blank, as though stricken by calamity.

Astonished, he looked at the broken windows. He rode to the little adobe building that housed the only store in the place, in which was also the post office, as the crudely-painted sign announced. He tied Reddy's reins to the hitching rack and went in.

There was a woman behind the counter, a woman hardly yet to be called middle-aged. She had a dull, apathetic look, and her face was white and drawn, even to the lips. She looked at him dully, without speaking; he could see a terrible pain in her eyes.

"Ma'am, I'd like to buy some paper and an envelope — and one stamp."

Mechanically, with slow hands, she gave them to him. He laid a five-dollar bill on the counter. She took it and put it into the cash drawer, closed the drawer. She turned off, pausing as though thinking. Then, slowly, she went back again, opened the drawer, counted out his change and laid it before him. All without a word.

Clint looked at her curiously. There was a small table back in a corner, and a shaky chair near it. Clint went back and sat down at the table. He took the stub of pencil from his chaps pocket, and wrote carefully in Spanish:

My good friend Señor Enrique Judson:
 Once you did a very great favour to a man who is my brother, although you know him by another name than that which I now use. It is for that thing that I cannot keep my part of the money paid for those horses stolen from you. I send it to you now, and I beg, Señor, that you will find it in your heart to think well of one who is nothing but a horse

123

thief and a stealer of cattle, as he thinks well of you.

Your friend,

Fulano de Tal.

He inspected the letter carefully, erased one capital letter and rewrote it. As in the note he had written before, the thin, sweeping lines looked purely Spanish, and some of the letters were formed differently from the usual English way.

He glanced over his shoulder. The young woman was standing behind the counter, staring blindly out through the window, two panes of which were broken — he noticed that the glass still lay on the floor underneath. She was an unusually tall woman, with a fine, slender figure, but something in the droop of her square shoulders showed the last depth of hopelessness.

Quietly, Clint slipped some bills from his pocket; there were few of them, but they were of very large denominations. Fifteen hundred dollars. He flattened the bills carefully, folded them in the letter, and placed them in the envelope. He licked the flap, and pressed it flat with his hand; one would hardly notice an unusual bulge.

Old Henry Judson — wouldn't he be surprised! And wouldn't he be puzzled as to who that Mexican was for whom he had done that supposed favour. But Clint well knew that old Henry, harsh though he usually appeared, seemed to have spent most of his long life doing good turns for those who were in trouble — Clint himself was an example; old Henry had picked

124

him up, a poor orphan boy, and perhaps but for Henry's harsh training Clint would not have been what he was; he had striven grimly to hammer his own high principles into young Clint's head, striven all the harder because he had seen that he had good material to work on. Yes, there would be more than one Mexican ready to lay down his life for little Henry Judson.

Clint stood up, the letter in his hand. He was about to ask the woman where the letter drop was, but something about her back kept him from speaking. He went to the corner that was fenced off as a post office. He found a little slit sawn in the counter under the window, and dropped the letter in. He turned politely, and raised his hat.

"Thanks, ma'am."

Her eyes came slowly toward him, but she did not speak. Clint was already in the doorway. His plan, the sensible thing, had been to spend as little time as possible in the town, to be unobtrusive, to speak only when he had to. But suddenly he went striding to her across the floor; he could not help it. He spoke quickly, gently:

"What is it, ma'am — tell me?"

Her hands raised almost to her face, flopped weakly, limply back to her sides. A little sobbing cry came from her lips.

"Oh, God!"

"What happened, ma'am — tell me?"

Clint had a hand gently on her shoulder; there was a lump in his throat, choking him. Never had he seen such blind, silent grief. Now she turned her large

125

brown eyes on him again, and the sympathy in his brought a film to her own. She spoke, slowly, as though numb:

"They came — last night. They burned the town. They killed — I don't know how many. They killed my husband."

"Good God! Who?"

"Pedro Durán. Ramón Costello — all of them. They robbed — they killed. They killed my husband."

There was a moment of silence. They stood facing each other. Clint's arms too were limp at his sides; his hand had fallen from her shoulder. He could not believe it, at first. And then he spoke softly, as though praying:

"Thank God!"

Again her eyes turned to him slowly; there was a dull question in them.

"Ma'am, I mean I killed both of them this morning — Pedro and Ramón. And some of their men. If I'd known, I — I might not have shot them through the head, made it so easy for them."

Her great brown eyes were fixed on his face, and for the first time some of the dullness went out of them. Presently she spoke:

"You — are Clint Yancey?"

"Yes, ma'am."

"The outlaw?"

"Yes, ma'am."

She turned slowly, mechanically — she was almost as tall as Clint himself.

"Come to the kitchen. I'll get you supper."

She walked like an automaton, or a sleepwalker. Clint followed her; it was not so much that he wanted to eat as that he hoped he could do something to help her. That lump in his throat was almost strangling him, and he blinked a time or two.

She picked up the stove-lid lifter fumblingly, and stood as though not knowing what should be done next. Clint spoke gently:

"Have you eaten anything all day?"

"No. I wasn't hungry."

He took the lifter from her unresisting fingers.

"Here, you go sit down — I'll get us something to eat. I'll make you some coffee."

He led her into the little store again, and made her sit in the old rocking chair. No one would ever have thought that the big, hard-faced Clint Yancey could be so gentle. The kindness in his touch seemed to break her despair. She reached up quickly and barely touched his hand, and then her own hand fell palm upward in her lap. But Clint noticed two tears creeping slowly down her cheeks, saw her eyelids tremble. Again he laid a kindly hand on her shoulder.

"There — cry. It's the best thing you can do."

A silent sob; her firm shoulder trembled under his hand, and her head sank slowly. Clint tiptoed quietly back to the kitchen. A cry, hot coffee, food — nothing could help much, but these were the things that could help a little. Poor young woman!

It was beginning to grow dark in there. Clint lighted the coal-oil lamp and set it on a shelf. He built a fire quickly, and while the stove was getting warm he

127

looked around. He found everything he might need except bread, and that he did not trouble to hunt for; like all cowboys, he had little liking for bakers' bread. He rolled up his shirt sleeves, scrubbed his hands, and set about making a pan of biscuits; he had put water on for coffee when he made the fire.

He shook his head a little, sadly, thinking. So that was why Felipe had been so long getting the bandits to Cinco Santos; they had been up here on this raid. They had murdered this woman's husband — and he had killed both the leaders, and others with them. He wished that he had it to do over, that he could be back there again — he would have left many more of them lying in the dust. They were a foul blot on the face of the earth, on the face of Mexico; this was not the first wife they had made a widow.

That family he had lined up against their adobe wall. They had stood there patiently, waiting to be shot down; they knew Pedro Durán and his ruffians. Poor devils! Clint liked Mexicans, even the peon, as do all who know them and speak their language. Gentle, trusting, polite, with that sad, wistful fatalism in their soft brown eyes.

And why should they not be sad and wistful! Clint knew something of their history: for long ages the ruling Aztecs had brought their ancestors in thousands to their teocalis, that their fiendlike priests, whose tangled hair was clotted with dried human blood, might cut their quivering hearts out with their flint knives — sacrifice to their foul gods. Then had come the Spaniards, with crosses on their breasts and with less

128

mercy in their hearts than the savage priests themselves. In the name of God and Gold they had slain thousands, enslaved the living. And now the bandits, most of whom called themselves revolutionaries and *patriotas*.

Clint opened the stove and pushed in fresh wood. His thoughts changed. Don Luis. Yes, Don Luis had sent Felipe for those bandits, perhaps had even dared to send orders to them; hard to guess what his connection with them was, but connection of some sort there was.

Why had he done it? Not to get back the money he had paid; the main purpose seemed to be to kill Tex Fletcher, and that would end the profitable business between them. No, it was something personal. Clint had reasoned all this out before, and always he came to the same conclusion: Tex had practiced some of his treachery on Don Luis, not thinking it would become known. And the handsome, languid young Don was a man who would never forget.

Clint nodded. Tex had a mortal enemy in Don Luis Cabeza de Vaca. And any man who was such an enemy to Tex should prove useful to him. That was why he had left Tex and the others; he was going back to see Don Luis, to talk to him. And if he was going to split Tex's gang, to take part of the men, he must lead them in rustling cattle; why else should they follow him? To drive rustled stock blindly across the border would be foolish; he would need to have arrangements made down there. Again, Don Luis. He would leave here as soon as he had eaten; he would ride by night only, and would steal up on the *ranchería* in darkness. He would be safe. Curiosity would make the Don willing to hear what he had to say, and once he had told his motives he would be doubly safe; the long arm of Don Luis would protect him while he was in Sonora.

He pulled the biscuits out of the stove and glanced at them approvingly. They were a light, golden brown. He put the pan in the warming oven and quickly set the table. He had a cowboy's speed in cooking, and during the short time he had been in the kitchen he had prepared a surprisingly dainty meal — never before had he tried so hard to make one appetizing. Surely she would eat some of that!

He went softly into the store. There were large windows there, and so there was much more light than in the kitchen — almost as much as in the twilight outside. He could see her face pretty plainly. She was still sitting in the same chair, but she had stopped crying now; she was looking blankly toward the open door, her face sad, but with some of that awful horror gone.

In her preoccupation, she had not heard him come in. He stood looking at her. She was much younger than he had first taken her to be — probably no older than himself; her wild, silent grief had made her look old. And suddenly, with a shock, he realized another thing; she had no trace of prettiness, but she was the most beautiful woman he had ever seen. Tall, splendidly-proportioned figure, and those great, melancholy brown eyes.

He spoke quietly.

"Ma'am, supper is ready."

130

She stood up immediately. It struck him that another of her size would have looked cow-like, while she was graceful, statuesque.

"Thank you, Clint."

She said it simply, without trying to smile; she would not be the kind to smile much at any time; her face was the too serious, thoughtful type. That, to Clint, was in her favor; he himself was slow to smile, slower to laugh.

He turned back to the kitchen. Suddenly he stopped. From somewhere down the road came the rapid drumming of many hoofs. He ran for the door, to reach his horse, but stopped again; he would let them pass.

Closer came the riders. The first swept into view, and Clint started wildly, his eyes sweeping the room as though vainly seeking an escape. Captain Donley of the Rangers! All of them! Why had he not thought; anybody should have known that they would all come dashing here to investigate that bloody raid.

Clint's heart was pounding until it seemed to choke him; he was holding his breath; he had one arm half raised and did not know it, could not let it drop.

All of them — the whole ranger force was tearing by on panting, sweating horses, their hard faces ahead. Here came Sergeant Wilson last. And suddenly Wilson turned his face, slid his horse to its haunches. His heavy shout came:

"Stop! Here's Clint Yancey's sorrel!"

Shouts; the rest of the horses sliding on their heels, whirling back. Guns jerking out of holsters. The commanding voice of Captain Donley:

"Surround the house, men! We've got him at last!"

Mutely, with white, drawn face, Clint stood there. He made no move to draw his guns, and it was too late to run; already, they had the house completely surrounded. And beside him stood that tall woman, a new horror in her great brown eyes, and her face suddenly pallid. The night before, she had stood over the riddled, bleeding body of her husband. Tonight, it would be the body of this tall, gentle young stranger who had come with mercy in her grief. A faint groan of anguish shook the woman as she stood there.

CHAPTER
THIRTEEN

Mona's Trick

The woman was first to move. She turned and ran to the kitchen, and the square of yellow light in the doorway disappeared; she had blown out the lamp. Then she was coming walking back in the gloom, to stand beside Clint again. The commanding voice of Captain Donley came:

"Yancey, come out!"

Clint noticed that he did not say, "Come out and give up." There could be no giving up; they wanted to riddle him with bullets as soon as he appeared in the doorway. Clint, who could see some of them through the windows, noticed also that they had not sought cover; they were sitting their horses in a circle around the little store, the most distance hardly fifty feet off, guns poised in their right hands. And he in there where they could not see him; he could empty three or four saddles before they could seek shelter. And they knew it.

Perhaps never before had the grim, desperate nerve of the Arizona Rangers been so exemplified; they did not fear Clint, although they well knew that he was one of the deadliest and fastest shots in Arizona — perhaps the fastest. Had it been the devil himself whom they had cornered there, they would probably have sat there just the same and ordered him to come out.

Oddly, a surge of pride swept over Clint pride in those men out there. He had been one of that band, and he had been accounted one of the best of them. But he did not answer; he feared that they might not know that there was a woman in there, that his voice might bring a shower of bullets through the windows. Instead, he whispered quickly:

"Run to another room; get down behind a wall!"

He saw the white blur of her face turn to him in the increasing darkness. She whispered:

"Are you — going out?"

Out! To be riddled before he had got a yard from the door!

"No."

"Are you — going to shoot?"

"No."

Of course not; why kill any of his old companions who thought they were in the right, thought him a thief, a traitor, everything contemptible? Anyhow, it would do no good; there were too many for him — thirteen of them, the whole force.

What was he to do? He did not know; he just stood there dumbly. If he did not answer, some of them would come in pretty soon — oh, yes, they were quite capable of that! And, standing in the doorway, they would begin shooting without stopping to see what he was doing. Nothing to do — nothing — but stand there

134

till they did come in. Then it would be soon over, and the honor of the force would be partly restored.

The rangers waited outside, guns ready. And with startling suddenness a trembling, vibrant whisper came from the woman beside him:

"Hold them out a while! Talk to them!"

Now she turned and ran down the store — she seemed fleet as a deer. She disappeared through a doorway, closing the door quickly after her. Clint judged that it must be a bedroom. Again came Captain Donley's military voice; there was finality in it:

"Yancey, are you coming out?"

Clint pressed back into a corner of the adobe wall, where he would be out of range of their guns as much as possible. He spoke to them:

"Give me a little time, Captain; let me think it over!"

He heard a grim voice that he recognized as Wendell's; it sounded almost casual as he spoke to another ranger:

"That fellow has nerve; hear how cool he talks."

Captain Donley answered:

"No use in thinking long, Yancey; we've got you."

Then the heavy bass of Sergeant Wilson:

"Yancey, is Mrs. Fernel in there?"

So that was her name; he had not even known it.

"Yes."

"Send her out, if you're man enough."

That stung! Clint's face flamed red. He called:

"Mrs. Fernel."

But she was already opening that door back there. She came running across the floor, and there was a dull, swishing sound that he had not heard when she ran back first. He peered, and he saw that she was in long, voluminous riding skirts. Above that was what seemed to be a man's blue cotton shirt, and she had a small Stetson hat on her head. He spoke quickly, reaching out to press her hand:

"Good bye. Take my horse — keep him; he's a good one."

She started to speak, but her voice caught. This young man spoke so casually, so quietly, as he gave her his horse before he was shot down. Her fingers closed hard on his, comfortingly, for an instant. Then she was hurrying to a window. She stood in the window, in plain sight. Donley gave his hat a quick tip, apologetically; he knew her fairly well, most of the rangers did, but it had happened that Clint had never been stationed in that part of Arizona.

"Sorry about this, Mrs. Fernel; we'll see to it that you are paid for any damage we do to your place. You can go to some neighbor's until it's over; you'd better arrange to stay there all night."

She answered; her voice was trembling:

"I — have a friend out in the country about two miles. I'll go to her place. This man says I can keep his horse."

Donley sounded relieved; perhaps he had been afraid that Clint would use the woman as a shield to protect himself.

"That's fine! It'll be just the place for you. Come on."

She left the window and ran back to Clint. Her hand seized his shoulder, shook it.

"Listen to me! Do as I say! I'm going out, but when I move my hand behind me, call me back — make me come. Say that you want me to find cartridges on the shelves."

"But —"

"Oh, do as I say! Will you?"

"Uh — yes."

He muttered it; he did not like the thing. And then she was opening the door. She went hurriedly about six feet, and Clint saw a movement of the fingers of her left hand. He shouted quickly:

"Stop! Wait! Come back here and find me some cartridges on the shelves!"

She hesitated; she seemed to give a little shiver, as though she knew that the sights of a gun were on her back. Shame swept over Clint. He was about to call to her to go on, to mount Reddy and ride away, but he remembered her beseeching "Oh, do as I say!" He spoke again, and there was little threat in his troubled, hesitant voice:

"Better come back and get me those cartridges, Mrs. Fernel."

She feared that he would fail her, call for her to go on. She turned and ran back through the door. In panic, she seized his elbow, hurried him back down the room. While they ran, she was whispering breathlessly:

"Put them on! I'll throw them out."

137

And then the bedroom door slammed in his face. He stood there staring at it in the darkness; he had not the faintest notion of what she might mean.

Almost immediately, the door opened a few inches, and something soft which she had thrown twisted around his legs and dropped to the floor.

"Put it on — quick, or they'll be suspicious!"

Her riding skirt! Clint held it in his hand, held it far out as though it were hot.

"I can't — they'll blame you — !"

"Oh, Clint! *Please!*"

It was the little wail in her low voice that made him do it, against his wishes. None too fast, he shook off his chaps, and removed his spurs. Then, slowly, with a feeling of repugnance, he began to pull the thing on. It was a puzzle to him; before he had got it straight, she was hurrying out, in another dress. Then she was tugging at the skirt, fastening the waist with a safety pin; it would not go around him.

"The hat."

He had it on his head, her small Stetson. His shirt was very much like that which she had worn; it would have to do. She hurried him back to the front of the store; he almost fell with those unaccustomed things twisting around his legs — but, after all, they were not so different from his wide bat-wing chaps. Captain Donley had shouted again, but they did not catch the words. She whispered:

"Is it dark enough?"

"Yes. Any darker, and they'd only look closer."

From the window, she called; they could not see her now, except perhaps vaguely:

"He — he says he won't let me go unless you give him half an hour to think it over."

"Ten minutes — no more!"

Donley did not sound quite convincing, but they did not take time to argue.

"He — he says yes." And then in a quick whisper to Clint: "Stand in the doorway a moment."

A last pressure of her hand, and she had opened the door, shoved him out there. Obedient, he stood there. She spoke directly over his shoulder:

"Wh-which horse — that sorrel?"

"Yes, Mrs. Fernel. Hurry up!"

Anybody would have been deceived; they seemed to hear the voice coming directly from the figure in the doorway, and then the figure started out. Clint was running in short steps; he could only hope that it would seem natural. Again the skirts twisted around his legs and he almost fell; but they would think it was only her excitement, her fear, that caused it.

He had the sorrel's reins, was untying them, and a ranger was swinging off quickly to help him mount. All the time, he kept his head lowered under the hat brim, but if that man came up to him, he was lost. He dared not swing on quickly, cowboy fashion, with the reins carelessly in his left hand and the saddle horn in his right. His right was grasping the cantle, and he twisted his left in the sorrel's mane.

Inspiration came suddenly — that ranger was hardly eight feet off. Clint's fingers dug into the back of the horse's neck. With a snort, Reddy whirled, and as he did Clint swung on clumsily; he did not have to act the part, for the wide skirts hindered him; he was not far from going clear over and off on the other side. Reddy was high-strung; these queer things excited him. He reared, plunged; he was on the point of bucking. The ranger leaped for the reins. If he had only known that it was Clint Yancey he was trying to assist! But the sorrel, a heel digging into his side, skittered away.

"Look out! Hold onto him, Mrs. Fernel!"

Two more rangers were dashing up to assist. Reddy tried to run, but Clint pulled him down instantly to a skittering, nervous lope. The rangers stopped. Clint heard a low exclamation from one of them:

"Say, but that woman can ride!"

And then he was loping down the road. Surprised though the rangers might be when they found that he was gone, they could not be as surprised as Clint was now. He had got away! He loped only a hundred yards or so, and then he leaned forward, spoke to the sorrel:

"Run, boy! Run!"

Reddy knew the words. Clint felt the saddle sink under him, and he faintly saw the long neck stretch out. And, oh, how Reddy could run! On the hard, sun-baked road, his hoofs sounded like the quick roll of drums. The rangers back there would hear it; perhaps they would wonder why Mrs. Fernel rode so fast, or if the horse was running away with her. But Clint wanted them to hear it; he had his plans laid.

Ten minutes later to the second, Captain Donley struck a match and looked at his watch for the tenth time. He called:

"Time's up! Come out, Yancey!"

From the window a frightened, forlorn voice answered him:

"He — he's gone. He wore my clothes —"

That she was there, proved it. A furious oath burst from the lips of one of the rangers before he could catch himself. For a second, all sat their horses as though paralyzed. Sergeant Wilson collected himself first.

"After him! He'll head for the desert!"

Horses whirled in the darkness, quirts flew and spurs raked. Down the road went the rangers, in a close-packed band.

Mrs. Fernel stood in the window, eyes wide and one hand over her pounding heart, as those wild hoof-beats died away in the night; she could hear them for almost a mile, until they went sweeping over the first low ridge. Now that it was over, she felt weak; she felt that she wanted to cry, but she did not. She groped her slow way across the dark store to the rocking chair, but changed her mind and went stumbling toward the kitchen. Would they catch him? Not likely.

She could not bear the darkness. She took the chimney from the lamp and struck a match, her fingers trembling; that she could light the lamp at all, after what she had been through, showed the stuff she was made of. In the yellow light, she stood staring at the stove, still hot, at the pan of golden biscuits in the warming oven. All that had happened seemed like an ugly dream; it could not really have happened.

She heard the cautious squeak of a hinge behind her, and turned, her palms going to her face, and a little scream rising in her throat. And her great brown eyes widened. In the doorway stood a queer, fantastic figure in a hastily-adjusted riding skirt and a small Stetson hat. Clint Yancey!

"Are they all gone?" he whispered.

She ran to him and placed her hands against his chest, pushing at him.

"Oh, go! They'll get you! Go!"

"This is the safest place — for the present. I hid my horse in the little shed outside."

"Oh, *why* did you come back!"

He had not meant to tell the truth, but it blurted from him before he could stop it.

"To see that you eat."

She stood with those great eyes fixed on him; for an instant it looked as though she was going to laugh hysterically; why, this thing was grotesque, and when he was in such danger!

"And," he added lamely, "to get my chaps and things."

They stood there a few seconds, and then he turned and went into the store. Very soon he came back, dressed as he should be. He was now the same polite, gentle Clint that he had been before the rangers came.

"Fernel, wasn't it, they called you — Mrs. Fernel?"

"Yes — Mona Fernel."

"Mona." He repeated it slowly, because he had never heard the name before.

"Yes, Clint." She said it gravely, as another cowboy might absently give his first name, the name by which he was accustomed to being called; that sad, lost look was beginning to come back to her eyes again. "I'm not hungry, Clint — really. You hurry up and eat; they'll be back."

"Sit down there."

She did. He took the coffee pot from the stove and filled her cup. Then he reached for the biscuits and other things, and set them before her. She looked at them and shook her head.

"I'm not hungry."

He was sitting down opposite her now. He had split a biscuit and was buttering it. Without even looking up, he spoke deliberately:

"All right! I'm not leaving until you do eat — and that's flat."

She stared across the table at him. It seemed utterly impossible that he could be mad enough to mean it; but a young man who had been mad enough to come back to make her eat could be mad enough for anything. To please him, she tasted her coffee; and when she set the cup down it was half empty, to her own surprise, but scarcely to his. She was starving, and did not know it.

"Biscuit?"

She took one, buttered it, and sat looking at it. Clint spoke sternly now:

"Ma'am, you *have* to eat; you can't sit and starve to death."

Slowly, each bite choking her, she began to eat. She had to humor him, after all his kindness. She did not eat much, but her fast was broken, and she had finished her coffee — a new color had come to her pallid cheeks. Clint was satisfied; he did not try to force her to eat more. He was drinking the last of his own coffee, and she was sitting looking at him hard, when she spoke suddenly.

"Clint, you are an outlaw, but you are not a bad man — you are too kind. I can understand why you should have to steal horses and cattle; but why did you take that bribe, and sell out the rangers?"

He looked at her with his mouth partly open; never before had he met anybody who would have asked such a frank question. She was merely asking for information; she implied that she was sure that there must have been some good reason for it. There was something so matter-of-fact about her tone that Clint spoke levelly:

"I did not sell them out, though there's plain evidence that I did. And I haven't, and never had, a cent of money that I didn't earn honestly — and I hope I never have."

She did not even look relieved; she looked almost as though she had been waiting for that answer, and had taken it for granted. She nodded. Clint jerked his eyes away suddenly; a pang of slight shame came over him. The food, the hot coffee, had brought out the full beauty of her grave, thoughtful face, and he had been

144

staring hard at it. He felt embarrassed; he felt like kicking himself for the indecency of it — and this poor woman not twenty-four hours a widow, broken-hearted over that brutal murder of her husband. The cleanness and wholesomeness of her mind showed plainly in her face, in her level brown eyes. She had taken him as her friend, her consoler in her sorrow — and he had unconsciously stared at her that way.

Luckily, she had not noticed it; she had her eyes fixed on the red tablecloth with its white pattern. At least, Clint felt sure that she had not. She asked a question:

"Where are you going now? The rangers will be between you and the desert — coming back; you might meet them."

There was nothing but the greatest respect in Clint's voice:

"I'm going back to Mexico for a couple of days; I have business there."

"Oh — then you'll be safe. But you'd better go now, Clint; we don't know how soon they'll come back."

That was true. He stood up and got his hat, started toward the kitchen door. She followed him, and held out her hand.

"Good bye — and I never can thank you for being so kind to me."

"But — how about what you did for me?"

"You wouldn't have got into that trouble only for helping me. Of course you'll come here on your way back from Mexico, and I'll get you a meal. I'll leave some blankets out in the shed, and you can sleep there if you want to; I'll leave oats for your horse, too. You will come here, won't you?"

"Y — yes, ma'am."

He could have kicked himself for promising. She pressed his hand.

"Good bye, Clint."

"Good bye, Mrs. Fernel."

He got his horse out of the shed, mounted, and rode off quietly in the darkness. He rode slowly, and his head was bowed. That tall, brown-eyed woman was still in the first paralyzing grief of the murder of her husband. And he loved her, and he knew it.

He would have slapped the face of the man who told him that his feelings were a fine, splendid thing that did honor to her, and even more honor to him; he thought of them only as the insult they would have been had he been beast enough to declare them. Nor was this twisted philosophy peculiar to Clint; it was part of the stern cowboy code to which he had been reared, this chivalry at which a knight-errant might have smiled. Hard-bitten, lawless men, these open-range cowboys — perhaps they needed these softening, childlike touches in their natures.

And not only did his feeling toward her seem indecent; he well knew it to be hopeless. The heart of that splendid, beautiful young woman was buried with her murdered husband. Had she not been so fine, so loyal, there would have been hope for him; but had she not been as she was, Clint would not have cared for her.

146

And so, hating himself, brooding, he rode among the barren, jagged hills, on either side of him the weird shapes of great cacti outlined against the brilliant stars. He saw himself in what seemed a revealing flash: a horse thief, a rustler — and now, worse; he had permitted himself to diverge from the stern code of his kind, the code which old Henry Judson had been to such pains to inculcate in him.

Poor Clint Yancey! There could be little doubt that he was potentially the most dangerous man in all Arizona — yet so ingenuous!

CHAPTER
FOURTEEN

Clint's Return

Clint Yancey thrust a little rounded pebble between his swollen lips and began to mumble it. He had picked it up a few minutes before, but it was so hot that he had had to carry it in his pocket a while to let it cool; it had burned his hand. The desert resembled nothing but a hot oven. There was no more air stirring than in an oven.

His eyes looked small, and red, and sore; he was peering ahead, leaned out over his saddle horn like a near-sighted man. He rubbed his bleared eyes and looked again through that white glare. Yes, that line ahead was the Silvermine Hills. He had taken three days to cross the desert this time; Reddy had been ridden hard lately and could not be forced. Poor Reddy; he looked gaunt, and drawn; alkali dust had caked in his sweat until he looked like a gray horse rather than sorrel. For once he was shuffling along with hanging head.

The heat of those three days had been ghastly, terrific. The air was thick and choking and seemed fetid, hanging dead as it was; the sky seemed a white-hot bowl inverted over the earth. And still there was a look of satisfaction on Clint's thickened lips as he saw all this; it meant that the summer rains would come at any time now, for this deadly, still heat always presaged them. He and Don Luis had counted on the summer rainy season as the best time to put their plans into effect; cattle could be hurried almost anywhere across the desert then; and even off it, it was convenient to be able to find water anywhere — it would let one follow an unpredictable course.

The sun was just setting when he turned in between two ridges, into the hills. There was a little seep a short distance up this wash, and he headed directly for it; the last two water holes on the desert had been dry, and the one before a vile, sickening thing from which he had turned away in disgust, and then turned back to drink. He had almost ridden on without drinking; if he had, he would not have been here now.

He saw another man come riding down the ridge toward the seep. Why, it was Billy Armour. Clint took only time for a brief "Howdy" before he pulled the bridle back on Reddy's neck to let him drink in comfort, the bit out of his mouth. Then he himself was stretched on the ground, drinking. The water was hot and tasteless, but he did not notice that, it was clear, and wet.

At last he stood up. He saw Billy holding Reddy's reins; he had pulled him away from the hole before he had drunk all he wanted. Clint gave a guilty start.

"Uh — thanks, Billy."

Billy looked him over from head to foot. He shook his head.

149

"Fine lookin' specimen you are! Wasn't warm out there, was it?"

"No. Oh, no! Say, Billy; take a look at my ears, will you — that left one isn't frozen a little, is it?"

Billy grinned.

"Well, you can take it, to joke that way! If a Gila monster lay on a rock out there five minutes, there'd be fried Gila monster."

They rolled cigarettes and lit them. Clint took the reins from Billy's hand and started to put the bit into Reddy's mouth. Billy spoke:

"Hold it a minute, Clint! You'd better not start toward town till dark. Me or Butch or Red Barclay has been watchin' for you a couple days, to head you off."

"Huh! What's wrong?"

"Plenty. There's a ranger in town lookin' for you."

"A rang — ! But Tex — !" gasped Clint in consternation.

"Tex," remarked Billy soberly, "ain't given no orders about him. Me, I'm thinkin' he passed out some hints not to bother him. In fact I think Tex don't love you any more."

Here was a nice state of affairs! To go back across the desert, the condition Reddy was in, was out of the question. So Butch had been right; Tex had him marked, for the name he had called him, for pointing a gun at him — but it seemed that he was going to turn him over to the rangers instead of killing him. This, Clint knew, was no new procedure for Tex; he had caused more than one of his men to get a life sentence, or the rope, as an easy way to get rid of them.

150

"Do you know," he asked presently, "what the ranger's name is?"

"Sure — Sergeant Wilson."

Clint stared blankly at him. Wilson, his pardner! He could guess what had happened; when the others turned back that night of his escape from Wacker, Wilson had kept on alone. It was just like him! Bull-headed — always ready to charge into something like an angry bear, without stopping to think whether he might come out of it alive or not; too much nerve, and too little sense to back it. With his pardner Lieutenant Yancey to hold him back until the right time, he was worth an army. They had been the ideal combination; alone, he would get himself killed inside of a month. So Sergeant Wilson and Tex Fletcher had joined forces against him — what a weird combination! Clint spoke broodingly:

"And all over me cussing Tex — I reckon Butch told you about it."

" 'Tain't that." Billy looked at him oddly.

"What, then?" demanded Clint.

Billy hesitated; there seemed to be something he didn't like to say.

"Uh — uh — It's over you strippin' Mrs. Fernel naked to get her clothes."

Clint's face flamed.

"I didn't do any such thing! Why, I wouldn't hurt a hair of Mona Fernel's head for — for —"

He had spoken a little too hotly; he saw Billy eyeing him narrowly, understandingly.

"I think I savvy a few things. Mebbe you wouldn't have to hurt her to get the shirt off her back?"

Clint turned on him furiously.

"Billy, one word about Mrs. Fernel — !"

"Aw, don't blow up! You can't tell me anything about what a fine woman she is; I know her. Did you know that she's Sergeant Wilson's niece — his oldest sister's girl?"

"Huh!"

Now Clint remembered hearing Wilson remark about having a niece somewhere down near the border; he had paid little attention at the time. But Wilson would have been just the same if he thought any decent woman insulted; in his chivalry, as in everything else, he showed more valor than discretion. Clint remembered one case where Wilson had almost beaten a man to a pulp for insulting a woman on the street — without waiting to find out that the woman was of such a class that to insult her would be quite a feat. Clint had had a bad time fixing that, although poor Wilson was ready to give the man his best horse to square himself.

"And," said Billy gravely, "I reckon there's something else you don't know — about Tex."

"What's that?"

"Funny you hadn't heard; everybody knows it. He's crazy about Mona Fernel, an' has been a long time."

"Why, the dirty — !"

"Uh-huh — he's all that, an' more. I reckon I don't have to tell you it's one-sided; but he swears he'll have her. Clint, why do you suppose Wacher got raided that way by them Mexicans? Dang little in that town worth stealin'."

"Why — I wondered; they couldn't have got much."

Billy stood scratching his head and looking at the ground. He himself could hardly believe what he was going to say.

"Well, somebody here got drunk an' let the yarn leak out: Tex fixed for that; he wanted Jim Fernel killed some way so it wouldn't look like his doin's. Reckon he didn't think there would be so many other people shot in the raid — mebbe he didn't care. He wanted Mona to be single."

Clint stood with open mouth and wide eyes. He knew Tex for a cold-blooded, treacherous butcher, but he could not believe that even he would go that far.

"Good God!"

Billy nodded very soberly.

"Turriblest thing I ever heard of anybody doin'. But he's so crazy about her he'd do anything to get her — he thinks he has her now."

Clint sat down on a boulder; he had a sick feeling. Billy stood over him, and presently he burst out:

"This rustling crowd! Gawd, but they make me sick, with their double-crossin', an' trickery, an' rottenness! Clint, if it wasn't that I said I'd stick with you, I'd light out right now an' go so far that nobody here would ever hear of me again. I'd make an honest livin', even if I had to herd sheep for two bits a day. Augh-h-h — it would turn a coyote's stomach!"

"Let's go," murmured Clint.

It was now growing dark. Clint walked slowly, with bowed head, to his horse. He slipped the bridle on and swung into the saddle, and they started off side by side toward town. They had gone half a mile before either spoke. Clint was the first to break the silence; there was a catch in his voice.

"Poor Jim Fernel — so that's why he was murdered."

He could see Billy Armour's face turn to him with a queer look on it.

"You didn't know about him?"

"What?"

"Why, he was one of Tex's spies — he's caused more than one honest cowman to be shot, down in that country, an' more than one herd of cattle to be stole from men that thought he was their friend. Jim Fernel was a low-down skunk. Tex roped him in — reckon it was easy enough — thinkin' it would give him a hold on Mona. But Fernel was scared stiff she'd find out; she'd have quit him flat in a minute. An' Tex saw that he'd better not say anything after all, or she'd never forgive him."

Clint swallowed hard; he was staring straight ahead into the gloom. So that was what Jim Fernel had been — that was the man over whom poor Mona was breaking her heart! Billy spoke hurriedly:

"For gosh sake, don't let her know; it would kill her!"

"I let her know!" groaned Clint. He would be the last one in the world to deal her that last cruel blow; it might wreck her mind. She must never know.

"But," he went on — he felt dazed — "those Mexicans were in with Tex; that would have them in with Fernel, too."

"Sure — that's it. The yarn is that Fernel signaled them when to come into town, not suspectin' that they were mainly to get him."

Clint turned, his face pale, and looked dumbly at Billy. He could not have spoken to save his life. So that was what Mona Fernel had been married to! His miserable death had been far too good for him.

Billy understood; not one word did he say on the rest of the ride to town. In the darkness, he led the way down the ridge far from any trail, and quietly took Clint to the old house which he had picked as a place to conceal Reddy; he had oats and water hidden there under some loose boards in the floor. Then, through dark back streets, past deserted buildings, he took him to the rear door of Butch's place and slipped him in. He spoke quietly to Butch.

"Clint's tired out; he missed a couple water holes on the desert. Don't bother him with any questions now; jest give him his supper an' let him go to bed."

Clint was indeed a sorry sight, with the thick alkali dust caked in his long stubble of beard, his clothes white with it, and his face drawn from thirst and heat, not to mention his troubled mind. Butch nodded gravely; he thought he understood.

"But Tex left word for him to go right up to see him as soon as he got back."

"Tex can dang well wait till tomorrow night — we'll say Clint jest got in then." He turned to Clint. "That is, if you want to see him; if you don't, I'll get you a fresh horse somewhere's to go back out on."

155

Sally Tolleson was setting the table. She was a large, buxom girl with a jolly face — she looked like anything on earth but a rustler's daughter. Clint glanced at the table and shook his head.

"I think I'll go right to bed, if you don't mind; I'm sure tired. I think I won't wait to eat now."

Billy Armour spoke with deliberation.

"Don't you? Well, I think you will. Shove up to this table."

"But, Billy —"

"Uh-huh — right here. I know you wouldn't hurt Sal's feelin's by not eatin' after all her trouble fixin' it. Them's beans — an' pass him the biscuits, Butch." Slowly, Clint picked up his knife and fork. He was remembering a night not long ago, when he had forced another to eat in spite of herself. The thought that came to his mind was not very original — it was that this is a queer world.

CHAPTER
FIFTEEN

Clint is Trapped

"No," said Clint stubbornly. "I'm going up to see Tex. I have to pretend to get along with him, for the present, if I'm going to stay in this town. And right here I'm going to stay till I'm ready to leave."

Butch wagged his shaggy head.

"Well, it's yo're funeral, Clint. But I'd guess it won't be a funeral, but a dive into one o' them old mine dumps durin' the night."

Billy Armour, the reckless one, grunted disgustedly.

"Aw, let him go! Clint's pretty good at takin' care of himself. Besides, there ain' no use in arguin' any more with him."

What twenty-four hours had done to Clint seemed almost a miracle. He had slept most of the time, except when he woke up to eat or drink. He had shaved, bathed, and those lines of the desert were out of his face already. In his neat cowboy clothes, freshly washed by Butch's daughter, he might again have been Lieutenant Clinton Yancey, ready for inspection.

There were four other men in the room besides himself, Butch and Billy Armour. Three of them were cowboy friends of Billy's who had come in to join him in that hare-brained attempt to play nester in the Silvermines; two others had decided that punching cattle for wages beat living here at the risk of one's life. These three were now ostensibly members of Tex's gang. Billy swore by them, but to tell the truth, Clint did not put much confidence in any of them; they were wild, staring-eyed young fellows who he judged might flop over to Tex in ten seconds if they took the notion.

The fourth here was of a different type. He was Red Barclay — nothing but a rustler, but neither Butch nor Billy had ever heard of his being in a single shooting scrape. The same easy good nature that had led to his being friendly toward Clint from the first made him friendly toward everybody. It was known that men in the town had pulled guns on him a time or two, but he had "kidded them" out of shooting. And, oddly enough, he was said to be a very expert shot.

He and Butch had been pardners for a long time; their dispositions were very much alike, so that was quite natural. On his return from the horse-stealing raid, Butch had hurried to be first to tell Red of the treachery that had caused his brother's death in the little pass; if Red had heard of it from somebody else, he would immediately have gone to Tex's rooms to shoot him — and undoubtedly got shot himself instead. Indeed, Butch had only held him back by divulging some of Clint's plans, and asking him to join them. Clint judged Red to be a man upon whom he could depend no matter what happened. Red had been sitting thinking; now he looked up.

158

"Clint, I got a good plan: There's seven of us here; how about us sort of droppin' over to the hotel one at a time, an' meetin' there; we can get around Tex an' riddle him full o' holes before anybody knows what's happenin'?"

"Red," said Clint earnestly, "I don't want to show who's boss like Tex, or anything that way, but I have certain plans I'm not telling yet. Anybody throws in with me will have to do what I say — and no more. Killing Tex now would ruin everything for me. If you don't like it my way, Red, we can shake hands right now, and you can walk out that door, and no hard feelings — I know you wouldn't squeal on us."

Without pausing to think, Red spoke quietly.

"O. K., Clint. I'm stickin' — an' doin' what you say, an' not doin' what you don't say."

Clint turned.

"How about the rest of you fellows?"

"We're stickin', Clint; yo're the boss." Every one of them answered in practically the same words.

"Thanks, boys — and if things turn out all right, you won't regret it. If they don't — well, I'll sink with you. Now, as I said, don't any of you follow me; I think I can handle Tex better by myself than to have a big shooting break loose."

He got up and buckled on his two gun belts — he always wore two now, crossed at the waist. He turned to Butch.

"Well, tell Sally *hasta la vista* for me, and that I sure appreciate all the bother she's gone to, washing and cooking for me."

159

Butch looked at him gloomily.

"Clint, you sound like you think you ain't comin' back alive."

Clint shrugged slightly.

"One never knows; this is all risky business. I expect to come back, but if I don't — I don't. Well, so long, fellows."

He put on his hat, straightened it, and strolled quietly out, pulling the door to after him. The six left sat looking at each other a moment; it was Billy Armour who burst out with what was on all their minds.

"Nerve! Pure, cold nerve! That feller's got it!"

Of course Clint kept away from the main street. He wound quietly through deserted side streets and dark alleys until he got behind the hotel. Cautious always, he crouched in some bushes a hundred yards from it, watching, peering into the darkness, listening for the slightest sounds. It was typical of him that he spent a full half hour there, scarcely moving a muscle; he always used the tactics of an Indian in this sort of thing.

At last he heard a faint, muffled cough — or perhaps a man clearing his throat softly; he barely heard it. But it came from an old deserted building ahead of him, and it told him what he wanted to know; the hotel was being watched. He wondered if it was Sergeant Wilson, but he suspected that some of Tex's most trusted gunmen had been called in to lie in wait for him.

Silently, he slipped back, to approach the hotel from another angle. There was a long row of low adobe houses, built one against the other, Mexican fashion. He climbed to the roof of the farthest one, and crept to the other end. He dropped without a sound beside a low wall, and on hands and knees followed beside this. Then he was in the deep darkness under the hotel wall, moving silently.

He knew of one room on the ground floor that had been ruined during some gun scrape since the rustlers took over the town; nobody would be using it. He crept to it, reached an arm through a broken pane, and opened the catch. Inch by inch, he raised the sash, and then he slipped through. The door was unlocked; every key had long ago been lost or thrown away, except some which Tex had bought or found for his own rooms. Clint felt sure that there would be no watchers inside the place, but still he crouched there a long time, his ear to the crack.

And then, his boots in one hand and his gun in the other, he was stealing up the dark back stairs; they led up from the kitchen, long disused. Only an instant's pause on top, and he hurried past Tex's door to the main stairs, and part way down it — down almost to the turn; any lower, and he could be seen from below. He sat on a step and pulled on his boots, and then he went strolling casually back up, and to Tex's door. He knocked.

"Come in!"

He walked in quietly.

"Hello, Clint! Uh — glad to see you back."

There was only a barely perceptible startled glance, and a slight break in the greeting, but Clint noticed them. No doubt Tex would have given a good deal to know how he had calmly walked up there without being seen.

Clint had his hat off, in his left hand; he glanced around for a place to lay it, and his eyes fell carelessly on a little table against the wall, not far from the door. At the back of the table were a few small specimens of ore and some other knickknacks which he hardly noticed. In front of these was a little tumbled pile — a few coins, a pocket knife, a dirty handkerchief and such things. Obviously, somebody had emptied his pockets there when changing clothes, and had not yet put the things into the other trousers pockets. Never had Clint's presence of mind showed so much as that he kept from starting at what he saw — a tiny thing lying in a heap. In fact he hardly let his eyes rest on it a second; he tossed his hat carelessly on the table and turned.

"Howdy, Tex. I hear you wanted to see me soon as I got back."

On Tex's invitation, Clint sat down. Now, both men were genial; both were pretty good actors in a case of this sort, and a stranger would have taken them for good friends. But Clint had taken two precautions; he had kept out of line of the window, so that he could not be seen from outside, and when he sat down it was facing both Tex and the bedroom door. He felt quite satisfied that Yavapai Slim nor nobody else was in there this time; again, it was but his usual wariness.

They talked of various things a while, until Tex suddenly looked up.

"Clint, the more I find out about you, the more I think of you. I don't know how our crowd ever got along all this time without you."

"What now?" asked Clint evenly; he felt like laughing in Tex's face. Of course Tex had figured out by this time that some watcher in front of the hotel had been careless and let Clint walk by — probably he would think that the man had gone across to the saloon. Tex nodded gravely.

"Yes, sir; Clint, I sure respect you. Most men would be too finicky to make a woman strip off and give him her clothes to get away in."

Clint waved it aside genially.

"Oh, I couldn't let a little thing like that stop me, Tex. The trouble about women is that most men in this country are too sort of respectful toward them — what the heck are they, after all?"

"That's what I always said; rougher you are with 'em, the better they like it. Take your case, for instance." Tex laughed. "Clint, a man o' mine coming in today told me you spent a night at her place — last Wednesday night. Don't that prove that women like bein' treated rough?"

Clint flushed now, and spoke with dangerous quietness.

"I did — I slept in that little shed behind the house, with my horse."

"Oh, sure! That's what I meant! As women goes — Mona Fernel's about the best of 'em. Not saying much, of course."

Never had Tex spoken more genially, but Clint saw the wicked snap in his dark eyes; he had trapped Clint into giving his feelings away, and done it neatly.

"Clint, about that raid the Mexicans made: Wasn't that the dirtiest piece o' work you ever heard of? Sure some low-down people in this world!"

Clint was getting sick of the thing. He raised his eyes and looked straight into Tex's.

"Tex, that's one time you spoke the truth; you should know."

Tex only smiled, and lowered his head to sit staring at the faded red carpet, apparently thinking over the lowness of humanity. And Clint, watching Tex, was thinking too. The Mexicans hired by Tex to kill Fernel — that was why they had been late returning. To be ordered by Don Luis's messenger to kill Tex. They did not care whom they killed, if they were paid for it for butchery was their trade. What a vile, stinking mess this whole rustling ring was, and everybody connected with it! Treachery overlying treachery — it reminded Clint of maggots working in rotten meat.

"How about a drink, Clint? I have the bottle setting in the window to cool; this weather's pretty near hot enough to boil whiskey in the bottle."

He stood up slowly and strolled toward the window. Clint grew tense; he was watching for some signal. But Tex only picked the bottle up quietly and came back, to sit down again.

"Here — have one."

"Thanks, Tex, but I think I'd better not. That rotten water out on the desert — or something — up-set my stomach." One thing he was not going to do, and that was to drink with Tex now.

"That's right; if you're off your feed, you'd better lay off this stuff a day or two."

Tex poured himself a drink and sat looking at it with a little smile on his face. Never had his great nose looked so like an evil beak of some bird of prey; there was something behind that smile that Clint could not understand.

"Clint, do you know where the Triangle K is?"

"Why, I've heard of it; never been there. Over north of Cuchilla, isn't it."

"That's right; old Dan Webster's place. I was figuring on starting out tomorrow to pick up a bunch of cattle there, but I'd sure like to have you along. Reckon I'll let it go a day or two, till you and your horse rest up a bit." He set his whiskey down, and chuckled. "Sure will be fun to be out with you again, Clint; us two work together fine."

Clint's keen blue eyes were fixed on the man's face as though trying to bore into it, to read Tex's mind. There was more villiany in that evil chuckle than in any other sound he had ever heard. If Tex had given a signal — but he had not —

And suddenly Clint's mind seemed to jerk. He had been a fool! Tex Fletcher had been too smart for him — that bottle taken from the window sill was the signal! The gunmen would be gathering all around the place, if not already gathered. Had he sat here like a fool and let his chance of escape slip by? But even then Clint sat thinking a moment, with hardly a change in his face.

Should he draw and try to kill Tex right there? No; win or lose, he was going to play his hand out as he had started to play it. He got up, not too quickly.

"Well, Tex, I reckon I'll be going."

He walked quietly across the room and picked his hat up from the little side table. He did it so casually that Tex could not be blamed for not noticing that he picked something else up with it, something so tiny that he held it concealed between his first and second fingers as they lay side by side. He turned in the doorway, putting on his hat.

"Yes, Tex; I expect to be in shape tomorrow to go anywhere I feel like."

Even Tex had to give him a glance of admiration; he knew that Clint knew of those outside, and the man was standing there with the door knob in his hand as calmly as if he didn't have a single care in the world. His eyes on him, Tex spoke regretfully.

"Too bad, Clint, about leavin' us, down there, to go see — your girl. But for that —"

"Good night, Tex; see you tomorrow."

Quietly, Clint closed the door behind him; he was not going to be tricked into standing there talking any longer, with that crew gathering outside to trap him. Then he was running on tiptoe down the corridor; his best plan, of course, would be to try to get out as he had come in. He already knew the way, and there was a chance that Tex's gunmen, not knowing how he had entered, would not yet be back there. He heard a faint sound behind him — Tex shouting something from the open window.

What would they try to do? Every effort would be made to take him alive, to turn him over to Sergeant Wilson. Tex would figure that would be more punishment than merely shooting him down; it would mean a life sentence, for selling out the rangers, and horse stealing. No, they would not want to shoot him if they could help it — or perhaps they might shoot at his legs. Well, he was not going to return the compliment; if he found anybody in his way, he would shoot to kill. The filthy pack!

He got downstairs easily, and into the empty room. The window was still open as he had left it. With hardly a pause to glance out, he threw a leg over and slid quickly to the ground — there were times for caution and slowness, but this was not one of them. He was hardly on his feet outside when a voice came from not more than ten feet off.

"Throw 'em up, Clint! We got you!"

He thought he recognized Terry Smith's voice. He was not sure, and he did not care. He whirled, and both his guns instantly spat little reddish jets toward the shadowy figure. A slight gurgling sound; the thump of a body falling over against the board wall of the hotel and then to the ground. Now, a gun in each hand, Clint was standing there, and little spurts of flame were coming out of the darkness around him.

CHAPTER
SIXTEEN

The Arrest

Clint stood only an instant, and then he went dashing toward the end of the adobes; if he could get up and run along the middle of those flat roofs, he might be protected from the men closer to him, and shooting at any distance was uncertain in the darkness. He saw a head and shoulders above the edge of the roof, against the sky, and fired point blank. He could see two arms thrown up, and the man came pitching down almost on top of him.

He leaped and caught the edge; it was not high. A shower of broken adobe rattled down on his hat brim; a bullet had clipped that edge between his hands. For the moment, there seemed to be but one man shooting; the corners of the house were between him and the others — but he could hear running feet.

"There he goes! Up on the roof!"

His long legs stood him in good stead now; he ran the length of the buildings in record time. He glanced down; there was a man crouched below him. He swept up an adobe block, perhaps fourteen inches square and five inches thick, swept it above his head with both hands, and sent it crashing down. The man collapsed without a grunt. He heard footsteps coming running, and as a man turned the corner another adobe met him squarely in the face; he too went over.

And then Clint swung himself down. Now, his hands free, he drew both guns as he ran. He whirled around a corner, and went racing up what had once been a business street but was now completely abandoned, blank store fronts on both sides. For a brief time there was a pause in the shooting, and then the pack turned the corner behind him. Yells of "There he goes!" broke out again, and shots. There seemed to be a dozen or so after him; probably a few loafers had joined hastily in the manhunt.

He was in a dangerous position, if ever he had been. It was too dark to see sights or to do good shooting, but the brilliant Arizona starlight would show him plainly as he ran. Again adobe sifted down on his hat; a bullet had grazed the wall above him. This would not do! Sooner or later — probably sooner — one of those bullets would drop him.

Most cowboys are poor runners; Clint was an exception in this respect. But not the only one; he heard the sound of feet catching up with him. In the middle of a stride, he dug a high heel in, whirled, and dropped to his knee, all in one motion. He fired before the other man had time to stop; he saw him pitch out on his face and slide toward him.

Then running again, with the pack after him, shooting, yelling; they were a fair distance behind now, and he could guess that, after that last shot of his, some of them were none too eager to get ahead of the rest.

Still, his only chance was to dart around the next corner and so be out of range a moment or two. Perhaps he could leap into some empty building around there, and they would not know which one it was.

That gave him his plan. He was within twenty feet of the corner when he suddenly whirled into a dark rectangle that once had held a door. In that faint light, those following would think that he had gone around the corner. On each side of the doorway were two wide expanses with jagged points of broken plate glass; the front of the store had been almost solid glass. Below the windows were walls of two feet high or so; he threw himself behind the one to the left, and lay there, a gun in each hand. He dared not try to run through the store and out the back; there would be a litter of broken counters and showcases, old boxes and things, and he would be sure to go crashing over it and fall — make a noise.

Here they came! Footsteps, jingling spurs, coming racing up the street — and past. He could hear the first men stop at the corner a moment.

"Which way did he go?"

"Down that way! Turned the corner!"

And they went running on, and more were passing the door. Now, he had better dodge out and go back the other way, before they came back to search for him. He rose to one knee; he was about to start out when he heard more feet coming. Two men this time — they seemed to be running more softly than the others. He crouched there against the door jamb waiting for them to pass.

They did not pass; they stopped hardly four feet from him. He heard a quick, low voice.

"Let's wait here till we hear 'em shootin' again; then we can run up there."

"Dang right we will! But what if they recognize us?"

"They won't; too dark. Anyways, I've stood about all Tex's trickery I'm goin' to — we can't let 'em get Clint."

"No — there's a white hombre, that Clint feller."

A pause, and suddenly a quick whisper from one of them.

"There's a shot! Let's go, Bud!"

They went running quickly but softly. For a moment, Clint was almost too surprised to move. Bud Haines and his pardner Newt Collingsby! Two of what he had considered the toughest young gunmen in town — and they were running to help him out on general principles; he had hardly ever spoken to either. A flash of triumph shot through Clint's mind. Tex Fletcher was losing his grip; he had gone too far with his treachery and trickery and his men were becoming disgusted — some of them. "A white hombre, that Clint feller." Why, those two tough young devils were friendly toward him, liked him; he had never suspected it.

Kneeling, Clint glanced out hurriedly through the broken window. There was nobody on the street that he could see; he started to get up, to run for the door. And as he straightened something hard poked deep into the small of his back. A deep bass voice spoke almost in his ear — it was murderous.

"I got you, at last! Damn you, Clint, here's where you get it!"

Sergeant Wilson! Clint's whole body gave a wild twitch, but it seemed that that twitch brought his hands high into the air; again his swift wits were working. Quickly, the words jumbling out, he spoke.

"Don't shoot, Wilson! I got my hands up — wouldn't shoot a man in the back with his hands up!"

"Oh, wouldn't I!"

The gun muzzle jabbed in viciously; it hurt. That throaty growl in Wilson's voice showed that he was almost mad with rage.

"Listen, Wilson! Look against the light — I have 'em up, high. All your life, to look back and think you'd shot a man in the back, when he had his hands up. Wilson, you're not that kind!"

Clint was not sure, but he thought the muzzle was not boring in quite so hard. He knew this man, knew how to handle him.

"You dirty, treacherous, horse-stealin' rat!" growled Wilson furiously, "what better you got comin'?"

"You can't do it, Wilson — you can't. You got to take me in alive, for trial."

There was a pause now. Clint could feel the angry tremble of the gun muzzle as it poked in. And soon he felt a tug at first one hip and then the other; there were two little clatters as Sergeant Wilson dropped his guns on the floor.

172

"Put your hands behind you — and I hope you try to pull something!"

Clint carefully brought his hands down, behind his waist. There were two little clicks, and the gun muzzle came away.

"Kneel down."

"What for?"

"Kneel down!"

Clint did; even handcuffed though he was, Wilson might shoot; he had little control of his temper, as Clint well knew.

"Open your mouth."

"Listen here —"

"Open it, or I'll bat you on the head with this gun barrel an' pry it open."

There was nothing else for it. Clint opened his mouth, wide, and a wadded handkerchief was rammed viciously into it. He felt the big square of black silk jerked from his neck, and this was bound across his face to hold the handkerchief in. It was strangling; it gave a sickening feeling to have his mouth stuffed full that way. Sergeant Wilson jerked the last knot tight.

"That'll keep you from shoutin' — I see you got pals might try to get you loose. Get up. Start back through the store."

The gun in his back, Clint felt his way with his feet, among the litter. Soon he was out in the starlight, in a little yard with a high board wall. Wilson's horse was there. He picked up the reins and led the horse, driving Clint ahead of him through the open gate. They went down the alley, and onto a dark side street. Wilson stood peering into the gloom until he saw a horse tied to a hitching rack. He drove Clint toward it, and picked up the reins.

"Climb up."

Clint could not, with his hands behind him; he made a motion with his head and shoulders. Sergeant Wilson seized him by the back of the waist and helped him, almost lifted him into the saddle. He tied the handcuffs firmly to the rear saddle strings. And presently they were drifting silently through dark alleys, Wilson riding and leading Clint's horse. He spoke only once, in a low voice.

"Best luck I ever had! I was on the corner there when I heard the shooting; I figured it was you they were after. When I saw it was coming my way, I dodged into the store to get you as you came by — all saved you was you running in the door instead of passing. Which was too dam' bad!"

When he had worked with Wilson, he had been the cleverer of the two, as well as the superior officer. It had been taken for granted that he was the one to evolve the plans, and that Wilson would follow blindly and do what he said — nothing could have suited Sergeant Wilson better; he did not seem to like having to think unless he had to. Now he showed a cleverness and competency that surprised Clint.

He got to the edge of town by the shortest and quickest route; that of course was to be expected. But then, with a high, barren ridge before him invitingly, he turned to the right. Riding in a slow, almost silent walk, he skirted the outside houses until he was directly opposite where he had come out first. Then Clint could see his head swinging, as he studied the ground in the starlit darkness.

At last he found what he wanted, a stony wash coming down across the old road he was now following. The little hollow in the road there was but part of the wash, and covered with loose stones. Without a word, he swung to his right and up, leading Clint's horse. There were great, loose boulders, but Wilson rode so slowly that the horses never slipped once to leave a scratch of a horse shoe — Clint himself had taught him that trick. He gave the horses their own time; when one wanted to stop to blow, he let him.

And after a long time of this struggling upwards, they were on top of the ridge, looking down upon the gulch and the little town that lay there, a few lights gleaming from windows. Again Wilson was letting the horses blow. He nodded down grimly; Clint could see his thick neck and heavy face against the sky.

"Now, let 'em follow that trail!"

And Clint knew there was nobody in Gulch City who could; he doubted if a Navajo tracker would have been able to find it in a week, if at all. Then Wilson was leading him directly away from the town — which also was directly away from the shortest route to ranger headquarters. If they kept straight on, when they had crossed the desert they would have days of riding circling it, to get where they were going. Certainly, nobody would think of following this way.

CHAPTER
SEVENTEEN

The Balancing Rock

They had to cross almost the whole width of the Silvermine Hills. It was just beginning to show daylight in the east when they saw the ridges ahead falling off to the desert. Clint made strangling sounds, kicked his horse to make it skitter and be hard to lead. For a long time, Wilson paid no attention, but the jerking horse was causing him too much trouble, and at last he came alongside, to growl venemously.

"All right — I'll take it out. They can't hear you now."

He stopped both horses, and, leaning over, untied the neckerchief from around Clint's head. He did no more; picking up the reins from his saddle horn he started on again, leading the other horse. At last, spluttering and strangling, Clint managed to spit out the gag. He waited a moment to get his breath, and then spoke in a sarcastic drawl.

"Nice, cool morning, Sergeant."

No answer; no change in that back turned to him.

"Look here, Wilson! You've got me, so I want to ask you why the devil you can't act like a human being. You're the same damned pig-headed —"

Wilson turned savagely in his saddle, and his hand dropped to his gun.

"Shut up!"

"Oh, can it! You know you wouldn't shoot me while I'm tied this way."

"Oh, wouldn't I!"

And Clint stared at him in disbelief. Why, the man might!

"See here, Sergeant — how much water have you, for two men going out onto the desert? It's a long way across, this way."

No answer.

"I only wanted to tell you that there's a shack and a little spring over to your left, in that hollow — it was Billy Armour's place."

Without a word, Wilson turned there. When they got to the cabin, he swung from his saddle, but before he entered he cut a length from his rope and tied Clint's feet securely under the horse's chest; evidently he was not taking the ghost of a chance of losing him. It did not take him long to search the little cabin, and when he came out he had a look of satisfaction on his face in spite of himself; he was holding a battered old canteen which he had found — he would have been mad enough to start into the desert with only one.

He would not even ask where the spring was — and it was some distance off. Nor would Clint volunteer the information; he sat his horse looking down with contempt on Wilson. He had not blamed the man for his enmity before — it was the natural reaction from such a close friendship as theirs had been, when he had seemed to find his pardner a traitor and worse. But this treatment of a prisoner was entirely unwarranted, and small minded, and Clint was coming to hate the man for a big bully.

Wilson found the spring at last, and filled the canteens — he had taken his own partly empty one too. He stood a while, anxiously watching the battered one he had found; it did not leak. Then he swung both across his saddle horn and prepared to mount. Clint spoke in a cold unfriendly tone.

"Wilson, try to act like a human being, for once in your life. Take my handcuffs loose and put my hands in front of me."

This was not a request; it was an order. Wilson glared at him. But he shook his gun loose and stepped close; he untied a little key from a buckskin thong at his belt and reached up. Clint, his feet fastened together under the horse, was helpless, of course; he quietly held out his wrists before him and let Wilson snap the handcuffs on again. At that, the man did more than seemed to be necessary; with a saddle string he cut from Clint's saddle, he lashed the connecting link of the handcuffs tightly to the horn.

"Thanks, old pardner!" said Clint sarcastically.

And so, in the first gray of dawn, they rode out into the desert. Again Wilson showed more cleverness than Clint had expected. Several miles away from the oasis stood a great hill — it seemed, rather, a huge, solid red rock that thrust itself up out of the sand; it was taller than it was wide. Some miner during the boom had named it the Devil's Furnace; and it might well have been a furnace, bare and burning under that desert sun. Straight to this went Wilson, as fast as he could get Clint's horse to lead. By the time daylight was strong, he was under it, slipping around close to its foot.

And then he turned straight out from the rock on the far side, often glancing back to make sure that it was directly between him and the Silvermines. Nobody could see them from back there. Clint himself could not have worked it better; he knew very well that there was now no possible chance of his friends following and rescuing him — even if they knew where he was. And, anyhow, they would probably believe him to be lying in the bottom of one of those old mine sumps by this time.

They rode without a single word. The sun rose, and the heat seemed even more terrific than when Clint had come in. He saw a tiny patch of white cloud hanging in the southwest, the first cloud he had seen in ages. They would begin to gather; it would rain before many days. But now this heat was unbearable.

Sometimes, when Wilson was not looking back, as he often did, Clint did a queer thing; he would hunch far forward in his saddle, straining his waist out and struggling to twist his hands back. It seemed that he was trying to reach his belt buckle. He struggled thus until he was red in the face, but he saw that it was no use; his wrists were tied forward, and only by breaking a bone could one of them be bent back. He gave up, and sat back in the saddle resignedly.

Noon came, and they plugged along steadily out there. There was no sweat on them, in spite of the tremendous heat; that scorched air dried any moisture before it had well escaped from the pores. Clint's tongue was getting thick and big in his mouth, but he would have died rather than ask for a drink. And Wilson himself must be suffering still more; he had never been able to endure hardship of this sort half as well as Clint — a man of his bulk never can endure it well.

Suddenly Wilson stopped his horse and drew Clint's up alongside. Clint saw his flushed face, almost feverish. He watched him unsling a canteen, draw the cork.

"Here!"

With an ungracious grunt, he held the canteen to Clint's lips, lowered it, brought it back up again. Clint had never tasted anything more delicious than that warm water trickling down his scorched throat.

And then Wilson was corking the canteen, slinging it back over his saddle horn; he himself had not tasted the water, parched though he must be. Impulsively, Clint spoke.

"Thanks, Wilson!"

"T'hell with you!" came a surly grunt, but Clint grinned a little at his back. Sergeant Wilson in many respects had the mind of a big, stubborn, spoiled child, but — he was white, in spite of himself.

On and on; now the Silvermines were lost in that waving, shimmering blur behind, and nothing but desert lay ahead. When the sun had set, and the air seemed almost cold in comparison to that baking heat, Clint spoke — it had been too hot to say anything before.

"Wilson, let's talk a while."

No reply; not even a motion of the back of Sergeant Wilson's head.

"Let's talk over how Tex got away, Wilson — and about that note you found. I might be able to tell you some things."

This time Sergeant Wilson spoke over his shoulder; his voice sounded very thick and hoarse; the poor devil had not wet his lips all day.

"All right! Tell me how he got away, if you didn't help him."

Just in time, Clint caught himself; he had almost spoken — this heat on his head must be making him groggy. He could tell Wilson, but he dared not. This silence seemed to be the answer Wilson had expected; he turned in his saddle, and there was a sneer on his flushed, dust-caked face, but he said nothing. A little further on, he turned again.

"What did you mean by treating Mona that way — stripping her and taking her clothes?"

Clint had remembered more of the things he had heard about Wilson's niece. Her mother had died when she was very young, and big, blundering Sergeant Wilson had taken upon himself the full weight of caring for her. Most of his pay had gone to send her to school, to clothe her; he felt an immense responsibility not only for her welfare but for every thought in her head — a big, clumsy, middle-aged bachelor of his kind would. And woe betide the man who he thought had insulted her! It was too grave a matter to talk of generally, and when he did speak of her it had been as "my niece";

Clint had taken it for granted that she was some young, unmarried girl, and had never connected "my niece" with Mona Fernel.

Now for the first time the full import of what she had done came shooting to his mind: with her uncle one of the rangers outside there, she had helped him, a stranger, to escape! Of course he could not answer Wilson this time either; it would implicate Mona Fernel, perhaps get her into serious trouble — at least with her uncle, if not with the law.

This silence was again exactly what Sergeant Wilson expected. With a bitter oath of contempt, he turned ahead. Clint, led a prisoner behind, stared at his broad back with a queer expression on his face. Now, he could explain everything to Wilson — and dared explain nothing. Good old Wilson! To Clint now, the man who had looked after Mona so assiduously was necessarily good, no matter what his brutal treatment of himself.

It was now almost dark. Wilson had ridden out of his way to cross a wide, low spot covered with strangely-shaped, wind-eroded boulders; why, Clint could not guess. Nor did he go straight through there; still leading Clint's horse, he was winding back and forth among the boulders, studying them carefully. At last he stopped, looking a long time at one in particular. Clint could see nothing strange in it; it was just another "balancing rock," of a kind common all over the Southwest, and particularly so in the deserts where the drifting sand eats fast. The round top of this one was about eight feet high, as big as a large dining-room table, and the little spindle of stone on which it balanced was perhaps a foot or slightly less through — this spindle was a few inches above the sand. The top of this roughly hour-glass-shaped thing would weigh several tons, and the bottom perhaps a thousand — or a million.

Wilson swung from his saddle and walked to Clint. He untied one foot, and his wrists.

"Get off."

Clint did.

"Now walk over to that balancing rock; back up against it and sit down."

Wilson had his gun drawn. Clint had nothing to do but to obey. When he was sitting, Sergeant Wilson brought the ropes from both saddles and began to tie his legs. Never had Clint seen a more complete job of tying a man — rope wrapped around and around, with a couple of dozen hard knots. But even then Wilson had the stubborn caution of his kind; while he laid out a scant, cold meal, he hardly ever took his eyes off Clint. He was not going to give him a millionth part of a chance of trying to escape. He even sat and fed Clint mouthful by mouthful, raising a canteen to his lips between bites.

The whole thing seemed brutal, uncalled for, to Clint lying there in that still scorching sand. But he noticed that Wilson ate little more than half as much as he gave his prisoner, and drank only about the same amount, although Clint had had water at noon. And then, the meal over, he untied that little key again from its thong. Carefully, cautiously, he unlocked the handcuffs, and stepped behind Clint.

"Turn and put your arms around that neck of rock."

"Huh!"

Wilson did not repeat it, but stood waiting. Slowly, Clint reached around with both arms. He felt the snap of the handcuffs on his wrists again. Wilson stood up, retying his little key to its thong, and spoke grimly.

"There! You didn't have nerve enough to say that Tex Fletcher got away without help, when he was handcuffed this way. Only that his arms were around a mesquite, and you're chained to the whole bottom of the desert. Let's see how you like that one, ex-ranger Yancey!"

He walked off deliberately, fed each horse a scant handful or two of oats, gave each a mouthful of water out of the crown of his hat. And then, with a last glare of contempt for Clint, he rolled himself in his blanket on the sand. It was not yet quite dark, but he had ridden all day and most of the night before; and he would want to get started again before daylight in the morning.

Clint, swathed in ropes, his arms around that stone weighing tons, lay looking at him. This man had been his friend for years, his pardner — and now he could expect more mercy from Tex Fletcher. Never had he seen friendship turn to such bitter enmity!

Darkness came, the stars shone brilliantly overhead, and still Clint lay there staring up at the sky. Far back toward the Silvermines, he heard the faint howl of a coyote; he wondered what it was doing out there in that barren land. He was aching all over, trussed up that way; his arms encircling the rock seemed numb and lifeless. Must be well past midnight now, and still he lay awake, staring at the stars with his eyes wide open. Wilson's prisoner — what a queer turn life takes sometimes!

CHAPTER
EIGHTEEN

The Key

Again Clint heard the coyote howl, very faintly this time. It must be going toward the Silvermines; probably it had been crossing the desert to get there. He tried to guess the time; he knew that it must seem much later than it really was, he lying tied this way with his arms around that stone. Really it could hardly be more than two o'clock.

He turned his head for the fiftieth time, to see Wilson lying wrapped in his blanket on the sand; farther off, he could see the two horses sleeping on their feet, their heads hanging. Queer business indeed; Sergeant Wilson, vengeful or cautious, had left him in just the same position that he himself had left Tex Fletcher that day when Tex escaped. Only that Tex had been handcuffed around a mesquite, and he had his arms around the spindle of a huge balancing rock.

How bright it was, for the middle of the night! The sky seemed to be an almost solid mass of brilliant stars, and the white sand of the desert threw back their light. He could plainly see an owl perched motionless on a high pillar of rock fifty yards away; the owl would be watching for lizards — he would find little else to eat out here.

Suddenly Clint jerked, and quickly turned his head again toward Wilson. He had heard a faint sound, the beginning of a snore. So Wilson was asleep at last; he could no longer keep his eyes open watching his prisoner. Clint had been waiting for this snore; he knew that Wilson had not been sleeping. Many a night, when they were rooming together, he had cursed that snore. More than once he had flung a boot.

Immediately, Clint went into action. He did a strange thing; he kicked his bound legs around; he seemed to be trying to raise them, to coil himself around that spindle of rock like a snake. Bound as he was, and cramped from lying, it was difficult.

At last he succeeded. He strained and reached with his manacled hands until he got his fingers twisted into the front of his belt. He worked them along the belt, careful not to lose his grip, until he felt the chain of his watch. Then he had a finger and thumb hooked into his watch pocket. And presently they came out; he let his legs drop, straightened them out on the sand.

He was slightly out of breath from the exertion, and he was struggling mightily not to have his breathing become audible in that desert silence. He lay still a minute or two. And then his fingers twisted back in toward the wrists. There came a faint click. He drew his arms around, unlocked the other handcuff. The snoring stopped, and Clint quickly flung his arms around the spindle of rock again, in their old position; he was again lying motionless.

He thought, lying there. Queer indeed! The evening before, he could have told Sergeant Wilson how Tex had got away, but he dared not — or he himself could not be trying to escape now; Wilson would have searched him for the key. There was that horse-stealing charge against him, and that letter of Tex's.

He had not begun to suspect even when Tex had told him that he could get out of any handcuffs the rangers put on him. But when the man showed him the bones of poor Carmody lying out there, where he had died of thirst, the thing had begun to dawn on him: Tex, going back some time to gloat over that poor remains of a ranger, had taken the key to Carmody's handcuffs. One would fit all the little intricate locks; it had to be that way, as one ranger often turned a prisoner over to another.

But no one except Captain Donley could have purchased one of those keys for a fortune; the company that made them was very strict; in their safe was a pattern key marked *Arizona Rangers,* and nobody but the manager of the company and one trusted mechanic was allowed even to see it. Captain Donley himself would have to go through a lot of red tape explaining why he might want a new key — it was on such caution that the company had built up its big business with law officers.

No wonder nobody had even thought that Tex might possibly have had a key! Not even Clint, after that remark of Tex's. But when he once suspected — knew, rather — his keen eyes had been searching every inch of

Tex's room for it. He had at last seen it, and managed quietly to pick it up as he reached for his hat.

Sergeant Wilson was snoring again. Clint drew his arms back and felt the knots on the ropes binding his legs. They were pulled hard as pebbles; it would take at least half an hour to untie them. He managed to squeeze a hand through the ropes and into his trousers pocket, and drew out his knife. A few slashes, and his legs were free.

The first thing, of course, was to get his guns; he had seen Wilson place them, with his own, under a corner of his blanket. He waited until the snore grew loud, and stole across hurriedly but without a sound — the deep sand made it easy to be silent. He cautiously, slowly, reached out a hand to feel under the blanket; he was crouched on one knee.

But there was one thing he had not thought of. The owl, perched on that tall rock, had turned its head to look at the strange, bent thing going hurriedly across the sand. Perhaps it was angry that its hunt for lizards was disturbed. Suddenly it let loose a strange, squealing sound — no bird can make queerer noises than an owl, or more startling. And Wilson, though snoring, had been tossing restlessly; probably he was having nightmares of losing this prisoner whom the rangers wanted so badly. His eyes flashed open, and a big hand darted out wildly and closed on Clint's wrist.

"Damn you!"

Clint flung himself back; he pulled Wilson almost clear of the blanket. Then, somehow, they were on their feet, sand spurting around them as they struggled,

189

locked together. The huge Wilson had the strength of an ox, as Clint well knew; it might have been the forelegs of a bear that were around him. Wilson was driven by a terrific fury that gave him double strength; he hated this old pardner of his who he thought had betrayed the rangers, insulted the niece he worshipped.

Wilson tore his right arm loose — Clint might as well have tried to hold a bull as that arm. The big fist came darting in an uppercut to Clint's jaw. Fortunately, the blow glanced a trifle, but at that it left Clint weak and almost limp. He did not strike back; all he tried to do was to hold those great arms, to keep the man from striking again. One more such blow, and he would go down unconscious, and he knew it. He had now but one hope; to prolong the fight all he could. This man's strength was far too great for him.

Wilson tripped over one of Clint's spurs — he himself was in his socks, although otherwise fully dressed. They crashed down on their sides. As though by mutual consent, they rolled apart, hurried to get up. For a moment they crouched, each on one knee, eyes on each other. A panic of rage came over Wilson; he knew that Clint could outrun him if he got off once; he feared that he would try it. But Clint remembered the three guns almost within reach of the other man, and he knew that one of them would be emptied into his back before he had gone fifty yards.

They came together like two fighting mountain lions. Wilson aimed a terrific blow at Clint's jaw; if it had landed, it would have broken the bone. But the wirier Clint slipped under it and, somehow, he again had

190

Wilson's arms pinned to his sides. The big man was swearing, grunting with rage, and with fear that his prisoner might escape. Back and forth they struggled. Wilson did not realize how far they had fought until Clint tripped him and sent him crashing backwards against the balancing rock, himself on top.

The thump of that head against the stone sent a twinge of fear through Clint; he was afraid he had killed the man. And then he knew that Wilson, though dazed, was holding his arm in a grip like a vice; the man was almost as rugged as the balancing rock itself. Up again, and the furious struggle went on, all the way back to where the blanket lay. Twice on the way back, Wilson struck Clint in the face, and both times his blows landed solidly. It had Clint groggy, but Wilson himself was still half dazed and had not been able to put his full strength behind his fist.

Gradually, Wilson's mind was clearing. He picked Clint up bodily and tried to dash him against the ground, hoping to knock the wind out of him and leave him helpless. But Clint got his legs around the other's waist, and they both went tumbling into the sand. Lying there, Wilson drove a savage blow for the temple. Clint jerked his head, and the fist caught him over the left eye, where the bones are thick.

And then, for the last time, they were back on their feet, charging into each other. Once more Clint dodged a smashing blow — it was clumsily sent this time. Wilson was panting wildly, and even in that weak light Clint could see the dark hue of his face; the big man was so out of breath that he seemed on the verge of apoplexy. And this was what the wirier, faster Clint had been fighting for all the time; he knew that it would have to come if he held out long enough.

Wilson saw it too; his wild, glaring eyes showed that he did. The impossible had happened; the smaller man was beating the big one in fair fight. But Wilson had one trick left. With his last strength, he dived in and seized Clint around the waist, lunged forward with him in his arms, and both sprawled headlong across the blanket. Clint did not realize what it meant until he heard a little metallic click.

Wilson had one of the guns! He had cocked it!

Clint slapped out wildly with a hand, and barely in time; the bullet kicked up sand within two feet of them. And again that click; the man was determined to get him if it was the last thing he did. Clint, struggling madly, got hold of the gun barrel. He felt it spring and quiver in his hand — another crash, the biting tang of gunpowder, and the bullet glanced off a stone and went zinging off out over the desert.

Now Clint had his fingers over the hammer; Wilson could not cock the gun again. They fought for it, rolling back and forth in a death grip. Three times more Wilson struck, with his left hand — once to the face and twice to the body; the big fist seemed to sink in three inches at each blow, but at that some of the strength was gone out of his arm now. A jerk tore the gun free of Clint's hand; it was swinging toward his stomach. Again that little click.

Clint, nearly blind with the exertion he had been through, twisted himself around. His doubled knee flashed up and caught Wilson in the pit of the stomach, with all his strength behind it. With a queer, sudden grunt, Wilson flopped over on his side, the gun falling from his fingers — Clint's boot kicked out and knocked it away.

He knew that he had only a moment or two before Wilson would recover. He tore the kerchief from the man's neck, made a quick knot on one wrist, and tossed him over on his back. By the time he got the other wrist tied, Wilson was beginning to struggle again. That strip of silk would not hold him long.

Panting though he was, and nearly blind, Clint ran to the balancing rock, and back. He had a handful of those pieces of rope. Quickly, he tied Wilson's wrists more securely, and then his legs. He stood up, swaying, and passed a forearm across his forehead. He went lurching across to that rock — he did not know why — and threw himself flat, to lie gasping for breath. Such a wild battle as that, he had never seen before, much less to take part in one.

Presently he drew out his watch, unsnapped it from the chain, and held it close to his eyes. He peered at it, puzzled, and then struck a match to see better. Why, it was only five minutes to twelve, and the second hand was still ticking merrily along; the watch was not stopped. There was no particular hurry now.

He lay about twenty minutes, then got up, straightened his torn clothes, and shook his two gun belts into place. He had been watching Wilson trying to wriggle back cautiously toward where the two guns lay, and he had purposely let him get almost there. Calmly, now, he walked over and picked up the guns, shoved them into the holsters. He found a canteen, drank a mouthful or two, and held the neck to Wilson's lips. Wilson only snarled.

"Damn you, Clint, I'd die right here rather than take a drink from you!"

"Suit yourself," said Clint coolly, and corked the canteen, laid it down.

He picked up the blanket, doubled it, and approached Wilson, who was now sitting up with his legs and arms tied. He waited, hoping Wilson would ask him what he was going to do, but the man would not speak. He laid the middle of the folded blanket on Wilson's bare head, brought the rest down around his shoulders, and tied it in place with some of the loose rope.

"Wilson, this'll blindfold you right. I'm going to take your guns and the full canteen and hide them a long way off, where you can't find them till daylight. That'll hold you here when I leave. And I'd advise you not to try to go back to the Silvermines, for two reasons. One is that some of that gang will put a dozen bullets through your carcass before you've been there ten minutes. The other is that I won't be there. Want to know where I'm going?"

No answer from that muffled figure.

"Well, I'll take the guns and canteen away."

Clint gathered them up. He spoke again.

"Oh, yes — I'll take your handcuffs too. I left them under that rock."

He walked over there, picked them up. And then, not moving his feet or making a sound, he quickly laid guns, handcuffs, and canteen up on a high ledge of the rock. When daylight came, they would be in plain sight, but Wilson would never think of searching there.

"Well, I'll be back pretty soon."

He turned and, empty-handed, walked off. He went a long way, taking a winding course through the sand; Wilson would be able to track him there even at night. He passed every boulder on the way; at some of them he stopped and shuffled his feet. A time or two he stopped and raked finger-marks in the sand; Wilson would dig there. He could imagine the man tearing furiously around, climbing boulders, digging with his hands like a badger. He found a wide patch of bare rock, walked onto it, turned, and came off a few yards to one side. Sergeant Wilson would crawl over every inch of that rock. In spite of his bruised face, Clint had to grin at the thought of it. And wouldn't Wilson explode when morning came and he saw those guns, there within his reach all the time! His language would almost melt the rock.

At last Clint strolled back. He was quietly smoking a cigarette now. He saddled his horse, and led it to where Wilson lay.

"Well, old pardner, I think you'll have a sweet time finding those things before daylight!"

He undid the blanket, and pulled it off. Wilson sat glaring at him.

"And, Sergeant, I'll tell you where I'll be about a week or two from now: when you hear of a big heard of cattle being stolen, go there as fast as you can — you'll be only about two days late to catch me and my boys."

"Yancey," Wilson's voice shook with rage, "I didn't think you — you — you —" He could get no further.

"Could lick you fair and square? Uh-huh — it was easy. And now do you want to know how Tex Fletcher got away from me? I've shown you that a man *can* get out of handcuffs without help."

"Agh-h-h!" Wilson roared like a wounded bear. "Somebody came in out of the desert and turned you loose — one of your dirty gang!"

"Think so? Well, look all around our tracks in the morning, and see if you find any others coming or going; that'll settle that. And I'd give a good deal to be at your trial for turning me loose — if you're man enough to tell about this thing. You'll notice I didn't hit you in the face, to leave any marks. It was your evidence, Wilson, that made an outlaw out of me. Well, will you listen to how Tex got loose, and about that note?"

"T'hell with you, Yancey, you rotten renegade! I wouldn't believe anything you said if you swore it on a dozen bibles!"

Clint shrugged.

"Reckon that's right — you wouldn't." He tossed something on the blanket. "Here's a knife; you can hunch over to it and cut yourself loose. But by the time you do it, and find your guns, I'll be a long way from here. Adios, sweetheart!"

He swung into the saddle, waved mockingly, and rode off into the night.

CHAPTER
NINETEEN

Showdown for Tex

The next night, Clint got back to Gulch City; he had hidden all day in the hills, not to ride in daylight. He had been lucky enough to find some old jerky which Billy Armour had left at his shack, and this and a jackrabbit he shot with his revolver made filling if unpalatable meals — he had slept most of the day, under a cedar.

He left his horse a block off, and went quietly to Butch's place from the back; he did not know what might have happened since he left. There was an old stable back there, a blank window facing him; he decided to go through that window and survey the house from the stable door. But first, with his usual wariness, he crouched under the window, listening.

And a very good thing that he did. Presently he heard the faint tinkle of a spur, as a man moved a boot. This was serious! Butch's house being watched meant that their plans had leaked out. Almost anything might happen now, the only thing certain being that it would be something unpleasant. At that, he was hardly surprised; he might have been surprised if one of Billy's three cowboy friends had not betrayed him. It was queer; they were the only supposedly honest men in his little band, and yet they were the only ones in whom he had never had confidence.

Of course he had to do something with that man in there, and he had to do it without the least disturbance; there might be other watchers around. At last he stood up and leaned openly in the window; he would be outlined against the sky for whoever was in there; this very openness was his best bet. He hissed softly, and called in a whisper.

"Come here — message from Tex."

He heard a grunt. As the man inside would see him, he was standing negligently with his left hand resting on the window sill and his right laid carelessly against the upper part of the frame near his head. The man could not see that he had his gun in that right hand, held in from the light, the wall hiding it.

"Now, what?"

He did not recognize the whisper, but a soft tinkle of spurs was coming toward him. As the man came near the window, his face became a gray blur, vaguely seen. Clint waited until he was close, and began to whisper slowly.

"Tex told me to — bat you on the head."

In the middle of it, his gun cracked down on the man's hat. There was not even a grunt; the man fell in his tracks. It had been so simple that Clint had a little grin on his face as he threw a leg over the window sill and slipped in. With the man's belt and neckerchief, and with strips torn from his shirt, he did a quick and thorough job of tying and gagging him, and then he dragged him into the darkest corner. He hurried to the door, and whistled softly a time or two. No answer; that meant that there was no other watcher, on this side at least.

He slipped quietly across the yard and entered the house — the door was not even fastened. He was surprised to find his whole little crew collected there, as though holding a council. But not as surprised as they were; their blank stares told him that they had never expected to see him alive again, after his mysterious disappearance. He unobstrusively studied the faces of Billy's three friends, but they seemed to look no more or less surprised than the others; he could see nothing to hint as to which was the traitor — and of course, to be fair, he admitted to himself that the thing might have reached Tex through some accident.

He quickly told them of the watcher he had discovered. Their blank faces told him that they realized how serious it was — there was not a man in the room who could safely bet a nickel that he would be alive in twenty-four hours. Or perhaps there was one, but Clint could not guess which.

"So what do we do?" asked Butch. He spoke calmly, but Clint noticed his eyes stray uneasily toward his daughter; that was all that he was worrying about; his own life had long ago come to be a thing of little importance to him.

"We get out, and mighty quick. Anyway, we have that rustling job all fixed up; it'll give us a stake, and a good one."

"You mean — get out for good?"

This was from Jake O'Dowd, one of the men he suspected. It might have been a perfectly innocent and natural question — and it might not.

"Haven't made up my mind yet. The thing now is to get away with that herd; I've made a good connection for selling it in Mexico."

Of course he knew what he meant to do, but he was not wanting to risk its getting to Tex. He did not ask for a consultation; he gave them quick orders.

"Get horses saddled; get them over where mine is hidden, and saddle him for me too. I have to go downtown to see a fellow, but I shouldn't be long. Take blankets and canteens and some chuck. And remember this: you fellows stick in one bunch, and if one tries to leave the rest, plug him — we can't risk having anything leak out."

"Why so danged cautious? Suspicious of us?" This came somewhat truculently from Ted Wynn, another of the three; he looked insulted, about ready to fight.

Clint glanced across at him keenly. Was he the spy of Tex's? Or was it merely his hot head? Butch cut in.

"Good idea — we're in a bad spot. Sally, git yore ridin' shirt on quick."

"Oh, yes!" said Clint. "Take my chaps over for me; I don't want to wear them and look suspicious down there."

"See here!" grunted Billy. "Let me go see that feller for you, whoever he is; I'd be a sight safer down there than you'd be."

"Thanks, Billy — got to do it myself."

He went quietly out the back door, and turned down the alley. Sneaking around would not do; his best bet was to walk around so openly as to take them by surprise; they would not know what to do about it. Besides, if they thought him unsuspicious they would believe there was no hurry.

This, he realized, was another case where nothing but sheer brazenness could carry him through. It was touchy at best. The point was that there were with him three men upon whom he could not rely; he felt certain that at least one of them would quit him, and all three might. That would exactly halve his little crowd — leave only four of them to rustle a large herd. It could not be done.

But he had long ago decided that the two young gunmen pals, Bud Haines and Newt Collingsby, would throw in with him if he could talk with them and show them that he had a big profit in sight — and they would stick because of personal loyalty to him. In fact it now was about a case of getting them or giving up all his plans — and getting out of Gulch City to stay out. He himself had to see those two tonight, or get shot trying. He did not like the thing, but he had to face it.

Clint walked boldly into the saloon opposite the hotel; he could display a surprising amount of "brass" when he had to. But he was hardly through the door when he wished that he had paused to listen first. The stony silence, the tension in the place, told him that he had walked right into the beginning of a gun fight.

Going in, he almost brushed Tex Fletcher, who stood at that end of the bar with a glass of whiskey in his hand. Tex nodded to him as calmly as though he had been expecting him.

"Hello, Clint."

"Howdy, Tex."

Tex turned his back — but the big mirror behind the bar would show him all that was going on in the room. Wondering what was happening, Clint glanced around quickly. He saw the two young gunmen he was looking for, Bud and Newt; they were together, as usual. He noticed that they had a look of quiet, wicked enjoyment on their faces, as though they had been thoroughly relishing whatever his entrance had interrupted for the moment.

And then, in the silence, came a mocking, sarcastic voice from the other end of the room; it was a good deal louder than seemed necessary in that stillness.

"Yes, sir, boys! Like I was sayin', I never yet turned rat on a friend o' mine, or got him killed to save my own skin. Whatever I may be — an' that's plenty, I admit — I ain't yaller down the back."

Clint caught his breath and held it. The showdown! He heard a quiet laugh, and turned to see Tex set his glass on the bar. Tex looked amused; he seemed to think all this a very good joke. One quick look at Tex's face, and Clint understood. Tex knew that his grip on the gang was slipping badly, that he had got the name of being a coward. Clint knew that he was not. He wondered what he would do.

There was no long wait to see. Tex walked slowly down the room, the smile still on his face; half way down, a blue puff of cigar smoke came casually from one side of his mouth. Clint edged over to Bud and Newt; he heard a quick whisper from Newt:

"Hell's goin' to pop!"

That man down there was Mike McCook. His own gang had been broken up by the rangers a few days before; had he come in here to try to recruit a new one from Tex's men? Or to make a daring effort to supplant Tex? Then Tex was stopped; he was still smiling.

"Pardner," he drawled quietly, "don't you think you're running over at the mouth a little too much?"

Mike pretended to be surprised to see him.

"Why, hello, Tex!"

Although Mike was of average height, and heavy set, Tex could look down on him from his six feet two. Tex spoke again, as calmly as though talking absently of the weather, not even bothering to remove the cigar from his mouth.

"Mike, I know some of my boys have been doing a little grumbling lately. I believe some of them got a notion I've lost my nerve."

Mike grinned wickedly; his own nerve had never been questioned, nor had there ever been reason to question it. He was somewhat of the Billy Armour type, but much older and farther gone in the rustling game.

"Tex," he drawled confidentially, "jest between the two of us, confidential, some are hintin' that you never had any — that it was all wind got you by so long.

Some say that you was just gettin' by with a good bluff — like this one yo're tryin' on me now."

Men began to steal quickly toward both front and rear doors. Tex turned calmly, but his voice snapped out in a way not to be ignored.

"Stay in here, everybody! I want you boys to see this, and spread it around — it's going to be good."

He turned back to Mike as though he had forgotten him for the moment. He half closed his eyes, and rolled the cigar absently across to the other side of his mouth.

"Mike, let's give 'em a little lesson in what sort of nerve we both have. Like I say, it'll be good — too bad only one of us can live to see the rep it'll bring. Let's see — we'll stand facing each other in the middle of the floor, and you'll draw your gun slow till the muzzle's within an inch of being out; I'll take that much handicap. Yavapai here'll snap his fingers when we're ready to shoot."

Clint heard a gasp from Bud Haines.

"He's crazy! Mike's streak lightnin'!"

Mike was flushed a trifle — it might have been from liquor. He looked slightly surprised; he really had believed that Tex was too yellow to stand up to a man of his reputation. But not for one second did he hesitate; he was going through with the thing almost as well as Tex himself. He spoke quietly and grimly:

"I'll take even draw, Tex; there'll be no argument about whoever comes through alive bein' the best man with a gun."

Tex laughed amusedly.

"I'm boss in this town, Mike, and everybody here does what I say — including you. Set? Start your draw, Mike."

Clint watched Tex Fletcher with fascination. That smile was still on his handsome face; he still seemed to think it a joke that anybody should "call" him. Carelessly, almost yawning, Tex raised both hands to straighten his hat on his head.

Perhaps Mike lost none of his nerve — nobody would ever know. Perhaps he was doing only what Tex himself had done many a time — taking an unfair advantage because that was habit with him. His gun had crept slowly up until it was almost out of the holster, and then, without waiting for Yavapai's signal, the barrel whipped horizontal like a flash. In the dead stillness, the little click of the hammer being thumbed back came suddenly, unexpectedly.

The crash of a heavy revolver. Mike tumbled over on his back, doubling up queerly. His gun went off, and a spurt of plaster came from the ceiling. Clint's eyes were very wide open; indeed, his mouth was partly open too. One instant, Tex's right hand had been touching his hat; the next, there was a smoking gun in it, level with his waist. It had been the most incredibly swift and smooth draw that Clint had ever seen — and while he was drawing, the smile had never left Tex's face; the cigar had actually been traveling across his mouth to the other corner.

"My Gawd!" gasped somebody. "He got him smack between the eyes!"

Tex jerked his thumb carelessly.

"Drag that thing out. Line up, boys — have one on me."

He slipped his gun back into the holster, and raised his head, his eyes sweeping the room mockingly. He laughed softly.

"Who thinks now that I'm losing my grip, or my nerve? If anybody does, I'll take him on, same terms — or any two at once. Oh, hell! why be a piker? I'll make it any four in the room, even draw? Well, who's it goin' to be?"

A wild-looking young fellow with black, curly hair looked at him with half closed eyes, and grinned.

"Tex, let's talk about somethin' nicer. Did you say somethin' about a drink?"

Two men, each holding a wrist, were sliding the body of Mike McCook toward the back door. The others were crowding toward the bar. In the bustle, Clint slipped through the door and out. That settled it; Tex was boss here, and there would be no more questioning his authority, no more disrespect. Clint's heart was in his boots; his carefully-worked-out plans were wrecked. Why, even he himself had a new respect, of a sort, for this outlaw leader — nerve the man had; the cold nerve of the devil himself.

CHAPTER
TWENTY

Outlawed by Outlaws

Clint had not taken three quick steps before the door opened behind him. He whirled, his hand going to his gun.

"Hold it, Clint!"

He had almost fired before he recognized the voice as Bud Haines's. Bud hurried to him, and spoke in a quick, friendly whisper:

"Git out of town, fast! We all got orders to git you."

Impulsively — he was almost desperate — Clint whispered back.

"I'm going tonight. But I've got a little gang of my own now. Want to throw in with us?"

It was risky to tell this. What if Bud went straight to Tex with the story? Bud spoke instantly.

"You bet I'll throw in with you, Clint! Tex has nerve all right, but he's a low-down snake. Yo're white."

Clint jerked his head up and stared at Bud. He had not looked for this quick decision. He was so surprised that he did not for the moment know what to say. Bud whispered again:

"I'll see Newt about comin' too — us two generally stick together in what we do. Hide — uh — hide between them two houses acrost the street."

He went hurrying back into the saloon before he was missed. Clint crossed the street quickly and squeezed himself into the narrow passageway. He waited there, taut with suspense. Probably, he thought, Newt would talk Bud out of it — the whole thing was crazy now, with Tex's unquestioned supremacy once more established. No, they were not coming, or they'd have been out by this time. With drooping shoulders, Clint turned to steal away. Perhaps never in his life had he felt so discouraged as at this moment.

It came to him that they might have to wait for a drink with Tex, not to arouse suspicion. This thought was but a straw to grasp feebly at; common sense told him that it could not have taken this long. He hesitated, glanced over his shoulder at the saloon, started on again.

Suddenly the door across the street burst open, and men came dashing out, jostling each other in their hurry. Clint heard shouts:

"Where's he gone to?"

And Tex's commanding voice:

"Scatter both ways, boys, and look for him. Remember, shoot quick when you see him, and shoot to kill!"

So that was it: Newt not only had talked Bud out of it, but had gone to Tex. Queer that they did not know that he was across here, crouched in the little passageway. Again came Tex's voice, calm:

"Five hundred for whoever gets him, boys. We'll have no double-crossers in Gulch City."

Tex having the nerve to apply that name to him! Or to anybody else, for that matter.

They did know where he was! Two of them were coming running across the street, six-shooters in their hands. What a situation! Outlawed by outlaws, a reward on his head!

Here those two came, straight for the mouth of the little passageway. Too late to run; they'd get him in the back if he tried it. It had to be fight it out. He stopped, turned back again, drew his gun; there was a faint, metallic click as the hammer came back. Whoever entered that passageway first would be out of luck.

Here came a man, running in! The gun muzzle came up level, and Clint's finger began to press the trigger. Once more, barely in time, came the words:

"Hold it, Clint!"

Sweat seemed to break out instantly on Clint's forehead, and his breath stopped short in his throat. Only by a split second had he avoided killing Bud. Newt's voice:

"There, pardner?"

"Newt! Bud! You're —"

They heard the relief, the thankfulness in Clint's voice. A barking little laugh from Bud; he sounded vicious if anybody ever did.

"I'm a tough — !" What he called himself was not nice. "What," he asked quickly, "do we do now?"

"Get horses and saddles. Meet me as soon as you can at the corner where the old dry-goods store used to be."

They were running back. He heard Bud's excited tone:

"He ain't in there; we looked well. Let's go up the street."

Then Clint was running through a dark alley, his gun in his hand. Five hundred offered for his scalp — within fifteen minutes, the whole town would have turned out to join in the hunt for him. Perhaps Clint was not scared, but he was never so near it before. Scared for himself, and scared for his futile little band of friends; they would be shot down like dogs, one by one, if they were caught. And the girl with them! He did not know what would happen to her; perhaps it would be better if she too would be shot down. He shivered a little; he wished her a thousand miles off. She could be nothing but a handicap. Outlaw's daughter though she was, she was but a quiet, feminine girl — soft, gentle, perhaps a trifle stupid, he thought. Probably she had never fired a gun in her life.

He shouted softly before he came to the old building where he had left Reddy hidden. His excited voice told that something had gone wrong, if the shouts from back in the town had not told that already. He could see dim figures hustling horses out in confusion; they were swinging quickly into their saddles, and even in that faint light their attitudes showed consternation, almost panic. In a moment he too had his horse out and was mounted; his chaps were thrown across the saddle, and there was no time to put them on.

210

"Quietl" he warned. "Keep to a fast walk; we don't want 'em to know which way we're going — they know about all of us."

They turned a corner or two in the dark, deserted streets of the old town, and Clint stopped them.

"Let's wait here. Two more joining us."

They did not like this halt, but nobody said anything. Two more joining, at this time! There must be two madmen in Gulch City!

The wait seemed ages in the tension, but it probably was not over three or four minutes at most. At last they heard two horses come clattering toward them, and the two riders looming up. Clint leaned out over his saddle, peering.

"Why — you — Is that Tex's big pinto?" he gasped incredulously.

A low, hard laugh of evil glee from Newt — he sounded like a young man who was game for anything.

"Shore is! And Bud has Yavapai's blood bay."

Bud spoke with overdone innocence:

"You said two horses, Clint — you didn't say what two."

Now the hunt for them *would* be on! That was a supreme piece of recklessness. On the other hand, the better his men were mounted, the better off they'd be. Perhaps those two wild young fools had reasoned this out; perhaps it was wisdom after all. Clint was starting off when he heard Billy Armour's grave, sober voice:

"Newt, how 'bout lettin' Sally ride that fast pinto — she's a gal?"

"Shore — shore!"

Newt caught the rebuke in Billy's tone and spoke in quick apology, ashamed of not having thought of it himself. He swung instantly from the saddle and reached up to help the girl dismount.

If it had been daylight, they would have caught a queer look on Clint's face. Since coming to this wild town, he had met some specimens of humanity whose lowness was almost unbelievable — and he had met some of the finest, most chivalrous gentlemen he had ever even imagined. There was one of them now, helping the girl from her slow horse to give her his fast one — because she was a girl. Clint spoke impulsively, and the warmth in his tone could not be overlooked:

"Newt, that horse is pretty light for a man — but we won't quit you, no matter what comes up."

Newt laughed softly as he swung onto the little roan.

"I know it, Clint. Why do you suppose I'm here with this crazy outfit?"

"Let's go, boys — straight up the gulch."

They went in a trot now, the girl in the center of the little band, the safest place. This part of the town, so far out, was completely abandoned; they did not see a soul. In a minute or two they left the last of the houses, and the sides of the gulch loomed high on each side, the summits sharply outlined against the steely light of the stars. They struck a fast lope, stirrup to stirrup. Clint glanced anxiously back at the girl. She was rising and falling with her horse as smoothly as any of the men; probably she had never ridden much, but she must be one of those to whom riding comes natural. That was a

212

relief, that she could ride well and would not delay them.

They were passing the same wash where Sergeant Wilson had turned up with Clint, when Clint saw one of his men swinging wide.

"Stop him!" he called.

The order was taken too literally. From within a yard or so of Clint, a gun barked, and the man pitched out of his saddle.

That shot was all that saved them. Tex, clever always, had sent men racing quietly to close the roads out of town. Those hidden in the bushes ahead thought themselves discovered. At that long range, their guns burst out; little points of red flame darted in the darkness up there. Clint was already shooting back at them as he whirled his rearing horse.

"Back! Ride for it!" And he added; "Get the girl in front!"

Butch grunted in a very tired tone:

"More comin' up behind us."

"Off the road, boys! Into the wash!"

It was a mad plunge in the darkness, through a fringe of bushes and down that steep bank. They came clattering down among the rounded, slippery boulders. One horse fell, but his rider helped him up with a swift kick and leaped into the saddle again. Down here, by crouching low over their horses' necks, they would be sheltered from the bullets coming from above. But they were being driven straight back into the town — and toward the other horsemen. Those below were running their horses now; the firing had of course been heard.

Butch turned his head; there was a little catch in his heavy voice:

"Sal, climb out the other side — run for it. Make a break for the desert an' try to git across. It's yore only chance, gal, an' — good bye."

And then, to Clint's surprise, this buxom, good-natured girl spoke quietly, firmly:

"I'm a-stickin', Dad."

Clint's face went white. Again his breath caught in his throat. So this was his bunch of rustlers and outlaws — and an outlaw's daughter. Most loyal crowd he had ever met — and he had got them into this.

The road wound along the bank of the main wash in which they were. Down beside the road were coming Tex's men, running from boulder to boulder, off their horses, shooting as they came. The clatter of hoofs below was still a good distance off; it sounded heavy, for one could not go very fast up such a slope. Still, it would not take them long to get up here. Clint and his little crowd had been forced down a few yards — a glance had shown them that the opposite bank was far too sheer for horses to climb. Clint slid from his saddle, and spoke quickly.

"Billy — Newt — Bud — come on. Rest of you shoot over the bank."

Leading them, he slipped as fast as he could up under the bank next the road. Before he had well started, he saw a head peering over through the brush. One of the others beat him to it; a shot, and the man came sliding down in a little trickle of gravel — they heard him groan feebly as they passed him. They ran only a few yards more and Clint saw a little gully beside him.

"Up here, boys. Charge 'em!"

With spurting guns, the four came running down the road. Newt and Bud were barking out shrill, Indian-like yells, and the rest joined in; it sounded like a dozen, at least. Taken in the back thus unexpectedly, the ambushers broke. A bare instant of uncertainty as they glanced back toward where their horses stood, and they were tearing down the steep road in panic. Bullets raked them as they passed the others; two of them were left behind. Clint shouted down:

"Come on — come on! Lead our horses up here!"

He leaped down into the wash, and met them part way. He flung himself ungracefully into the saddle and sent Reddy scrambling up the gully to the road, the rest following. Now those hoofs behind were very close, and a few shots were beginning to click off the rocks near them.

"Go on!" he ordered. "We four drop back!"

Those in the lead raced up through the standing horses of the ambushers. Clint waited until the last was through, and then turned to the three near him — they were sticking, all right.

"Shoot those horses — got to do it!"

He himself was firing. One horse leaped over the bank to die at the bottom of the wash; two more were left lying squarely in the road.

"Come on, boys!"

"Hell, they got us!" growled Bud disgustedly. He seemed more peeved than anything else.

"Come on, I tell you!"

They went clattering up, bullets ricocheting off the stones around them and whining weirdly into the night. And then the shooting behind was dropping back; there seemed to be some confusion back there.

"Huh?" grunted Billy in astonishment.

"The horses — the blood," answered, Clint quickly. "They can't get their horses by. Hated to do it — but better horses dead than us — and the girl."

An oath of astonished admiration burst from Bud Haines — he thought he had heard of all the tricks.

They caught up with the others near the head of the gulch, and again all eight of them were loping up together. They reached the top, and Clint made them stop a moment to let their horses blow — any how, he wanted to listen. Down below, the pursuit was on again, but there was a raggedy, uneven sound to it, as man after man forced his panting, shying horse up the almost perpendicular hillside and then around, down to the road again — the wind was blowing from the wash across the road, so that they would have to go high up to get their horses past. Clint picked up his reins.

"That settles 'em — let's go. Let's cut back along the top of the ridge over 'em, just behind the sky line."

They had gained such a good start that, with the ridge between, the pursuers could not hear them riding fast. And by the time the crowd got their sweating horses up to the head of the gulch, Clint's little band was well away. Clint rode in the lead, setting the pace. On a stony hillside facing back, he would only trot, sometimes even walk; down the far side, he would put his horse to a dead run. He swung up a last high ridge and stopped on the summit. He looked down; the desert lay before him, white and ghostly in the cold, brilliant starlight.

"Who's missing?" he asked; his voice sounded strained.

Two of Billy's friends were — they knew what had happened to one. The third, Jake O'Dowd, was there, and both he and Billy were very silent and inclined to hang their heads; it is bitter to find that a pardner is a traitor. It seemed almost incredible that not one of the others had even received a scratch — of course Clint's quick wits were largely to thank for that. Clint was listening. He could not hear a sound behind. And suddenly he heard Bud drawl absently to Newt, in a low voice:

"You know, I feel jest like robbin' a bank or somethin' tonight — jest to see if I couldn't stir up a little excitement."

Clint turned toward him with a hard little grin on his face, but he said nothing. He was wondering if those six men sitting their saddles around him were not the toughest, most reckless rustlers in all Arizona. They'd do! He touched his horse gently with a spur and went trotting down the ridge ahead of them, leading them into the desert.

CHAPTER
TWENTY-ONE

Billy's Home Range

Although it was almost midnight and the rain flailing the windows, Butch Tolleson stood up heavily and reached for his hat. He threw a wistful glance around the neat, orderly little sitting room. His eyes fell on the big Bible on the centre table and he quickly averted them; long though he had been a rustler, there were still some things that made him uneasy. He turned to the neat, motherly little old woman who sat with her knitting in her lap, and the thin, weazened old man with his glasses pushed up on his forehead.

"I'm shore sorry, but I jest can't stay all night. I got to be goin' now."

"It's a turrible night to be out in, Henry," said the old man, getting up and shaking his gray head sadly. Butch had not been called by his right Christian name for so long that it gave him a queer feeling.

"Can't be helped. Well, thanks a heap for promisin' to take care o' Sal till I come git her."

The old couple shook hands with him and saw him to the door, and Sally put her hands on his shoulders and gave him a little peck of a kiss; it nearly killed her to know her father's trade, but she loved this great, awkward bear of a man.

Hoofs went sloshing quickly off through the mud, the sound dying. Old Mrs. Beasley turned gently to the girl.

"You pore dear! It must have been terrible on you, riding in this rain — you're soaked! How long since you left that — that town?" She could not bring herself to say the name of Gulch City, known for its evil.

"Why — over two weeks." Sally did not like to answer questions, but those cousins of her dead mother's were so kind, and seemed so good, that she could not find it in her heart to appear uncivil to them.

"And where were you since you left the desert, honey?" asked the old lady kindly.

"In — a cave."

"A *cave!*" She threw up her hands in horror.

"Why, it was the opening of an old mine we camped in — there were a lot of abandoned mines around there."

The old man spoke softly.

"Ma, you'd better put her to bed; the pore child's all tired out, an' wet to the skin."

"Why, the pore dear! I'll give you our spare room upstairs, honey. Come this way."

A few minutes later the old woman came slowly back down the stairs alone. She sat at the table, and for a long time there was silence. Suddenly she burst forth.

"David, it's a cryin' shame, an' that's what it is! A nice gal like Sally Tolleson, an' a cousin of ours, bein' raised by a — a cattle rustler!"

219

"It's that, Ma."

The old man spoke broodingly. The two looked at each other, and looked away again.

"Ma, that cave — an' them old mines — Must be over beyond Cuchilla, the far side o' the T X range; I don't know nowhere else sounds like it. An' — there must be more of 'em in that cave, or Henry wouldn't start back at night like this. An' wantin' to git rid o' the gal."

"Pore Sally! I — could give her a good home; she'd be like a daughter to us, David. An', after all, she's our cousin, an' we owe it to her." Her voice rose virtuously, angrily. "'Tain't right, a rustler raisin' her!"

A moment of silence, and the old man spoke in a low voice.

"Mebbe — mebbe I'd better —"

He got up slowly, glanced at his slicker on the wall, and looked at his wife.

"David," she said, "it's our plain duty to pore Sally. We *got* to do it."

The old man spoke broodingly, to himself.

"There'll — be — big rewards for 'em."

"You should be ashamed of yourself, David!" The withered cheeks of the old woman flushed, but she did not meet his eye. "It's pore Sally you should think of, her not gettin' Christian raisin' like a girl should — she'd be happy with us, with Henry where he couldn't touch her."

Old David Beasley said nothing, but he seemed to have a hard time to keep his head up as he reached his slicker from the wall and went out, toward the stable.

Butch sloshed along in the darkness on his tired horse. He was soaked to the skin, cold water streaming down his back. He was shivering, and his teeth chattering, and his hands blue in their buckskin gloves. But he was thankful in his heart; Sally was in kind hands. He had not looked for those old cousins of his dead wife's to be so friendly; he had doubted if they would take the girl in at all. When he married Sally's mother, they had been bitter; they had refused to speak to either of them. But, then, one gets gentler with age — maybe he'd better let Sally stay there with them, if they wanted her; it would be a good home for her, where she could be respectable, there on the little farm. He'd miss his Sal, but he had to think of her good.

Toward morning he managed to steal a fresh horse from the corral of a little ranch he was passing; he had looked for it to be a lazy old night horse, but it turned out to be pretty fair. The morning sun was blistering, but he welcomed its heat on his back after that night. When afternoon brought the usual thunder and rain again, he found a sheltered spot under a ledge of rock; here he ate some cold, hard biscuits and some cold beef that was beginning to taste queer. He slept until dusk, and went on.

At two in the morning he was back with the others. With numb hands, he managed to strip off his streaming clothes to the skin; he crept into his blankets, smothering a groan. He was getting too old for the rustling game, and he had to admit it at last. Lying there, he thought of what he would do if he had to live his life over again — it would be very different, and

221

poor Sal wouldn't be ashamed of him. But he was almost exhausted. In cold and misery, he soon fell asleep.

And next evening, sitting by the camp fire, he was the same genial, good-natured Butch as always, so far as anybody could see; he seemed almost a father to those young rustlers. The fire was well back around a bend in the mine tunnel, so that its light would not shine out. There were wide cracks in the stone roof, through which the smoke worked up; those cracks seemed to run in a network all through the high divide; they absorbed the smoke in their windings, so that no trace of it showed on top. Billy had led them here; he, boy-like, had found and explored this tunnel when he was punching cattle for the T X. The cave at the mouth of it, making a good hiding-place for their horses, was what rendered it desirable.

Clint came across and sat down by Butch. He rolled and lit a cigarette, and passed the makings.

"When," asked Butch, "do we lift that herd? Ain't there been rain enough to make mud outa the Mojave?"

"Couple days more — pretty near any day. I want the feed to get a little better start." He turned to Billy Armour, the only other who happened to be there at the moment. "Say, Billy, tell me how you happened to go *bronco*. Reckless as you are, you look like you could be honest if you set your mind to it."

Billy rolled over on one elbow on his blanket. Quizzically, he blew thick smoke out his mouth and sucked it up his nose, then released the whole thing in a burst through sun-hardened lips.

"I'm jest nacherally tough," he grinned.

"But what started you out?"

"Oh — that. I was punchin' cattle for the T X, right here on this range. I took a notion I didn't like the color o' the range boss's hair, so I perforated him good an' plenty. Then I lit out with a bunch o' T X cattle — an' a few of other brands that run into the herd an' I didn't want to hurt their feelin's by chasin' 'em out rude." He yawned. "I always could drive cattle better by night anyways."

Suddenly Butch flared up — his face flushed quickly. He turned to Clint.

"Don't believe a word that young devil tells you! I'll give you the straight of it. Did you know that the T X runs nothing but rustled cattle it buys from Tex? The pick o' his Mexican cattle — big money in turnin' 'em over."

Clint nodded.

"I know more than you do about it, Butch. Nearly half what it has right now is good stock of Don Luis's — Tex didn't exactly steal 'em, but he was back of the stealing, and made the deal with old Simms. That's what got us nearly killed in Mexico; the Don found out about it — more of Tex's double-crossing."

"Well, I'll be — blamed!" Butch whistled. He was trying to stop swearing lately, and remembered about it as often as one time in twenty. "Well, Jack Harrington, the T X range boss, took all the best horses out o' Billy's string an' give 'em to a new hand that was a pal of his. When Billy heard about it, he blew up on the spot, an' quit — old Simms paid him off, Jack not bein' around the ranch at the time. Anything wrong in quittin' sudden that way?" he challenged.

"Why, no! Believe me, I'd quit pronto if a foreman pulled a dirty trick like that on me."

"Well, Jack didn't see it that way. He met Billy in a saloon a couple days later, an' started to call him every dirty name he could think of for quittin' when they was short-handed; he thought he was only a kid an' he could get away with it."

Billy nodded agreement, and put in sweetly.

"Uh-huh. We was both roarin' drunk, like I usually was."

"Will you shet up!" Butch almost shouted it at him, and his big hand closed on a heavy stick of wood beside him.

Billy grinned innocently and winked at Clint. "Sure!" he told Butch gravely. Butch glared at him, and went on.

"If this young ijit had give himself up an' stood trial, he'd likely have come clear, even with Simms's money against him — I don't reckon that old skin-flint would have spent a cent on the case, even if Jack *was* his nephew. Old Simms is president o' the bank, an' Billy didn't dare try to draw out his five hundred he'd saved. So he lit out for the hills an' started rustlin' T X cattle to git even. And — and mebbe a few others."

"In fact," yawned Billy, looking very bored, "any as wasn't tied down — an' they don't leave cattle tied down around here."

224

"Billy, did I say — !" Butch growled like a peeved bear.

"Oh, 'scuse me, Butch, for interruptin'!" Billy looked innocent as a newborn babe, but he cast a droll glance toward Clint.

"Who else did you kill?" asked Clint; his face was sober.

Billy scratched his head, and began to count silently on his fingers. When he had got to fifteen or so, he looked up at Clint with surprise on his broad face.

"Blame it, Clint, I can't think of anybody else, offhand."

"And a fine bad man you are!" scoffed Clint at him.

Billy looked embarrassed for a moment by his lack of murders, but nothing could disconcert him long. He sniffed right back at Clint.

"And one hell of a fine rustler boss you are! Why, us goin' to clean up on T X cattle, an' sell the Don's back to him, looks a dang sight too like honest rustlin' to suit a tough hombre like me."

"They won't all be the Don's, by any means; we take everything we can run off, without looking at brands."

Butch was poking fresh wood into the fire. He spoke quietly.

"Clint, like I been tellin' you, there ain't no kind o' rustlin' can git us in more trouble than this we're figurin' on — we should of kept clear o' Wayne County, like everybody else in our game does. We know danged well that Sheriff Jim Dukes is right in with Simms an' Tex; it's their money keeps him in office. I'll bet my saddle Tex found our trail headin' this way, an' sent

Dukes word to look out for us — Tex would rather see us sent to the pen for life than shot; it would last longer."

Clint absently kicked a coal back into the fire.

"I thought of that — but nobody knows where we're hiding. We can make a quick raid an' get out."

"I dunno — I dunno. Course nobody knows where we are, but — I still think this ain't safe."

Clint stood up and stretched.

"Safe? Well, you know, Butch, I've about got to the point where I'd feel scared if I found myself mixed up in something safe. It wouldn't seem natural to me any more."

They faintly heard a sound of hoofs on the mine dump outside, and immediately the flap of chaps and clink of spurs as a man came running back through the tunnel. Red Barclay, his face redder than ever, burst around the corner.

"Say Clint! I was scoutin' over west of here, like you sent me. Say, I saw three men ridin' around, an' one of 'em too big to be anybody only Big Jim Dukes, the sheriff. An' on my way back here, I saw two more bunches o' men ridin'. Say, the hills is full o' deppities an' posses, an' they're lookin' for us!"

Butch glanced up at him with his mouth open, but he hardly looked surprised; he had come to expect this sort of thing to turn up always.

"Somebody squealed!" he grunted. "Now, who could it be?"

Clint whirled to him; the thing in his voice was not far from anger.

226

"Butch, there are no squealers in our bunch, and I want everybody to know it! Something else made 'em suspicious that we're around here."

All the others had come running. They looked badly disconcerted, but hardly scared, as they crowded around Clint.

"What do we do — get out?" asked Newt disgustedly.

"No — we rustle those cattle. We take the T X to about the biggest cleaning a cow outfit ever got."

"How?" asked Red Barclay. To judge by his tone, he seemed to think that Clint had gone slightly crazy.

"Why — blamed if I know. I have to figure it out."

He turned and walked slowly toward the entrance. He heard the low, reckless laugh of Bud Haines behind him.

"Give him time, boys — give him time! That hombre can figure how to steal this tunnel, divide an' all, if he gets them brains of his to workin'. I'm bankin' on Clint Yancey to pull a rustlin' job that'll — uh — make Arizona history."

"Oh, I've seen dumber!" admitted Newt with a slow grin. "Tell you what, fellers: let's start a game o' cooncan — who's got the cards?"

"I'm busted flat, since last night," admitted Billy sadly.

"Heck," Newt waved airily, "that don't matter — we can settle up out of our split from them T X cattle when Clint sells 'em."

"O. K.," said Billy, and they began to spread a blanket on the floor, to squat around it.

But Clint turned back.

"Whose night is this to go out and get chuck? Jake O'Dowd's, isn't it?"

Jake and Billy had taken turns, they being the only two who knew this range. A friend of theirs who was trying to buck the T X with a small outfit had purchased the things they needed and kept them at his cabin; one sackful a night, carried before a saddle, was all the men needed. Jake glanced longingly at the cards, and got up.

"Uh-huh. Clint, Muggins said he's afraid they're gettin' suspicious of him, buyin' so much chuck all at once. I'd hate to get him in trouble; the T X only wants an excuse to send him up, or shoot him."

Clint thought a moment.

"No, we don't want to get him in trouble — he's been mighty handy for us, and you say he's strictly reliable. Tell you what — has he any good horses?"

"One pretty fair one; rest of 'em skates."

"Well, steal that best one tonight — you might pack in a good bunch of chuck on him this time. Then Muggins can go running to the sheriff tomorrow yelling about his horse being stolen; that'll square him, I reckon. Of course he'll get him back safe."

"Sure — that's it. I'll have Mug help me rope him an' pack him, an' make shore I steal him right."

Again Clint turned down the tunnel slowly, and a second time he turned back — quickly, this time. He spoke almost excitedly.

"Say, steal a saddle with him — if Muggins has only one, take it anyhow. I've got a notion."

Bud Haines was riffling the greasy cards. He spoke meditatively, the brown cigarette dangling from a corner of his mouth.

"Notion? Didn't I tell you fellers he would? Cut 'em, Butch."

CHAPTER
TWENTY-TWO

Baiting a Sheriff

The next afternoon, Clint himself went out on scout; it was a dangerous job now, for the country was alive with horsemen in little groups. He was riding the "stolen" horse and saddle. Hardly two miles from the cave, he saw one of these bands afoot, inspecting the mouth of an old mine tunnel. That settled any doubts he might have. Somebody had given the sheriff information about his approximate hiding place, and his camp was sure to be discovered within a day or two. It also proved conclusively that none of his men, nor "Muggins" Brown, had turned traitor — if one had, the exact location would have been known.

He was covering the hills in sweeping semicircles and zigzags, with the stealth of a raiding Apache. He had already inspected two bands of men from far closer range than they would have believed possible; he seemed to be looking for somebody among them. Trotting along now, smoking a cigarette, his odd, keen blue eyes were darting restlessly in all directions; hardly a jackrabbit moved within a mile that he did not know of it instantly.

He was following a bare side of a ridge. Squarely to his left, the crown of a hat appeared over the ridge across the draw. He drove the spurs in. A leap or two of the horse, and he was behind the only bush on the whole hillside, a thin, spindly algerita. He tumbled out of his saddle before he was through sliding to a stop; he opened his mouth and dropped the cigarette, and swept off his big hat. Then, with a jerk or two on the bit, he had the horse facing directly into the algerita, behind it — it took constant pulling to keep him head on.

Horse's ears, especially when they are pointed forward to other horses this way, are easily seen. He quickly broke a twig off the algerita and trust it into the top of the bridle. Before he stopped, he had known that there was a patch of bear grass a little farther up the ridge; it was of very much the color of the algerita, and the two would blend together, the horse's head not appearing above them against the pale ground.

His eyes crinkled up with amusement as he stood there. There were five men sitting their horses on top of that ridge now; he could even faintly hear them talking. Shading their eyes with their hands or hat brims, they were scanning every inch of the country for miles around with infinite care. Clint, his hand on the bridle, grinned slightly. It often seemed to him that most men might as well be blind, for all practical purposes — they could see so little. Now he himself, had he been one of those, would have concentrated first on this algerita; a steady stare at it would soon show movement if there was any. If he didn't mind a little noise, he might have thrown a casual shot at it for good measure. Possibly

231

there were no eyes up there as good as his own, but the worst there could have found him in a few seconds, had they been trained to know what to look for.

Here they came, angling down the ridge, the click of hoofs coming to him. He jerked the horse around to the side of the bush falling behind them. If one of them looked back — really looked — he could see a good part of the horse's head against the bare ridge now. But they rode blissfully on, determined to find Clint Yancey if it took a month. Clint was so amused that he almost laughed.

They trotted up the ridge he was on, and their backs bobbed slowly down behind it. There was a streak of recklessness in Clint that made him enjoy this sort of thing; he was chuckling softly as he swung up into his saddle.

He rode almost to the top of the ridge. He was holding his hat in his right hand, and he went up only far enough so that his eyes could see the backs of those men going down. When one twisted in his saddle to glance back carelessly, Clint did not duck. He did not make any move — movement is what attracts attention. He just sat there, his eyes crinkled sarcastically.

They were dropping down, and he went up a few paces more to keep them in view. And then he saw a group of men coming down the next ridge, to meet them. Three in that band — and the leader riding a huge, powerful buckskin. Now buckskins are reasonably common, but most of them are fairly small and chunky; there would be few in Arizona of this size and build — he had almost the lines of a racer, but sturdier. That must be Sheriff Jim Dukes's famous buck. And the rider was big enough to be the sheriff; and the sun flashed on something on the left side of his shirt.

Yard by yard, Clint rode up, until he saw the two groups meet beside the wash. They were talking, shaking heads. Each would be assuring the other that there was no sign of rustlers in the direction they had come from. As Clint expected, they soon separated, one group turning up the wash, the other down. Clint trotted swiftly to the summit, where he sat his horse outlined against the sky. He had rolled and lit another cigarette, and he sent a thick puff of smoke skyward.

The thing tried his patience; why, those groups rode twenty yards apart without seeing him. He was deciding just how to act, thinking the whole thing out coolly, as usual. It seemed to him that his best bet, not to arouse suspicion, was to play the part of a bold, bad bandit — to seem entirely reckless. It was a new rôle for Clint, and he was surprised to find that he enjoyed the prospect; the thing was going to be fun, of a sort. He took his cigarette from his mouth, cleared his throat, and shouted down mockingly.

"You gents! Is that Mister Jim Dukes, sheriff of Wayne County?"

Both groups stopped dead, and their astonished faces turned up to him. They were so surprised that he had to repeat the question a second time before he got an answer.

"I'm Sheriff Dukes. Are — are you — ?"

"I'm Mister Yancey, of Gulch City. Didn't happen to be looking for me, did you, Sheriff?"

There was a note of relief in the shout that came back.

"You mean yo're goin' to give up? We'll treat you right, Yancey."

Clint laughed derisively.

"On how tall a cottonwood? Sheriff, I just dropped over here to tell you that you couldn't catch me on a bet; you might as well gather up your men and go home. I'll promise to be out of Wayne County in twenty-four hours — that fair enough?"

There was an excited consultation down there; the two groups had drawn back together gradually. Most of them, Clint knew, would be cattlemen — and voters. Still, the answer surprised him.

"Will you promise not to steal any cattle around here, if we give you a chance to get out with your men?"

This was in another voice, an older man's voice. Clint shook his head and laughed down at them. He was playing his part to a T.

"Well — nothing much only T X's. I'm going to clean out half the T X herd tonight."

At this piece of brazen impudence, a savage roar came up from the last speaker. Clint guessed immediately that the man was old George Simms, owner of the T X, and Tex's friend. Fine! Nothing could be finer! Clint could have hugged himself. He shouted back in a drawl.

"Why, Mister Simms, you wouldn't mind a little thing like that, would you? I don't suppose I'll be able to get over half your stock — you'll have lots left."

234

The thing that came back up to him this time did not sound at all nice. He shook his head reprovingly; against the skyline, they could see that headshake very well.

"*Mister* Simms! Don't you know that swearing is sinful? You'll never go to heaven that way. But, then, they say you're such an old skinflint, and run with such bad company, that you'd never get there anyhow."

This time the sheriff spoke again, and the fury in his tone showed Clint that he was producing the effect he wanted — getting all of them fighting mad.

"Clinton Yancey, I'm callin' upon you to ride down here an' give up! Everybody knows you belong to the Tex Fletcher gang — you an' them fellers with you. I've swore to bust up that gang if they ever stole a single dogie in this county; they're dirty crooks!"

Oh-hoh! thought Clint — so that was it! That was one reason why all this showy effort was being made to catch him. The voters of Wayne County would not know of his split with Tex, so if Dukes could kill or capture him and his men, it would seem plain proof that there was no crookedness in the sheriff's office. No, not catch him — things might come out in court. Dukes would not want any of them alive, to talk.

Clint's eyes had been missing nothing. He saw another group of riders come dashing toward him; they had seen him sitting up there. They were still nearly a mile off, but it was time to be moving on. He laughed down again.

"Sheriff, let's play tag — I'm it; try to catch me!"

He whirled his horse too suddenly; it was not as well trained as Reddy. The quick touch of the rein and spurs made it rear high and paw the air. While it was balanced thus on hind legs, Clint swung off his hat mockingly — it looked like a last piece of daredevil recklessness.

"Adios, Sheriff — and Mister Simms! I'm on my way to round up those T X cattle. Try to stop me!"

A shower of bullets came up. Clint had figured on whirling and leaping out of sight before they could fire, but he was lucky enough not to be hit — they were trying to start their horses and shoot at the same time, and that did not make for a good aim. Then he had the horse turned; he was out of sight behind the ridge.

They had to put their horses up the steep slope, while he could fly rapidly down. When they reached the top, his back was a good distance away, and he was riding like the wind. And were they coming after him now! The way in which they tore down the ridge showed that they did not care if they killed their horses; the thing was to get Clint Yancey — dead.

Clint had not drawn a gun, but those behind were firing steadily. Of course they could have no hope of hitting him at such long range; he knew that they did not expect to, and most likely were not bothering to aim at him. What they were doing was signaling every group of riders in the whole countryside to close in on him. And the popping of other guns, some near, some almost out of hearing, told that the signal was spreading.

There had been no rain that day, although Clint had seen heavy thunder showers all around. The ground, parched so long, had soaked up the former rains; it gave ideal footing for his horse, neither muddy nor dusty, but packed well. He had taken this into his calculations, otherwise he would not have dared to start this race so far from camp. Lobo, at first, ran almost as smoothly as Reddy.

But before he had gone a mile, an uneasy look began to grow on Clint's face. Already, Lobo was getting a sort of right-hand pitch to his gait, and the quivering of his chest against Clint's legs was becoming uneven, spasmodic. Looked pretty bad; he had overjudged the horse on his looks, and on short runs to test him; that deep chest was not living up to its promise.

Glancing back anxiously, Clint saw that the sheriff on his powerful buckskin could catch up with him easily — but that Dukes appeared none to anxious to get ahead of the others. And small blame to him; why, alone, come to close quarters with the dangerous Clint Yancey, when the whole crowd was due to overhaul him in less than a mile more? They were gaining steadily; there was no mistaking that.

And here came another crowd, directly toward him! Clint saw them as soon as the first horse appeared around the bend of the draw, but he kept directly toward them. They were slowing up already, drawing their guns. Perhaps they knew what Clint meant to do, but they could not stop it. He went straight on until he was opposite a low saddle in the ridge to his left, and then whirled his panting horse toward it, up the slope.

237

As he expected, the two bands kept to the draw, to follow him through the saddle; the higher, steeper parts of the ridge would wind their horses too badly.

He dashed through the saddle, Lobo now staggering and floundering, sweat streaming down him. He went barely far enough to make sure that there were no men ahead, and he slid the horse to a stop, jerked out his carbine, and ran back. He threw himself behind a pile of boulders, and with one as a rest, took careful aim. A horse beside the sheriff's toppled, its rider flying over its head as it went down. He swung the muzzle, and dropped a horse in the lead of the other band.

Both crowds slid to a hurried stop, turned back the other way. But not far. Now, part of each band was swinging up the ridge to come around him; some were crossing in front, out of range; a few, including the sheriff, stayed where they were. Clint crawled backwards quickly, the boulders hiding him from the men. Those few moments of rest had given Lobo back a little of his wind. Still, Clint only struck a long lope as he went down the saddle on the far side.

He had a good start before the first man appeared on the ridge behind and saw him. There were shots, and shouting, and presently the sheriff, as Clint had expected, came racing through the saddle on his buckskin. There were six men with him, all well mounted on horses that had had a short rest.

Another mile, and they were again coming within shooting distance. And here came a crowd swinging in from the right, to join Dukes and the others; Clint had barely got past in time to avoid being caught between them. Poor Lobo was on his last legs; he was lumbering along — willingly, it is true, but with nothing more left in him. Another half mile, and he'd go down under Clint.

Now, Clint was riding beside the foot of a high divide. Ahead lay a pile of broken, bluish stone, sprawling down to the level ground. He raised his voice.

"Out, boys! Hold 'em back! My horse — all in!"

His men had heard the shooting sweeping toward them and they were outside already. They sprang to their feet on the edge of the flat place crowning the old mine dump. Each had a carbine, and knew how to use it; bullets came singing over Clint's head from in front. He glanced around, to see men throwing themselves from their horses, running for cover — but they were drawing carbines first. And here came another band, down the divide!

Poor Lobo thudded, staggering and heaving, toward the mine dump; he was in no condition for that treacherous climb up. Clint sprang from his saddle, whipped out his carbine, and stopped to give the horse's neck a quick pat.

"Poor devil, you did your best!"

It was dangerous, with bullets coming flying from long range, but he whipped out his knife and cut the cinch, jerked off the bridle. Now the horse would go; saddled, he would have stood there and most likely got shot. And then Clint was scrambling up that high, steep slope of broken rock, chance bullets clipping around him; perhaps nobody had ever before climbed a mine dump so quickly. He threw himself over the edge and lay panting; he saw that the others were lying down again, near the edge, with carbines before them — they could not be seen from below, nor hit. The wild, reckless eyes of Bud Haines swept over him, first in concern, looking for blood, and then with a sort of grin in them. Bud nodded at him.

"Shore a nice day, Clint — but it missed rainin'."

Clint gave a short-winded grin back; after that climb, he had no breath to answer. He crept out, his hat off, and peered carefully over the edge. He got glimpses of men coming running from cover to cover on all sides — why, it looked as if every man in the county might be here! And there had been some coming down the divide, too, to take their stations above the cave.

"Fellers," said Newt, "an infant mouse couldn't sneak out through that crowd. You got to hand it to Dukes for bein' a good organizer."

In twenty minutes or so, the Sheriff's voice came from behind a rock not more than fifty yards off below them; he was careful not to show so much as the brim of his hat.

"Give up, you fellers! We got you trapped; you can't get out no way!"

"No, but we can sit here, and you can't drag us out," answered Clint. He sounded surprisingly cool.

"We can starve you out — we don't care if it takes six months!"

"Will you promise not to shoot if we come out?"

"I won't promise nothin' for what some of the cowpunchers might do — they're not my men. You lost yore chance to give up, Yancey."

"If that's how you feel about it, come up here and get us. But I can beat you, Dukes; I'll promise plenty for the first we get sight of."

Clint turned to his men.

"All right, boys — devil 'em. Madder you get 'em, the better."

Billy, of course, had a personal grudge, and concentrated his efforts on old Simms. The old man seemed to have a vicious temper — he actually kept up with Billy in bad language for almost fifteen minutes. But Billy was a positive genius at that sort of thing; with casual pauses for puffs at his cigarette, and with winks at his companions, he poured out a stream of sarcastic invectives that would have made a saint turn purple; he accused old Simms of more forms of low-downness and crookedness than Clint had ever thought to exist. And Newt and Bud were not far behind in what they said of the sheriff and others; they punctuated their remarks with an occasional shot at a boot or hat that showed. Jake O'Dowd was only fair at the thing, and Red and Butch soon gave up, outclassed.

Presently it was sunset. Clint turned over from where he had been peering.

"I'm going in and get something to eat. I think you fellows can handle this a while."

"Sure, Clint — go ahead," remarked Billy gently.

Clint crawled back; he did not stand up until he was almost in the mouth of the tunnel. He started in, but before he had gone two steps he tripped over something; he went plunging forward, hands out, barely keeping from falling.

241

A deafening din broke out ahead of him in the closed tunnel; two or three shots that almost blended into one. Wildly, he clawed the air, got his balance, whipped his two guns out. Why, all his men were outside — somehow, part of the posse had got in here!

Another shot, with hardly a break after that first burst. He fired at the flash, leaping backwards. He was against the light; they could not help getting him before he reached the mouth.

CHAPTER
TWENTY-THREE

The Trick

Clint had fired but one shot; he was running backwards with both guns pointed, waiting for another flash to shoot at. Why they had not got him, framed as he was against the light, he did not know. He was scared, more scared and startled than he had ever been before in his life — perhaps partly because the thought was running through his head that all his men would be killed, as well as himself. A last leap back, and he threw himself sidewise; he now had the angle of rock between him and whoever was in there. Blankly, blinking, he turned.

The first thing he saw was young Billy Armour. Billy was on his back, kicking his legs in the air and making queer noises. For an instant Clint thought he had been shot — and then he saw that Billy's howl were not of pain; the crazy young devil was strangling with laughing.

And there sat Bud and Newt, leaning against each other weakly, holding their sides. Jake O'Dowd had his back turned, but his shoulders were jerking up and down. Poor Butch and Red were doing all they could to keep straight faces, but they seemed on the point of bursting — a loud guffaw finally did erupt from Red.

Clint knew that his own scared face must have been a sight. He managed to blurt:

"What — ? What — ? They found the way through, and — !"

Billy got up. Still choking, he beckoned, and walked straight into the tunnel. Clint followed, putting his guns timidly back into the holsters; he walked on tiptoe, and seemed inclined to shy like a horse, to Billy's amusement.

"Cuk-careful, Clint!" gasped Billy. "Don't fall over that thing again."

What he called "that thing," Clint now saw, was a single strand that had been untwisted from a lass rope and stretched across the entrance near the ground. As his eyes became accustomed to the lesser light, he saw more strands of rope, and pieces of white twine, running crazily through the air before him. Billy led him back from the opening and pointed a twitching finger to a six-shooter tied solidly to a big stone, its muzzle toward the roof. He had to stop to hold his sides, but he finally managed to explain.

"You said I'd have to stay here to keep shootin' an' hold 'em around. So I thought up this, an' me an' Bud fuf-fixed it, an' — haw-haw!"

"You blamed fool!" Clint glared at him angrily.

"But," explained Billy, "we *had* to make shore that it would work! You see, when you fall over that first string, it pulls the trigger. Then the bullet cuts another string an' drops a rock hangin' from the roof that fires the second shot with a string. That rock falls on a

244

jackknife lyin' open across another string lyin' on a stick, an' —"

If trying to follow the maze of twine had not made Clint dizzy, the explanation would have; a more weird contraption he could hardly have imagined in a nightmare. Billy solemnly went through it all a second time, making it less clear than ever — but giving Clint time to get over his anger, which was the clever Billy's real purpose.

"You know, Clint," he remarked gravely, "it's shore lucky that Newt had a double-action gun — it would have taken jest twice as many strings to fire a single-action, countin' strings to cock it every time."

By now Clint was grinning for he would hardly have been human if he had not. He shook his head at the round, red, innocent face before him.

"You blamed young fool! But it only went off three times."

"Uh-huh — that's why we had to test it out; lucky we did. Now, I think if I run this piece o' rope across here, instead of —" Suddenly he turned, with the naïve anxiety of a child on his broad face. "Clint — say, Clint! — I don't have to stay back here all by myself now, do I, with this thing fixed?"

"No, you don't; this'll hold 'em, even if it fires only one or two shots. All we want is to run 'em out if they start creeping up during the night — make them think we're all here."

"Uh-huh — that's how I figgered," agreed Billy with relief.

He knelt down, doing something to the gun tied to the stone.

"Hold on, Billy!" Clint seized his shoulder. "Leave it pointing up — no use in killing any of them; killing deputy sheriffs is bad business. Besides," he added, "if I've got Dukes down right, he'll talk some innocent cowboy into coming in here first, to see what happens."

Billy turned to look up over his shoulder, and nodded grave agreement.

"Dog-goned if you ain't right, Clint! We don't want to kill any innercent cowboys, do we? Only want to scare one out of a year's growth, an' make him go runnin' over the side o' the dump an' break his fool neck. Uh-huh!" And he bent over the gun to fasten it as it had been.

Clint hurried back and ate — the rest had eaten before he came. He would not risk going through Billy's invention again, but he called to the others. They popped a few shots through the gathering darkness, and crawled carefully back to join him — all but Billy and Bud seemed as suspicious of the contraption as himself, and tiptoed through it with held breath.

"All right, Billy — you lead; here's the lantern."

In single file, they went down the tunnel. A good distance from the end, Billy pulled himself up to one of the many cracks, and the rest followed. How Billy had first found his way through that honey-comb, Clint could not imagine — only a reckless youngster would have risked getting lost in the maze. During their stay, he had explored it a second time, marking the walls with the burned end of a stick.

There were places where Clint had difficulty forcing his shoulders through as he crawled on his stomach — poor Butch, the bulkiest, groaned and swore as they dragged him through by the wrists. And there were spots where it seemed that only a miracle kept the roof from caving down and trapping them — once they found the crumbling skeleton of a mountain lion pinned under a fallen boulder; it might have been there a thousand years or more. They had but one period of relief: in one place there was a cave the size of a small room, and here they stopped to rest a few moments and feel uneasy about what was coming.

For Billy, the passage was all too short; he was very proud of this old discovery of his and of his place in front as guide. But by the time he blew out the lantern, and they saw feeble light ahead of them, everybody else had had far more caves than he wanted. They crawled out, forcing themselves through thick, thorny brush. They were now on a ledge high up the far side of the divide; it was much steeper on this side than on the other. A gentle nicker that Clint recognized as Reddy's came from a little thicket of Apache plume. Clint heaved a sigh of relief.

"They didn't find 'em, up here. Well, let's saddle, boys. Hope we get down without breaking any horse's legs."

"What if it don't rain?" asked Butch anxiously.

"Well, as I said, we'll have to crawl back there again, and hold 'em off till it does rain at night. But it's going to — see that lightning off there, and smell the air."

"Lord, but I shore hope it does!" Butch mopped his face and glanced uneasily back toward the opening he had come out of.

There was a moon in the first quarter, almost directly overhead. So much light made it dangerous for them. Riders would be coming from miles around, as word got out that the outlaws from Gulch City had been trapped — this would be the greatest piece of excitement the district had ever seen. But they rode with caution, and two hours later they were standing in thick cedars, looking out on a great herd of cattle spread all over the grassy flat, some lying, some moving sleepily back and forth. They could see men riding slowly around the herd, and up on the side of a low hill were little points of red light where other men sat smoking.

"Not bad!" gloated Butch, his eyes on the cattle. "I never thought I'd be in on the rustlin' of a bunch this size."

"I uster punch cows for Brad Terry," remarked Red Barclay. Terry was the man for whom this herd had been gathered; he intended it to stock a new range he had taken over, in the Brewster Valley country, near Antelope Creek. Perhaps he did not know why old George Simms had been willing to sell him so many cattle at such a more than reasonable price; perhaps he suspected, but thought it none of his business — there was a good deal of such let-alone in Arizona, or rustling could not have flourished as it did.

Clint was inspecting the sky more than the herd. The moon still shone, but the heavy black clouds had crept up from the horizon and toward it. From those clouds, lurid flares shot frequently, although the true storm had not yet broken forth. Slowly, the rumble grew louder. Between thunderclaps, they could hear the faint, distant popping of guns — the night-herders kept loping to the top of that little hill and peering toward the sound; they seemed excited, as though wondering what was going on.

Clint turned his horse away from the little rock pool at which it had been drinking.

"It's nearly on us. All right, Butch!"

"Uh — think I can get away with it?" asked Butch nervously.

"We-ell," Clint smiled faintly, "you're the only really respectable-looking man here — you'd pass for a preacher. They'd know Billy or Jack. You have to try it."

"Uh — all right," sighed Butch.

With uneasy face, he turned his horse. There was a little sandy flat back there behind them, hidden by the cedars from the night-herders. Butch leaned forward and spurred. He went flying across the flat as though in a quarter-mile race. He whirled the horse, came back again; he turned again, and dashed away, his quirt flying. Three times he went the length of the flat, and then Clint motioned to him to stop. He slid his panting horse — a man of his weight makes a horse pant easily. All the others came running. They had their hats by the brims, full of water from the pool. This they dashed over the horse.

"That hind leg!" snapped Clint, and Billy heaved a hatful against it. Clint gave a last glance over the animal, and spat out: "Get going, Butch!"

Butch's quirt sang, and he tore madly out into the flat, toward the night-herders. He was yelling at the top of his voice.

"Boys! Hey, boys!"

There came sudden shouts, and several of the men dashed to meet him. They saw a big, honest-looking man on a panting, apparently sweat-drenched horse — must have come a long way.

"What's up! What's up!"

"We got Clint Yancey an' his bunch cornered in an old mine! Old Man Simms said for all of you to hurry over there, before they git away from us!"

"But — the cattle!"

This seemed to be the range foreman, judging by the anxious glance he threw toward the herd.

"The Old Man said leave 'em go to hell! They won't go far at night, an' we can bunch 'em again in the mornin'."

"That's right," corroborated a grizzled old fellow.

The foreman raised his voice joyously:

"Boys! Let's go! They got Clint Yancey cornered!"

Yells burst forth; this would be a million times better than the sleepy job of night-herding. Men came dashing from all around the herd. The foreman, his face flushed with excitement, waited until they were all there, then swung his quirt high.

"Let's go, boys! Ride like the Comanches was after you!"

As they went tearing madly off, Butch called piteously after them:

"Wait for me, boys! Wait for me! I want to be in on it!"

"Wait, hell! We ain't waitin' for nobody!" taunted the foreman over one shoulder.

Butch plugged doggedly after them a short distance, but they seemed to outrun his exhausted horse easily. He winked at the horse's ears, gave a low, heavy guffaw, and pulled on the reins — they were out of sight now. He turned and loped easily back to the flat, and on his face was the virtuous look of a man who has done his difficult task well.

A little crowd of riders was already sweeping from the cedars. Ropes were swinging across the backs of the surprised cattle — no yells, yet. Clint called excitedly:

"Push 'em, boys! Push 'em!"

He glanced anxiously at the sky. They got the cattle to their feet, bunched, and started. It was dark now, those heavy clouds over the moon.

Suddenly the storm broke in full force — instantly, without warning. A sheet of green light flared and flickered around them. A tall cedar that had been standing on the edge of the flat a moment before lay shattered in splinters. The deafening crack was brief, and then they heard the howling moan of rain sweeping toward them, a cold wind ahead of it. Before its sound had drowned all else, Clint's last shout rang out:

"Don't try to hold 'em! Let 'em stampede! *Let 'em stampede!*"

A moment of darkness between flashes. Clint's mouth opened, and he stared in awe; he had heard of this weird thing before but never witnessed it. On the tip of each horn in the big herd glowed a ball of fire big as a tennis ball — bright, whitish-green, perfectly round. He knew it to be St. Elmo's fire — a fairly common phenomenon in some parts of the world — but that did not lessen the gruesome effect it produced on him at first sight of it. The lights were bright enough for him to see eyes rolling in terror beneath the white horns; the cattle were nearly insane with fright at this thing they could not understand. An almost human moan came from one of them.

Then, a single low bellow from the middle of the herd, as a tremendous flare of lightning came; it made the St. Elmo's fire disappear temporarily, but threw up the long white horns in startling relief. Stampede!

Wildly, the herd tore down the flat, Clint riding madly at one side of the point. Butch was on the other. Both were frantically waving slickers; they were trying to hold those demented cattle to a course; but they might as well have tried to wave a river in flood aside. But it did not matter; they had managed to start them in approximately the right direction and they were going straight — straight over everything in their path.

Now the cold rain struck, in a wild deluge. Instantly, the men were wet to the skin, water streaming down their legs inside their chaps. Again the unearthly flames showed on the horntips. This, Clint knew, was going to be no ordinary storm; it would be one to be talked of for twenty years. And soon it was howling around them like a thousand devils, roaring, trying to pluck them from their saddles. The frenzied cattle plunged on, eyes bulging and shining. And in that beating torrent, a track could not have been found ten seconds after the last cow had passed. A wild night — a fitting night for such reckless men, on such a reckless errand!

A sickening flash showed Bud Haines racing past Clint. He shouted something that the wind and rain tore from his teeth and smothered. But on Bud's face was a wide grin, teeth white in the lightning. And Clint flung back the grin from his own streaming face. By morning those cattle would be — who could even guess where?

CHAPTER
TWENTY-FOUR

Six-gun Equation

All Arizona was in an uproar. Tex Fletcher had played the greatest coup ever heard of in the rustling game; he had practically bankrupted the big T X by one daring blow. And his right-hand man had given notice of exactly when the cattle were to be stolen, and then stolen them! Tex had made a mockery of law and order; things had reached a terrible pass. Not that Arizona had ever resembled heaven — but this was entirely too much! And the sheriff, with all his force and a huge posse, within earshot of where it happened!

Sheriff Jim Dukes had been forced to resign hurriedly — there had even been talk of lynching him; he had left the country during the night. Hugh Pendexter, the new man, had promised to fire every deputy as his first act in office. He could not find one to fire.

The Legislature was in session, as it happened. There was a bill up to disband the Arizona Rangers, and it was certain of prompt passage. The ranger force, created to do away with rustling, had proved a monumental failure — as well to send children armed with pea-shooters out to stop it. The rangers kept off the streets; cat-calls were flung at them, and one could not arrest a man for that even if one had the heart left, and could hold one's head up to see him. Some were talking of asking Washington to declare martial law and send federal cavalry in, as had been done in Indian uprisings; this thing just could not go on any longer. To call it a disgrace was to put it far too mildly.

But nowhere was there more turmoil than in Gulch City, Tex's headquarters. Tex had gone almost insane with rage. To get the blame, and not the game, would drive almost any one insane. The reward for him had been increased to ten thousand, and many of his chief men now had up to five thousand on their heads. He had got wildly drunk; he had been in two gun scrapes and killed two men. Now he was sober again, and all the more dangerous for that; it was hardly safe even to speak to him.

And the crowning point had been the return of those seven men from Mexico. They had come riding splendid, silver-mounted saddles, wearing new six-shooters ornamented with silver and gold, and with fine, hand-made bits and spurs. They were dressed like cattle barons, and they threw money around in fistfuls of yellow-backs. They had told openly what Don Luis had paid for the cattle, and everybody said that he, Tex, had been getting the same ridiculous figure, and keeping nearly all of it himself.

And those seven resplendent, wealthy figures had been in Gulch City many hours before he had even heard of it — the plot sprang up before they were well in town, and spread like wildfire. Almost all the

255

younger, more reckless men had been dazzled; they had quit Tex and gone over to that double-crossing, treacherous ex-ranger. He might have known what it would mean to permit an ex-ranger to live in his town!

But his older, trusted men stuck, in a body. They could see that there was something wrong, that it was only a brilliant flash in the pan. And they knew that the very feat that had dazzled those younger fellows was the worst blow that had ever been struck at Arizona rustling; it would stir up public sentiment. It would be a miracle if rustling on a large scale was not ruined forever — at least there would have to be a year or two of lying very low, only cautiously rustling a few head here and there until this excitement died down.

Strange! The ranger force had failed to make even a noticeable dent in the rustling rings — and here it seemed that an outlawed ex-ranger might have ruined the game!

But perhaps the bitterest pill for Tex Fletcher was that he could no longer call Gulch City his town. Only half of it was his now; the wide, sandy main street was a no-man's-land where one could appear only to be shot down in his tracks from some building on the other side. Tex had boarded up his windows facing that street, after all the panes had been shot out. The windows of the saloon across the street were also blocked with thick layers of boards, but he could hear the loud merriment going on in there almost day and night — some young fellow had a guitar, and there was a great deal of boisterous singing. Obscene singing, it seemed to Tex.

They had one song, frequently shouted in dinning chorus, that drove Tex to frenzy; he had bitten more than one cigar clear in two as it came yowling across. It was an adaptation of the doleful *Cowboy's Lament*, and it ran thus:

Beat the drum slowly an' play the fife lowly,
Sing the dead march as they carry him along,
Take him to the desert an' pile the sand o'er him,
For Tex he was two-faced an' he got by too long.

In his town! This was the chorus, the mildest part. The other stanzas are not printable — a cowboy's language is not always prudish — and if there was any form of treachery or trickery of which they did not accuse him, it was of such an abstruse kind that even Tex himself had never thought of it.

And there was a dirgelike ballad that Billy had composed to the air of the old Arizona classic, *Billy Benero:*

They was racin' through the night,
Three pore boys that shore was white,
But that dirty Tex was treacherous, as now I will
recite.

This told the incident of the pass near the Kite Cross in lengthy detail.

But Billy's masterpiece, in surprisingly good meter, related how Clint Yancey had several times saved Tex's life at the risk of his own, only, each time, to have Tex make a traitorous attempt on his life, until finally the loyal Clint, his high sense of honor outraged, had been forced to turn against his faithless chief and take over the leadership of the gang, after a mighty gun-battle with Tex — that this last was a trifle premature did not seem to worry Billy or any of the others in the least.

Even the clever Billy was only vaguely, instinctively aware of it — and Clint not at all — but this howling of invective-filled songs in chorus did more for the homogeneity of Clint's men than a thousand well-put, logical speeches could have done. Such is human nature.

And through it all — on the north side of Stope Street — walked the quiet figure of Clint Yancey, the hero of this desert epic, the admiration of all these reckless young outlaws. To one who had known him all his life as a quiet cowpuncher, a still quieter ranger, Clint was an astonishing figure now. He could not help knowing the value appearances would have on these wild young fellows of his, with their incurable romantic streak. Had he gone around in shabby, run-over boots, he would still have been their hero — but not so much so.

Still, it was with mortification and with a flushed face that he first appeared on the street in those clothes with which his friend Don Luis Cabeza de Vaca had presented him — the Don had ordered them for himself, and they had just come, new, from Mexico City and never been worn; the two men happened to be of the same tall, slender, erect build, so the fit was faultless. The immense, steeple-crowned sombrero must have cost a sum well up in three figures, and the little braided jacket was almost as valuable. Clint had balked at the skin-tight trousers, with its hugely-flaring bell bottoms and their green silk inserts — until he saw how ridiculous his plain trousers looked with the rest of the outfit.

When he first went out with his great, silver-mounted Chihuahua spurs clinking loudly, he held his breath for a roar of laughter to go up. Possibly he saw a faint twinkle in the back of Butch's eye, but for the others, they were overcome with awe and envy at this gorgeous sight of their leader; they spoke to him in low, deferential tones. Billy Armour offered him six hundred dollars cash — all he had left of his rustling money — for the rig, though how he expected to get his squat frame into it would be hard to explain.

And the queerest thing of all was that within a week Clint was pretty well accustomed to the rig — all but the weight of the elaborate sombrero, with its wide band of gold and silver wire; he wished that he could clap on his worn old Stetson, which was comfortable, and let it go at that. But he was head of a wild gang of reckless young outlaws, and he had to live up to the part; he had not Tex's imposing height and fierce nose to carry him through. In short, Clint now appeared the ideal leader for this wild band; his quiet, rather cold reserve, and that eternal watchfulness of his odd, piercing blue eyes were the crowning point.

And that cunning psychologist, Don Luis Cabeza de Vaca, had known that all this would come to pass when he presented Clint with the suit. In that sense, he was using Clint as a tool to destroy the man who had proved treacherous to him. But it was a tool he feared;

259

he was, now, perhaps the only living man who knew the immense force behind the calm, rather cold face of Clint Yancey; strong as he was, the Don knew himself the weaker of the two, and wanted Clint for a friend. All of which Clint never once suspected. Had he been asked to describe himself bluntly and baldly, he would have done so as a rather stupid, muddling cowboy — this was his true opinion of himself.

It was eleven at night, and Clint was sitting in his room with Butch and Jake O'Dowd. His new room was over the saloon. There was a door partly open, leading out into the narrow corridor.

"Yes, sir!" said Butch emphatically. "It was us swingin' them cattle round halfway between the Silvermines an' the range country that fooled 'em; we was goin' through the dryest part o' the desert. We could only have done it right after them rains an' find water, an' a few bites o' brush for the cattle to eat, drivin' 'em loose-herded that way."

Clint wrinkled his forehead; he did not seem so proud of his plan now.

"We had more luck than sense. If I'd known the desert as well as I do now, I'd have known that it doesn't rain out there always when it rains near it. And the rain failing all at once, after that one big storm. Why, we had to practically run 'em the last three days — they were skeletons when we turned them over to Don Luis."

Jake laughed.

"And the Don just glanced over them, and said '*Está bien!*' and paid you on yore own count! I don't see yet

260

how he figures he can make any money on 'em at the price he paid — but that's none o' my business."

Clint's and Butch's eyes met knowingly, but they said nothing. And then, in a moment of silence, came a dry drawl from the open doorway:

"Howdy, Clint."

Jake's hand flashed down to his gun, and Butch's jaw dropped. Even Clint started, but he collected himself and answered quietly:

"Howdy, Yavapai. How did you get in?"

"Rode in a circle clear round town an' sneaked in from this side. Climbed the shed roof an' in through that back window in the hall."

Yavapai Slim was rolling a brown cigarette with both hands. He turned to strike a match on the door jamb, and that, purposely, gave the others a full view of his back. He had no six-shooter on, nor could there be any in his somewhat tight clothes; he wore no coat. Clint, suspicious, eyed his hat, and he carelessly took it off to pass a hand over his thin, sandy hair; they could see that the crown was empty.

"Pretty holster you got, Yavapai," remarked Clint.

"Shore is — present from Tex last Christmas; real hand-carved leather."

Yavapai, with a sidewise glance at Clint, picked up the empty holster and pressed it flat casually; there was no knife or small gun in it.

"Clint, I come over to throw in with you."

The thing sounded astonishing, not to say suspicious, but Clint spoke quietly without change of expression:

"Why? Think Tex is licked?"

"Naw — not yet. But he will be, when I tell you what I know."

"What's that, Slim?"

"He's fixin' to clean you out tonight. He's leavin' only a few men to guard the street, an' leadin' the rest of 'em around, horseback, in a wide circle to take yore side o' town from behind."

"Something like army fighting, Slim!"

"Uh-huh. He sent me in ahead to spy things out for him."

"As the man he trusts most?"

"Shore." Yavapai spoke as though that should be taken for granted.

"You're doing a good job — coming up here to see me personally." Clint smiled dryly at the tip of his cigarette.

"Kinda!" Yavapai saw the smile and chuckled. "Clint, I got it all figured out. They're goin' to start off in one bunch, up that big side gulch they call Markham's Wash, an' then swing wide around town. If you can get yore men over there in time, you'll have 'em trapped."

"Real military tactics, as they call 'em — sounds like a pretty good plan. What time will they be there?"

"Well, they figure on closin' on you jest before daylight."

"Apache Indian style."

"Uh-huh. I figured I can go back to Tex an' tell him yore men is all asleep, an' nearly all of 'em dead drunk besides. When we start up the wash, I can go ahead to scout; I can slip over to yore side an' give you warnin'.

Course," he added, "I know you'll do the right thing by me, Clint, for doin' all this for you."

"Oh, sure!" Clint agreed readily. "I understand that you were Tex's main killer — you might know how many fellows are lying in those old mine sumps."

"We-ll, I was his main man. But I'll do anything for you, Clint, that I did for him." He said this with a knowing grin that was almost a leer. "The point is," he explained, "I been seein' a long time that Tex was losin' his grip — too tricky. I seen that there'd be more money in it for me to throw in with you. Besides, I always kinda liked you, Clint."

"Yavapai," inquired Clint, "what's the use in telling a dam' lie like that? You loved me like you did a snake since that time I ran over you before everybody."

For the first time, Yavapai Slim looked a little bit put out; he did not seem to think that remark very good taste. He tried to grin again.

"Oh, well, what's that got to do with things anyway? Business is business. You don't suppose I ever liked that dirty, two-faced skunk of a Tex Fletcher, did you? I never knew when he'd get me killed myself." He answered Clint's quick, sharp glance; "Oh, shore! I had to pretend to like him — that's business too."

Clint sat in thought a moment, and looked up at him.

"Yavapai, how would it be, when you fellows are riding up that wash, if you got Tex out in front with you, friendly like, and put a bullet through his back for me when he wasn't looking?"

Yavapai nodded twice, obsequiously.

"Shore! Shore! Yo're the boss, Clint — I got to do anything you say. Glad to, Clint." His slitty eyes fixed craftily. "But I'd expect you to pay me extra for that — to give me what I got comin'."

Clint turned and quietly tossed the stub of his cigarette through the open window. He turned back, his face hardly changed.

"Yavapai, I've a good notion to give you what you have coming right now — that's a bullet through your stomach. Of all the dirty, tricky, sneaking killers I ever saw, you're the rottenest by a long way. Now you know where we stand, you two-faced rat."

Yavapai's face flared suddenly dull crimson; this was the last thing he had expected.

"You — you mean, Clint — ?"

"I mean — get out, before I do plug you. Go back to your treacherous boss and knife him in the back if you want to. But remember — next time we meet, it's shoot on sight. Get that, Yavapai?"

Yavapai, just inside the door, was trembling with rage. Never before had Clint seen so much evil in any man's eyes, not even in Tex's. The slim fellow was mouthing with fury; it seemed that his twisting lips were going to foam. He could hardly speak, but he raised a trembling forefinger.

"Clint Yancey! You dirty — ! I try to help you — I try honest — !"

"Honest!" spat Clint; he was not hiding the disgust on his face. "You never did anything honestly in your whole rotten life. I have a tough, wild crew, but a rat like you isn't fit to curry their horses. You — Get out, quick!"

Clint stood up; obviously, his intention was to throw him out on his head, and instantly. Yavapai's shaking hands grasped blindly at his thick neckerchief of black silk. And suddenly his hands came away. The stubby muzzle of a derringer in his right was pointing at Clint's chest.

"All right — all right, Clint Yancey! Take it in the guts! Tex will pay me well for it! I tried honest — honest — honest —"

Clint stood there calmly. He had been caught off his guard; who ever would have thought of a derringer hidden in a neckerchief? He heard a coyote-like snarl from the man opposite him:

"Shore! Draw, one of you fellers there! This is a double-barrel; one bullet ketches Clint Yancey in the belly, an' the next the first o' you to make a move — I can be through the door before the other gets his gun out."

Clint turned slowly and saw Jake O'Dowd's tense face. He knew what it meant. He spoke in a low voice:

"Don't try to draw, Jake; it's no use." He turned back again. He was a trifle pale, but there was a tiny smile on his grave face. "So you're going to gut-shoot me, Yavapai, are you?" he asked almost humorously.

"Yes, damn you! But first I'll have the fun o' tellin' you jest what I think o' you. I never had no use for you, you dirty ranger —"

He spat out a stream of wild, almost incoherent invective, his face flaming and his thin lips twitching jerkily. All his hate toward Clint came out now — all that Clint had always known. Clint stood with that hard, calm little smile on his brown face, but he was hardly listening at all; he was thinking quickly. He looked up suddenly.

"Yavapai," he interrupted, "suppose I offered you five thousand dollars, cash, gold, right now?"

Yavapai Slim stopped speaking with a jerk. There was the sudden crash of a gun. Yavapai toppled forward quietly into the room, his derringer going off as he fell. He struck the floor with a thud, and lay there, motionless. Yavapai Slim, gunman, would never move again.

Butch, his wide-open eyes fixed on Clint, sat frozen. He had seen many a shooting scrape in his wild life, but never anything like this. From his unmoving lips came queer, unbelieving words:

"An' — an' he had a gun on you!"

Clint stepped toward the figure on the floor, and stood looking down at it almost pityingly. He slowly shook his head.

"Butch, I'm not a well-educated man; I've had to make my own living since I was a kid. But I always liked to read when I had time, trying to learn a little. I remember reading in a Sunday paper about a thing called the personal equation — ever hear of it?"

"Uh — no. What is it?"

Butch sounded interested. Whatever it was, it sure seemed to help a man's shooting, which made it important in his world.

"It's like this: when a scientist is timing something, say a running horse, to find out when it passes a certain point, he presses a button on a stop watch when he sees it pass there. But nobody is able to press it exactly as the horse passes — he has to see it pass, and then make himself press the button. So they find out about how long it takes for any certain man to press it, to get the time down to split seconds."

"But, about shootin'?" asked the practical Butch, who had been following with wrinkled, puzzled forehead.

"I was banking on Yavapai's personal equation being pretty slow — the time it would take him to switch his mind away from the five thousand dollars I'd put in it, and to see me starting to draw, and to tell his finger to pull the trigger."

"You — bet on that stuff! And you won. And you say you ain't eddicated, or smart!"

"Yes, I won." Clint said it wearily; his nerves were relaxing, letting down, after the tension. He turned, wondering why Jake O'Dowd had not spoken. He saw him sitting still in his chair, his face ghastly white and a queer, meaningless grin spread across it. There was a thick stream of blood pouring down the lower part of his blue shirt, down over his trousers, and dripping steadily to the floor. Clint leaped to him.

"Jake! Good God, did his stray bullet get — !"

Jake nodded weakly; his head was sinking slowly down toward his chest. His voice came in a low, hoarse, distant whisper:

267

"— got me, Clint. I — I'm done for. I been pretty — pretty wild an' reckless — Clint, I played square with you. I tried — tried to be — be — white — white —"

He was toppling from his chair, slowly. Clint seized him in his arms, and Butch leaped to the other side. Together, they gently laid him on the bed. Jake's eyes were dimming, a film coming over them. He moved a hand feebly.

"Clint — pardner — shake. I been a tough son —"

As Clint's fingers touched his, he felt a little quiver. Jake O'Dowd was dead, lying there. Clint had the cooling hand in both his; he was almost as pale as the dead cowboy.

"Jake, you *were* white! I never met a squarer —"

He stopped with a gulp; those ears could not hear him — it seemed impossible to believe it! Butch was standing over them. His mighty chest heaved, and he wiped under his eyes with a corner of his neckerchief.

Vaguely, if at all, they heard a shout from the head of the stairs — a quick inquiry as to the cause of the shooting. Now, booted feet came clattering rapidly along the corridor, and men burst excitedly into the room. They saw Yavapai Slim lying dead on the floor, and a cry of exultation went up; he had always been the most thoroughly hated man in the town. Clint moved away from the bed and pointed silently.

They were a rough crowd, but somebody took of his worn Stetson, and one by one, slowly, all their hats came off. Jake, newcomer though he was, had been well liked.

"Yav — Yavapai got him?"

"Yes."

Clint felt Butch Tolleson nudge him, and followed him into the corridor. Butch led him a little way down past the closed doors. They passed Yavapai's six-shooter lying on the floor, cocked, ready to be picked up. Butch was excited now; he whispered quickly:

"Clint, here's our chance! Gather the boys, and we'll go over and trap 'em in the wash. We'll clean 'em out!"

Clint thought, saying nothing, his head bent and his forehead wrinkled. Finally he pushed a door open and entered one of the empty rooms. He struck a match and lit a dusty lamp. He slowly put the chimney back on.

"Sit down, Butch."

He himself took one of the broken chairs, and sat staring at his boots. On his face was very much the look of a chess player carefully studying his opponent's last move, and trying to decide his own next move from it.

"We orter hurry!" grunted Butch impatiently. "It'll take a long time to get the boys all together, and get saddled, and get over there. We orter have plenty of time."

Clint rolled and lit a cigarette, slowly. He let it go out after two puffs, and sat looking at it with wrinkled brow. At last he seemed to wake up. He took another match from his pocket, and relit the cigarette.

"We're not going over."

Butch gasped in horror.

"But, Clint — man, yo're missin' the finest chance you'll ever have. Yo're crazy, man!"

"Will Tex try that thing of coming around us when he sees that Yavapai doesn't get back?"

"Huh!" A pause. "I never thought o' that. Why — I reckon yo're right, Clint — like you always are."

"Did he ever mean to?"

"Huh! Well, Yavapai meant all he said, didn't he?"

"Sure. But don't you think Tex is too clever to put much confidence in a man like Yavapai; he knew better than anybody else in town what he was. Do you think he'd have told him all his plans, and then trusted him over on this side?"

"But — blame it all, Clint! — what *was* it all about, then?"

Butch looked subdued, baffled, almost scared; such chess games were too deep for his mind, and he realized it. Clint was smoking quietly now. Although he did not know it, he was in his element, and looked it — quietly at ease.

"If I don't miss my guess a whole lot, Tex has some trap set for all of us over here, to clean us out — maybe he wants to get us out of town so that he can cross the street and seize this side. Well, we're staying on this side of Stope Street. When Yavapai doesn't get back, I don't think there's a chance in a thousand that he'll try to come over, but I'll put a few extra men on guard anyway. If it does no other good, it'll keep our men stirred up against Tex."

Butch got up.

"Well, I see there ain't nothin' to the old sayin' — that two heads is better than one, even if one of 'em is a sheep's head. I'll let you do the thinkin' from now on, an' tell *me* what to do."

"Wait, Butch. If we did start around there, how would we go?"

"Huh? If we ain't goin' — Well, the sorter logical way would be for us to make a wide sweep around. Shore — around back o' the ridge on our side, to that low gap in it down below town. Then across through the gap opposite, in the other ridge."

"Past the old Horned Toad Mine?"

"Uh-huh. Shore. Only easy way to get around. But why you askin'?"

"I've been thinking a little more about things Tex might try to do; never hang onto the first thing you think of, Butch, any longer than it takes to think of something more reasonable. Then where? Past that old dug-out in the side of that ridge — the old powder house of the Horned Toad?"

"Shore. And then up the —"

Butch stopped dead, his mouth flying open first, and then his eyes, which were fixed on Clint. He blinked, hard.

"Huh! An' it's half full o' dynamite left since minin' days!"

"So I've heard." Butch's face was such that Clint had to smile slightly.

"Well — let's go, Clint."

Butch led the way out, his head bowed. What he seemed to think of his own wits, compared to Clint's, was not much.

CHAPTER
TWENTY-FIVE

Clint Outwitted

Two days of stalemate; the forces were so evenly divided that neither side wanted to risk a battle — at the best, it would have got too many men killed, whoever won. And then one morning after a great deal of waving of a white flag from a window, the hand holding it out of sight, there was a shouted parley. It seemed that Tex wanted to come across to talk to Clint. That, of course, was fair enough, and nobody objected; as a matter of fact, both crowds seemed to be getting pretty tired of this matter and ready to reach a compromise of some sort. The meeting was arranged for one o'clock, to give plenty of time for word to go around that there was to be no shooting.

That was a busy morning over the saloon. Billy Armour knew of Tex's ornate rooms, and he soon persuaded others that the dignity of their leader could not be allowed to suffer by comparison, since it represented their own dignity also. There were a fairly large sitting room and bedroom at the front of the hall; they had belonged to the saloon owner, but had suffered heavily since his leaving — it might have been either a cyclone or a few free-for-all fights that had occurred there. Billy led his gang, with a battered pail and a mop made from a torn shirt. He sent others running to commandeer the best furniture on their side of town, with vague promises that it might be returned later. Somewhere, he found a green carpet, and he showed amazing skill in placing things over the holes burned in it by cigarettes. When, puffing and proud, he at last called Clint to inspect his new quarters, Clint stood staring in the doorway; the thing was complete even to a potted cactus in bloom in a vase on a side table.

"And," said Clint, "you waste your time trying to be a rustler!"

"Ain't bad, is it?" agreed Billy; modesty did not seem to be one of his overpowering virtues.

A young fellow came running up the stairs and toward them. Billy turned to meet him.

"Oh, you found one! All right, Clint — get them clothes off an' go to bed."

Billy took the thing from the other — a flatiron!

"But, Billy — !"

"No, I won't ruin 'em — see what I done to this joint. Clint, ain't you got no pride? — look at them wrinkles!"

So when one o'clock approached Clint was an almost dapper figure, and certainly elegant; the nearly-new clothes looked entirely new. He stood inside the saloon door, with Billy peeping through a crack. Billy turned excitedly.

"Here he comes! Let 'em see you!"

Clint opened the door. He saw Tex standing on the hotel porch across the street, then crossing it and coming down the steps puffing a cigar calmly. He waited until Tex was half way across the street, and then stepped out quietly to meet him.

"Hello, Clint."

"Howdy, Tex."

Tex reached out a casual hand, and Clint took it; under the circumstances, he had to. They went walking back toward the saloon door side by side.

"Staying pretty hot, Clint."

"Yes; the real rains played a joke on us this year and didn't come — yet."

"They won't; I know this country."

Tex nodded to the few men in the saloon — Clint had forbidden a congregation there.

"Howdy, boys."

Courteously, Clint permitted Tex to go up the stairs first, and followed him. He went down the hall and opened a door, stepped back to let Tex enter. Tex cast a quick glance of surprise around the room, but said nothing; there could be no questioning that it was better than his own, even if it lacked some of the gilt and red.

"Sit down, Tex. Have a drink?"

Tex sank into the comfortable chair which Clint pointed to; he would not know that the one Clint took had a bag of sand stuffed under the seat to make it look plump — Billy Armour had given Clint definite instructions which he dared not disobey. Billy's triumph was that Clint poured their glasses full from a genuine cut-glass decanter which somebody had dug up somewhere. Clint threw his big sombrero on a side table and crossed his elegantly-clad knees.

"Well, Tex, what did you want to see me about?"

Tex set down his whiskey glass.

"To ask you to come back; this fight business will get neither one of us anywhere, only ruin both of us, and the boys with us. All I ask is that I'll be the boss; we'll split fifty-fifty on what we make. How's that?"

"Doesn't suit me, Tex."

"Didn't think it would. All right; we'll be equal pardners in everything, and whoever gives an order first, it sticks, and the other backs him up. But of course we'll talk things over first when we're both here. Can't find anything wrong with that, can you?"

Clint took another sip of his whiskey, and set the glass down. He spoke politely.

"Only that you'd get me shot in the back before long."

Tex did not look offended; he took it as merely a business remark.

"Well, then, what do you suggest? You know the kind of shots nearly everybody here is; you know how many either of us would have left if it comes to a fight."

"It's too bad," said Clint.

"Oh, all right! Clint, I don't claim to be any angel, but getting all that many men killed — well, the thought of it makes me a little bit sick."

"Sure," Clint nodded. "It would be about as sickening as that raid on Wacher."

Tex saw those cold, keen blue eyes fixed on him, and flushed slightly; he saw that Clint must know something about who was behind that raid.

"Well, here's the proposition — and there's not a man in Gulch City can't say I'm not fair when they hear about it: We call all the men of both sides together, and we talk to 'em in turn, an' put our cases before them. Then we'll let 'em vote on which of us they want, an' whichever of us loses gets out and stays out. And we'll have it understood before the vote that if he's not out inside of an hour he gets planted. Well?"

Clint was cornered, and he knew it. The men of both sides were sick of the split, and hardly one of them wanted open battle. Tex, with his imposing figure, was one of the most convincing and apparently straightforward talkers Clint had ever heard; while he was facing one, it was hard to believe that almost every word he spoke was a lie or a deceit. He was the old leader, and Clint knew that already some of his men were regretting their hasty action in jumping over to the new, since now it promised nothing but warfare with no profit. And the fact that he himself was an ex-ranger would be played up for all it was worth — it would be made reason to mistrust him.

"I'd sure hate, Clint," said Tex with a worried look on his face, "to see any of those poor boys killed in a fight."

There was an example! Who would believe that, if it meant a profit for him, Tex would have laughed if they all got killed? But if Clint refused, his men would turn from him overnight — and who could blame them?

276

"How many men on your side now, Tex?"

"Don't know exactly."

Tex grinned, faintly, dryly. He was telling Clint that he had a majority, and daring him to do anything about it. And not one of Tex's men would be likely to vote for Clint. But there was no use in thinking it over any longer — trapped he was, by this master of trickery.

"Very well, Tex — a vote let it be." He nodded, as though he thought it a good plan.

"When? Where? Wonder if there would be a row if we got our men together to talk to them?"

"Might — they're a hot-headed crowd." As a matter of fact, Clint did not want his men mingling with the others, and talking to them; Tex did not know how restless some of them were becoming or he would not have said that.

"Well, we'll both talk to 'em separate then, an' take separate votes; we can have 'em walk to different sides of wherever they're at, so's we can both count 'em, an' no arguments about it."

"Where'll it be, and when?"

"Why not tonight? How about that old livery stable up the street?"

"It happens to be on your side of the street, Tex, and all my men would have to walk across; something might happen to them out in the open. Why not the old theater opposite it? Or — tell you what — why not have my side meet in the theater, and yours in the livery stable?"

"O.K. We'll talk to your side first — if enough of them come over we won't have to bother with the others; they're old hands of mine. What time?"

"Oh — say about ten o'clock tonight. I want a little time to think of what I have to say; I know you've been figuring out your arguments for a couple of days anyhow. And we must give enough notice to make sure of having everybody there. Well, that settled?"

"Sure — anything suits me, to avoid a lot of killing."

"Another drink, Tex?"

"No, thanks, Clint — reckon I'd better be going."

"To give a preliminary talk to any of your men you're not sure of. Fair enough! I think I'll circulate around a little among mine." Clint laughed. "Why, it's just like running for mayor, or something! Pretty queer business for Gulch City!"

They strolled down the stairs together, and Clint went a third of the way across the street. Tex turned with his cigar in his mouth, and chuckled.

"Clint, I suppose you know I'm faster with a gun than you are. I'd have settled it all by plugging you up there in your room — only that I knew you had somebody hid somewhere covering me, to drill me if I made a break."

Clint grinned dryly.

"You judge people too much by yourself, Tex. As a matter of fact, I didn't; there was nobody within hearing of us, even."

"No! Well, the smartest of us makes mistakes — I wish I'd known. Well, see you tonight."

"Adios, Tex."

And they parted, each walking slowly back to his own side of the street. But once Clint was inside the door he sprang to life. He called his first little crowd, those who had been with him at the rustling of the T X cattle, and led them up to his room. He told them what had happened. Billy, in spite of his being the youngest, and his being given to a good deal of tomfoolery, was the cleverest by a good deal — Clint had long ago learned to respect Billy Armour's quick and sound wits.

"Clint," he said, grave for once, "yo're sunk! How did you let him trick you into that, smart as you are?"

"Because," said Clint ruefully, "I'm beginning to think he's a good deal smarter. What would have happened if I'd turned the offer down?"

"Bet he was hopin' you would! You'd have been sunk worse — the boys would all have been sore at you, and likely most of 'em would have sneaked across Stope Street in the dark tonight.

"So — what do we do?" asked Butch; he looked very gloomy.

"We all get our heads together here, and think up everything we can against Tex, and every low-down thing he ever did in his life. Then, when we got it straight in our heads, we start around among the boys, talking to them like we never talked before — all real confidential."

"And," said Bud Haines, "we have to get together on Clint's good points, and be ready to tell everybody what a fine feller he is — which ain't missin' it much, takin' the dang fool sorter on the run."

Clint looked a trifle foolish.

"Well, if I have any good points it wouldn't do for me to run around bragging about them. Let's settle the other first, and I'll start out while you boys talk over the other thing. Now, are you all sure we've got the best plan — just talk common sense to 'em, and be sure everything we say is the truth? We're not going to try to kid them."

They all nodded agreement; it seemed the most logical plan in the world. Which showed how little they knew about politics; they should have served plenty of free liquor and talked nonsense, trying to whip the men into a rage by meaningless mouthings, and making promises that could not be fulfilled.

Electioneering for peaceable votes! It was a queer thing indeed for Gulch City, the rustlers' town, as Clint had remarked. But it was going on only on one side of Stope Street; on the other, Tex sat in his room, puffing a cigar and chuckling.

CHAPTER
TWENTY-SIX

The Panic

As a gatherer of votes, Clint soon felt himself a complete failure. Having set out with the fixed purpose of being a convincing talker was perhaps what ruined him; he could not remember what he had meant to say most of the time, and when he did remember it, he felt that he had not said it in the right way. And he had not the slightest doubt that he would make a perfect fool of himself tonight when he got up on that old stage and tried to make his first speech. It never occurred to him to do the logical thing — to go around being a good fellow and buying drinks, and say nothing about the coming vote, and nothing against Tex or for himself.

So, very soon, he slowly mounted the stairs and went back to his room. He threw himself into a chair and sat with his eyes on the floor. He knew that Tex, always cocksure, always ready with his tongue, would plead with those boys to be true to their old leader who had stood by them so long, and not to side with — a former Arizona Ranger! Nor would this be all; it seemed certain to Clint that Tex would have some plausible accusations against him. No, just one accusation — some big one that could not be disproved on short notice. Perhaps a forged letter from Captain Donley of the rangers; something of that sort, but no telling what.

And this, after all his weeks of work, of planning, of danger, was to be the end — sent out of Gulch City, laughed at. And he would no sooner be out of that refuge than the rangers would manage to arrest him; Tex would help out a little on that too. He had made a mistake; he had tried to buck a man who was more clever than he, and he had lost.

He sat there an hour; two hours. He rolled and smoked cigarette after cigarette. At last his door burst open and Butch came in indignantly.

"Clint! Why the blazes don't you get to stirrin' around? Ain't we got little enough chance anyways, without you jest settin' here like a bump on a log, an' doin' nothin'?"

He had never seen the good-natured Butch so nearly angry.

"Sit down, Butch; I want to talk to you."

"Blazes, you know how I'll vote! Go talk to some o' them young rattle-heads!"

"Sit down."

"Oh, Lord!" Butch threw himself into a chair and mopped his face with a red handkerchief; it was plain to be seen that he had given up his last hope.

"Butch, I've sure been thinking — I'm pretty near dizzy from it."

"Oh, shore! Yo're good at that." Butch was sarcastic.

"Tex can get the biggest vote."

"I — reckon."

"But here's what I want to know: wouldn't that be a little too straight and open a thing for Tex to even think of?"

"Huh?"

"Wouldn't it be a lot more like him to pull a trick of some sort, to make sure of it?"

"But — he doesn't have to."

"Makes no difference; it's not his nature to do anything the square, outright way; he wouldn't think of that."

Butch scratched his graying head and wrinkled his face.

"Blamed if I don't believe yo're right! But what would he try to pull? The way it's fixed, he couldn't crook the votin'. I can't see —" he trailed off.

"I can't either, and I've been trying to figure it out till my head is spinning. Let's go poke around-town."

"Where?"

"I don't know — just around."

They got up, and Butch came over and put his big, hairy hand on Clint's shoulder. He spoke pleadingly.

"Listen here, Clint. Yo're smarter than Tex — heck, everybody knows you are! Think what he's trying to do; you dang shore can, if you set yore mind to it."

He looked so earnest and convinced that Clint had to smile — a pretty sickly, discouraged smile.

"But the trouble is, Butch, that I don't happen to be a fortune-teller. Well, let's go." And with a worried sigh he put on his sombrero and went out.

At a little after half past nine that night the men began to drift toward the old theater. Nobody felt like going around to the main entrance on Stope Street, where they could be seen from the side of the street; they came dawdling along to the two side doors, and that at the back, in ones and twos and threes. They were surprised to find one of Clint's old men at each door, to write down their names as they entered; those men seemed very businesslike about it. What did the names matter?

Somebody had hastily given the seats a rough dusting — they looked streaky. And what big kerosene lamps were left had been lighted and swung from the ceiling. Nobody had bothered with the footlights, and most of them were broken anyway; one of the large lamps had been hung from the ceiling of the stage. But the lights were few, and it looked gloomy in there, with dark corners full of cobwebs. A few years before, this place had been well lighted, as fourth-rate actors trod the narrow stage and spoke their pieces in harsh voices. And there were one or two, now famous, who could have remembered this little mining-town theater with a smile. In the profession, the Golden Shell Theater in Gulch City had been the last outpost.

"Time is it, Shorty?" a man called across the floor.

"Five to. They'll be along pretty quick."

They were sitting in small groups out toward the stage, booted feet sometimes cocked up over the seats in front. They were talking and smoking.

"Here's Clint!" somebody shouted.

He came in through the side door, Butch with him. It was pretty dark there, but Clint's clothes identified him instantly. He went down the littered aisle and found a seat near a chatting group, but took no part in the conversation; he seemed very thoughtful. When they spoke to him, he answered absently, and was silent again.

"Ten o'clock! Where's Tex?" asked somebody.

Clint did not seem to notice even that. Now, he pulled his watch out and looked at it every little while. A man stood up and started for the door, grunting disgustedly.

"Hell, I'm goin'! I knew there was some sort of fake in it."

He got to the door, and gave a tug at the handle. He looked surprised. Suddenly he turned and yelled:

"Try that other door over there!"

A man raced to it, tugged, threw his shoulder against it.

"It's — barred on the outside!"

"We're locked in! They got us!"

Panic broke out. Men were running, falling, cursing. Somebody jerked his gun out and fired all six shots into one of the doors. Clint went leaping from his seat. He sprang on the stage, shouting at the top of his voice; somebody would be killed if he could not stop this panic.

"Boys! Boys! Listen to me!"

His five original men were shouting too, from different parts of the place.

"Stop a minute! Stop an' listen to him!"

"We're done for!" yelled someone. "They'll set fire to the place!"

Clint's voice rang out commandingly; he was getting scared of this thing.

"Stop it! Sit down! It'll be all right!"

They looked dazed; one would never have expected that reckless crowd to take it so. Somehow, he got a reasonable amount of silence.

"Go sit down, boys, and listen to me!" he pleaded. "I tell you it'll be all right. If anything was going to happen, wouldn't it happen to me too?"

Nervously, with heads jerking to look around, some of them sat down. Clint stood under that smoky lamp on the stage.

"I heard one of you ask if I'm the man barred the doors. I did not — but I had a good notion they were going to be barred, so I hid an axe in here to chop one down when I'm ready."

"Let's have it, quick; they'll get us!"

A man started running toward the stage, but Billy Armour reached out a boot and tripped him, then sat on him. Clint had meant to talk to them, but he saw that it could not be done; not one of them would hear a word of what he said. They were beginning to stand up quickly again, and another voice came.

"They're all around us!"

"They are *not*!" shouted Clint. "They're as far from here as they can get, and I'll show you why. Come this way, some of you fellows."

He turned to one of the wings, and they came leaping onto the stage to follow him. He led them into a small, dark store-room, packed almost to the ceiling with old boxes.

"Throw this stuff out."

They stared at him as if they thought him mad, but Butch began to heave things through the door, regardless of shins in the way. In a moment or two part of the floor was clear, and they saw an old trap-door with an iron ring sunk into it.

"Come on, you fellows — but put your cigarettes out, and walk mighty careful!"

They followed him in a mob down the very steep, unrailed little stairs. They found themselves in a dark basement — it smelled musty.

"Now, boys, I'm going to light a match — but the sooner I blow it out again, the better I'll feel."

There came a scratching sound and a yellow flare. A gasp of horror went up from all the men at once — the floor was piled high with small wooden boxes, and here and there lay a metal drum of a kind most of them had seen before. Something like a piece of heavy white cord ran out through the wall near the joists; it had been cut off short inside and a box full of wet sand placed under it. Clint reached up and plucked it from the wall.

One wild glance at the smoking, spitting end. A man whirled and went sprawling, and another fell over him. They fought to get back to that stairway, and they fairly boiled up through the trapdoor. Butch, his hands in his pockets, stood up there grinning, well back out of the way to let them go by. Billy Armour was whistling *The Mocking Bird* innocently, with one eye cocked at the ceiling; he had never looked more angelic.

Back in the theater, they waited for Clint to come, and crowded around him.

"That axe, Clint! Let's have it!" They walked on tiptoe when they had to move.

"Wait a minute, boys — there's no danger. Every bit of dynamite out of that old powder house is down there, but I cut the fuse before you got here; it ran out through a hole in the wall, with a big box over it so's it wouldn't be noticed. Some fine men of our side sneaked up and barred the doors when we were all in here, and then lit the fuse. Well, see what Tex had all fixed up for you boys?"

The growl that went up was not very loud, but never had Clint heard so much menace in human voices. Now was his time!

"Boys, I'll throw my cards on the table. There's nothing to this rustling game. I'm quitting and giving up to the rangers — they'd get all of us sooner or later anyway. But I have a plan. Let's capture that dirty skunk across the street, and all his rotten pack we're able, and take them in with us. If that's not good for a few pardons for us — well, I'm due for the longest sentence of any of you. I'll take my chances; how about you?"

Nobody noticed that the first prompt cry came from only five men scattered around; it was contagious, and voices joined in. But, as Clint had expected, there were dissenters. He was ready for it.

"Fair enough! Anybody that wants to come with me, comes, and anybody that doesn't, doesn't. Those not coming can get out of the Silvermines and leave word with me who's to represent them, where he'll get his mail, and under what name. If we see that we're likely

288

to get pardons, we'll write, and the rest of you can come in and give up — or do what you want to."

"Listen, Clint," said a dry-faced young fellow. "I ain't fool enough to stick my head into a trap like that. But we all know yo're on the square with us. If you got a plan to ketch them dirty — across the street, we'll help you; then we light out till we see the hole card. How's that?"

"I couldn't ask any better! Now, the axe is —"

"Hold on!" shouted somebody. "Here we're fixin' a plan like that, an' how do we know there ain't another spy o' Tex's in here listenin' to us?"

Billy Armour took his cigarette out of his mouth and looked carefully at the ceiling. He spoke absently.

"Oh, shore! Jest waitin' here to be blowed sky-high!"

"That's the point!" said Clint triumphantly. "We got every one of your names as you came in, and the list is open to anybody to look at. We can bank on each other — the few not here will have to do some tall explaining about the barred doors if we see them this side of Stope Street again, which isn't likely."

At last Clint produced the axe which he had hidden. It was no big job to break down a door; they went to it with a will. Clint led them around to the side of the building and turned over a big, empty packing case. He struck a match, and pointed.

"I pushed the good end of the fuse out again, so you'd see the layout. There's a dynamite cap on it inside, and one stick of powder."

"Say!" exclaimed Billy. "Let's light it, and see what would have happened to us if Clint hadn't got wise."

At first Clint was not inclined to favor the notion — just the notion Billy would have got! But then he saw that the object lesson would have a good effect in tightening his grip on the men. And there were plenty of empty houses in Gulch City; a few blown up would not matter.

"Go ahead."

"Hey!" somebody yelled. "Let me get out of here first — I got more sense than that crazy Billy!"

They scattered and ran. Billy lit his cigarette, and then coolly stooped and touched the match to the fuse. There came a little hissing splutter, and a tiny stream of blue, acrid smoke poured out of the hollow end. Billy stood up and yawned.

"Well, I gotta go see a feller about a pet horned toad."

He went strolling casually off, his hands in his pockets. He was getting "a big kick" out of this thing.

Three or four minutes passed. Suddenly a terrific explosion rocked the little town. Clint was lying behind an adobe wall, peering through an open window. The upper glass came flying in over his head and struck the floor behind; he ducked, and popped his head up again.

"Gawsh!" He heard an awed voice from the other window.

A big stone crashed through the roof and tore into the floor behind him; he should have got much farther off; he had never seen an explosion of this magnitude. His ears were ringing; he was almost deaf. Clatters and crashes outside, as things came raining down. And then, silence.

He climbed through the window, and ran forward. He could see other figures running too. He scrambled over wreckage of houses, and at last stood by the edge of the gaping hole; there was no sign of the theater. A long silence, as more and more men joined the group. At last he heard a bitter voice.

"An' — an' that's what our pal Tex would have done to us!"

CHAPTER
TWENTY-SEVEN

The End of
Gulch City

Nobody thought of going to bed; there was too much excitement. They stood around the hole perhaps an hour, and then strolled in a body back toward the saloon. They were hardly in there when a man came running through the rear door, shouting excitedly.

"Say! The old livery stable opposite the show house is on fire!"

They all ran out to the back, and found places from which they could see the red glow up there, still small. There were guesses as to what had started the fire — something flying through the air after the explosion, of course. They could hear men yelling beyond Stope Street, and the banging of guns — the fire signal of the Southwest. Then there came an excited shout from across the street.

"Clint! Where's Clint Yancey! I want to talk to Clint!"

"Tex himself!" somebody exclaimed.

Clint ran to a spot from which he could yell across and still not be exposed to a bullet.

"What do you want?" he called.

"That you, Clint? Say, Clint, will you call the fight off while we try to put out the fire? It'll burn the town down! We'll both be ruined!"

There was hurried advice from the men crowded behind.

"Don't do it, Clint! The wind is straight to the hotel — it'll burn him out."

But Clint had been thinking, all the while he watched that growing fire; he suspected that it was already out of control. He shouted back:

"Sure! I'll let nobody shoot at any one around the stable fire — anywhere else, look out!"

A man swore disgustedly. Clint turned.

"Boys, it's what we want. Each of you get his horse saddled as quick as he can, and we'll meet here. Take all your stuff on your saddles. Get chuck and canteens of water."

"What for?"

"Do what I tell you — no time to explain things."

There was a brief hesitation, and one of them spoke up:

"Come on, fellers! He fooled Tex once tonight — Clint's all right!"

Clint himself ran to get Reddy. Half the men were there when he got back, and soon all were gathered, sitting their horses. They were close enough to the mounting fire that the red light showed faintly on most of their faces, but a few were in shadow.

"Boys, make sure of who's here — that there's nobody that wasn't in the theatre."

There was not; either spies had not had time to get back or they thought it too dangerous.

"Boys, here's what we do: surround the town. Lie up on the sides of the gulch with carbines; close both ends. But set the houses all around the edges of town on fire first — the place will go anyway, so it'll only make it a little quicker. Get Tex's men coming out — take them alive."

"Alive!" came a bitter growl. "After what they tried to do to us!"

"Yes, alive! Can't you see that taking them in alive would mean a lot more to us than going in and saying we'd shot them? Shooting them might only have meant a personal row."

"He's right!"

"Butch, you take men and stop the lower end of the gulch. Billy, get the upper end. Bud and Newt, the sides, and Red comes with me. All set? Let's go!"

The band scattered in a run. Looking back, they could see frantic figures dashing around the livery stable — as if that could do any good; two houses next it were already on fire."

And presently a ring of flame sprang up quickly all around the old town — in that semi-desert climate, everything was powder-dry. Clint watched in awe from high on the ridge. Now the whole middle of the town was blazing fiercely; that ring was also widening, creeping in. He could even see some of his men on the far ridge as they darted from one boulder to another, seeking those which this light showed to be safest; they looked strange and red, running across there, tiny

THE END OF GULCH CITY

figures like flies. There was a roar from the flames that was loud even up on the ridges. The heat sent smoke and sparks shooting wildly straight upward far into the sky, and a cool, steady flow of air swept down by Clint, going to replace that sent up.

There was wild excitement in the town below; he could see men, red figures, running in all directions, half blinded by smoke and dazed by heat; some were flapping at their clothes where sparks had fallen on them. They were racing to get their horses, to gather up their other possessions. And then a shout from near Clint:

"There go some of 'em!"

He saw half a dozen, bent low over their horses' necks, run wildly through a narrow gap in the flames, and tear up the side of the ridge. In that roar from the flames, he could not hear any shooting; perhaps there was none. He saw the riders stop suddenly and throw up their hands. Then two or three men were running from behind boulders, ropes in their hands, while their companions from their shelter kept the men covered. They had to make quick work of it, for two more had broken through the same gap, one hatless, the other without his chaps.

"Here they come, Clint!" warned Red.

"Get 'em! I want to keep watch."

Two were coming up here. Confused, nearly blind — it was easy to capture them. He saw a solitary man farther down go scrambling up the hill-side afoot, his hands over his head. There were a few women, mostly Mexicans; the men were permitting them to go through the line, but most of them sat down just beyond it, gazing lonesomely back at their town.

That was only the beginning; they kept rushing out singly, in pairs, in little bands — never an organized force. A few held out until it seemed that no human being could live in that wild furnace down there. This was the very thing that had made the capture so easy; if they had had the slightest resemblance to order, if they had got together at the beginning and tried to burst out in one band, there would have been a bloody battle, and those not killed would certainly have escaped. But among Tex's men there was nothing but confusion and panic; Clint remembered how close to wild panic his own men had been earlier in the night, and could understand this.

The last stand was in a few adobe buildings that seemed to be fireproof — those men in there must be on the verge of smothering to death in the smoke pouring in from all around. And then, at nearly three in the morning, a shout went up all around the ridges:

"There they go!"

Fire had eaten its way through the ends of the rafters; the windows began to glow red. A few nearly blinded men came staggering out of the adobes, gasping and choking, seeking the nearest gaps in the flames, to go running wildly. They were the hardest-bitten of the whole crew, mostly men who knew that they could expect no better than prompt hanging if they were captured. Only three of them had horses to lead out, and as it happened they charged straight up toward Clint, where he sat Reddy — he had had most of his men hide their horses, but he wanted to be able to race quickly from one part to another if he had to. Here those three came! Shouts were flung down to them:

"Stop! Stop! Throw 'em up!"

They saw that they could not get through. One must have grunted something to the others, for they slid their horses and leaped from the saddles, jerking at their carbines. They meant to die. Lead raked down on them; two of them fell beside their horses. The third threw himself flat behind a stone not much larger than his head, and began firing quickly.

Reddy reared high, plunged down the hill. Clint sprang to the ground, his heart in his mouth, but there was no time to look at the horse. He whipped out a six-shooter, but before he could fire he saw the man roll to his back from behind the boulder; somebody else had got him. Clint turned to Reddy; he was almost afraid to look. But a glance showed him that it was no more than a moderately severe, fairly deep flesh wound in the thigh; it would be healed in a month or so, but meanwhile he could not ride the sorrel. He heaved a sigh of relief and turned to watch the scene below.

When dawn broke slowly, Clint stood looking down on what yesterday had been Gulch City, the rustlers' town. Nothing was left of it but here and there an adobe wall sticking up lonesomely, roofless and doorless. There were no more flames, but smoke came curling slowly up everywhere. He tried to identify where the hotel and the saloon had stood, but it was difficult. Gulch City was no more.

He walked through the bound, sullen prisoners for the third time, although he knew that it was useless. Tex was not there. Indeed, he had not expected to find him; if he had been there through the fire he probably would have kept some sort of order among his men, and perhaps got most of them out safely. It was the lack of leadership that had made it so much easier than Clint had expected. Now, too late, the prisoners could see it — Tex's treachery had sold them out; he had abandoned them to save his own skin.

Clint spoke to one of them:

"Where's Tex?"

The man glared at him, and suddenly bared his teeth like a snarling dog.

"The — must have run when the livery fire got going well, after he'd sent us to fight it."

"He," said Clint soothingly, "probably didn't go far, at first — he'd lie up on a ridge ready to come down and boss things when he saw that it was safe in town."

The language the man ripped out almost made Clint blush. From another of Tex's men, Clint had taken a horse that he judged might suit him; he had his own saddle on it. He mounted, and went around giving instructions.

"Butch, you take charge of getting them in. Turn them over to the rangers and tell them what happened."

"I ain't goin' in."

Clint was surprised; he had not expected Butch to be one of the men to hide out until they knew that pardons were assured — but, then, Butch had a long record as a rustler. Clint had promised the men not to try to force anybody to go in and give up; he even kept from looking disappointed now.

"You, Billy — will you take charge?"

"Huh? Ain't you goin'?"

"Yes, but I have something to look after here, first, and there's no food left for all of you to stay here. I'd like for you to take them in, Billy."

"Think I know why yo're not comin' now. Shore I'll take 'em in."

"Good! Red, Bud, Newt — will you help him look after things? Whatever you do, see that nobody's let loose a minute only you boys on the list we made last night. How many else going?"

Perhaps a dozen hung back.

"Very well, boys. We'll let you know how things look — but if there's a jury in Arizona will send any of you up, I'm sure making a bad guess."

He turned and shouted:

"All right! Everybody get going right now — every minute you spend here is wasting chuck, and you have very little of it. Drink all you can at the last water holes, and fill the canteens. Head over to the north; it's the quickest way across the desert, and the most water, even if it is out of your way. Billy, take good care of Reddy, and see that none of the other horses kick him in that sore leg. Well, good luck!"

He watched the cavalcade go trailing off, Billy Armour in the lead, trying not to look very important. He heard a rough oath.

"Blazes! I'm stayin' with the gang!"

One of the dozen who had hung back went loping to catch up with the rest, and two more followed him. The others hesitated, and one of them spoke presently:

"Clint, I'd go too, only that I have a pretty bad record — I killed a deppity sheriff over in Willoughby. So have the rest of us here. But," he added quietly, "I'll go in and give up if you say so."

"I'm not telling you what to do, Lefty — use your own judgment."

The man hesitated, and at last turned his horse back the other way.

"Adios, pardner; we'll let you know where we're hidin' out."

"Adios, boys. We'll do all we can for you — and for ourselves."

They rode off silently. Clint turned to the one man left.

"Aren't you going with them, Butch?"

"Who? Me! I'm goin' with you to help you hunt Tex — I know what's on yore mind. I want to help you to take him in, the dirty — , even if they hang me as soon as I get there."

"Butch, I hope you don't feel sore when I say that you're the first real, lifelong crook I ever ran around with. And you're about the whitest man I ever met."

"*Phuh!*" snorted Butch. "If I'd seen any other color stickin' out o' you, you'd find me a heap different. Well, where's he gone to?"

He turned his head and stared in all directions, as though that might help him solve the mystery of Tex's disappearance. Clint did not answer, so Butch went on:

"He'll get across the desert quick. My guess is that he'll head for Californy — I heard yarns that he has a whole lot o' money cached in some banks over there, under another name."

"N-no," Clint slowly disagreed. "He'd never get through; he's blamed with the T X rustling we did, and all Arizona is wild about that — it won't be so wild when we tell them that old Simms was a pal of Tex's and had all rustled cattle on the outfit."

"Then — where *is* Tex?"

"I think we can ride to the desert the shortest way, and pick up his trail easy enough; he'll have left it plain for me purposely."

"Why?" demanded Butch incredulously.

"To lead me out there. He has a night's start, and the best horse — or maybe he doesn't know about Reddy. Butch, I've ruined him, and burned his town, and tied up every one of his men and sent them in to the rangers. Tex couldn't live another happy day unless he leads me into the desert and leaves me to die of thirst, to get even. I'm going to see if he can do it."

"He dam' shore can!" burst out Butch. "If you are crazy enough to try to catch him. No man ever lived — not even old Cactus Markham — knew the desert better than Tex Fletcher."

"I know that. So you lope off after Billy and the rest."

Butch wagged his graying head pityingly at Clint, and then he sighed.

"Well, let's start lookin' for Tex. I said I was stickin' with you, whatever came up."

He turned his horse. Clint saw from Butch's face that arguing would be no use. Together, they rode slowly off toward the desert.

CHAPTER
TWENTY-EIGHT

The Meeting

Two men staggered up the side of a butte, leading gaunt horses that they could no longer ride; the horses were weaker than the men.

"I tell you," Butch croaked argumentatively through swollen, cracked lips, "he only went up here to see if he could look back an' see us — he knowed you'd follow him."

Clint looked at him with bleared eyes.

"We got to stick to his trail; see the queer places he found water, this last couple of days. Or is it three days we been out, Butch?"

Butch stopped to rest, leaning against the still scorching wall of rock; the sun was just setting. He wagged his grizzled head, puzzled.

"I thought it was four — I dunno. Uh-huh; he found the water — an' ruined every hole after him so's we'd have none. Gawd!" he burst out. "What wouldn't I give for one teeny thimbleful o' dirty water, to rensh my mouth out with!"

There was a crack circling up the side of the rock, and they were following it although they could see no hoofprints there. And Clint had insisted on circling the whole butte to make sure that there was but one trail entering and one leaving — Tex could not be lying up there to ambush them. Clint, who was leading, stopped and stared at something lying in the middle of their path. A dead coyote — not dead a day. Its mouth was open and its tongue hung out, black and swollen.

"Got caught out here. No water."

Butch only blinked at the dead coyote; talking was too much effort. They went slowly up and up, until at last they came out on the flat place on the summit. Butch's eyes nearly popped out.

"W-water! A spring!"

They stared at each other. It could not be true — why should there be a clear spring up here? And why had Tex not destroyed it? But a spring is not so easily destroyed as a tiny water hole that would be dry until the next heavy rain.

"Huh!"

Clint followed Butch's eyes. Stretched there was the skeleton of a man, and around it other skeletons. And there were twisted pack saddles, and other things.

"Prospector," said Butch. "Got here some time it was dry."

They dropped the reins of the horses they led, and hurried forward. At the edge of the water, they could see the prints where Tex had knelt to drink — prints of knees, of boot toes, and of fingers. Butch grinned.

"Here's lookin' at you, Clint!"

But his grin ended in a wince, and he raised his hand to his mouth. It came away bloody; his lower lip had cracked open. Thirsty though he was, he drew back

304

with a smothered groan from the tiny spring; he would not get blood in the water until Clint had drunk first. Clint noticed it. He stooped quickly, so that Butch would not have long to wait. He heard Butch mumbling.

"Lucky we found it. Couldn't make it to any other water. Thought we was done for."

Clint's lips almost touched the water — already in imagination it was trickling down his throat, the sweetest thing he had ever tasted. And suddenly he jerked. He paused an instant as though undecided. And then he stood up, shoved Butch away as he stooped quickly to drink.

"It's — a poison spring!"

Butch sat back on his haunches, horror on his face.

"Hu — how you know?"

"That dead coyote — an' the prospector an' his burros."

"But — Tex drank! I'm goin' to drink it! Hell, man, I'm thirsty, an' I'm goin' to —"

He was almost babbling it, a wild light in his eyes. He was stooping again. Clint seized his shoulder and flung him away; he fell on his back.

"Have sense man!" Clint snapped it. "He didn't drink — he left those marks to fool us, to get rid of us."

Butch sat up. He put his arms around his knees, and stared broodingly down into that limpid water.

"No, we can't let Tex fool us, Clint. We won't die of his poison water — we'll thirst to death!"

And Butch laughed wildly, rocking back and forth. Partly, Clint knew, it was the fever that comes with such thirst as theirs — but partly it was stubbornness, Butch's dogged fighting spirit. That heavy, middle-aged man had ridden beside him, plugged along on foot beside him through the sand, with never a grumble. Butch looked over now at Clint, his eyes bloodshot and shrunken, but without the light of craziness in them — yet.

"Clint, we can prove it. Let the horses drink."

Clint had been holding them back. He shook his head.

"Let 'em drink, Clint — we got to shoot 'em anyways. We couldn't let the pore critters thirst to death — only us can do that!" And Butch laughed again; he was not far from the breaking point.

Slowly, they stood up. They pulled off saddles and bridles. With rolling eyes, the horses threw themselves toward the spring. They drank — and drank — and drank. And at last they slowly turned away. The two stood watching them. They went a few feet off, and one reached his lips tentatively toward a little patch of yellowish-green brush. But he stopped, raised his head, and looked out into the growing darkness. He twitched, staggered. And then his back humped up and he moaned. The men waited a few moments more, to be sure, and then their guns came out. There were two shots up there on that butte.

"Well, Clint, we don't drink — can't give Tex the satisfaction. Oh, but that feller knows the desert!" Butch looked at Clint. "Ten dollars, pardner, to shoot me too."

His heart heavy, Clint peered into those shrunken, red-rimmed eyes in that lined face. He looked a long time, and sighed in relief. What he saw was not madness but a faint twinkle.

"Butch, you're all right!"

"Shore I am — so're you, Clint. Well, let's go — I hope we pass out where that — can't find our bones, to laugh at 'em like he does at pore Carmody's."

They went to their saddles and began to untie the little packs behind the cantles, their dwindling little hoard of food — they had rationed themselves to a mouthful or two a day. A man can go long without food, but not without water. And then Butch heard Clint's voice; it sounded strangely quick and eager.

"Butch! You've seen saddle-blanket whiskey that Mexicans make back in the mountains."

"So you got it now!" sighed Butch, and added harshly; "Clint! Come out of it, dang yore hide!"

"No, Butch! I mean steaming whiskey up into a saddle blanket, an' then wringing the blanket out — it's a kind of still. There's a few sticks to make a fire, and the prospector's gold pan to boil water —"

Butch sat back on his haunches, his swollen mouth open.

"You mean — But would it get the poison out?"

"One way to find out," said Clint quietly.

All through the night they slept in turn, one awake gathering little sticks, breaking up the bleached pack saddles, using their own stirrups — and often pausing anxiously to wring out that damp saddle blanket stretched above the steaming pan. When daylight came, there was no more wood. Their lips had shrunken almost to normal size and their faces seemed to have filled out slightly — but there was only a tablespoonful or two in one canteen, the other still empty.

"Butch!"

"Huh?"

"The hills — the range country! See it 'way off there?"

"Do we quit — or keep on?" Butch would not even offer a suggestion.

Clint thought a few moments.

"Butch, you go in there; I'm keeping after him. In case — in case — uh — I don't come back, you might tell the rangers I was after Tex; they'll know then I didn't double-cross 'em."

Butch picked up one pack and threw it over his shoulder.

"Aw, come on! I said I was stickin'."

"But, Butch, they *have* to know! Man, that's all I've been working for all the time — to clear my name, and the rangers'. It's my job, not yours. And if you won't go tell 'em you're no friend of mine."

"I think I savvy, Clint — and you'd live as long without me. Longer; take all this grub an' water. And," he grinned, "don't swaller it all at once an' founder yoreself."

"No; we split it; it's a long way to —"

"Aw, shut up! You gimme a pain."

They went together to the foot of the butte. Butch thought of something.

"Oh, say, Clint! There was a name burned into one o' them pack saddles I used last night. We found out what happened to old Cactus Markham. Pore ol' Cactus!"

"Think you can make it in, Butch?"

"Wish you didn't have to go no farther, Clint. Gawd, but it's gittin' hot already! Well, good luck to you, pardner."

"Give my regards to Sally — an' the boys. Adios."

Clint turned. He could see those hoof tracks winding off into the sand.

Next day he found Tex's dead horse; the wheeling buzzards led him to the place, and saved him four or five miles of tracking. The ground was black with the bloated creatures; they flapped heavily upward. He could not look at them; he did not like to think now of buzzards, those scavengers of the desert.

He went to the horse. There was a piece of skin hanging down from a thigh, and the straight edge showed a knife cut. So Tex had provided himself with meat — why had not he and Butch thought of that? But this stuff now, lying twenty-four hours or more in the scorching sun, fouled by turkey buzzards — he turned off, averted his eyes from the birds hopping out of his way, and plugged grimly on. Now there were not hoofprints before him, but boot tracks. This was better.

That evening he found where Tex had piled dry sand into a tiny water hole at which he had drunk. Scraping with his bare hands, Clint found bedrock four feet down. There was a little bowl-shaped hollow in the rock. He thrust his handkerchief into that, and once in a while removed it, to suck it. He slept, and when his blistering mouth woke him up at two in the morning, the little hollow had seeped almost full. With his hands, he scooped up enough to half fill his canteen, and the rest he mopped up with his handkerchief, to squeeze it into his mouth. In the starlight, he found those tracks and started walking again. During the night, he crossed an old trail that Tex had made a day or two earlier, with his own trail and Butch's over it.

In blazing noon sunlight, he saw the trail gradually come closer to a wash it had run beside; it turned into it, and did not go out the other side. Clint followed the stones of the wash a hundred yards or more, and stopped suddenly. This was too plain a trail for such a place! Twice he had found faint prints of boot heels. He stood there, staring at the hot stones.

And suddenly words pounded through his head: "Clint, can you leave a false trail on the desert?" That was what Tex had said when he showed him the bleached bones of poor Ranger Carmody.

Clint turned back. He passed the place where he had entered the wash. He went a hundred yards, two hundred — not a trace of a trail. He kept on, almost half a mile. Now he was bent over, examining the stones one by one. At last he found a faint white scratch on one; a nail in a boot heel must have done it; there would be nothing else. On half an hour more, and there was a toe mark where sand had blown in a thin film across a flat stone; it was hardly noticeable. He kept on.

And suddenly he stopped. He did not know which way Tex had gone; there was no way to be sure. Tex, the poker-player, the expert gambler and judge of men — how smart had he judged him, Clint, to be? It all depended on that. All he had left was to out-guess Tex, to try to read his mind better than Tex could read his.

Clint laughed queerly. Suddenly he raised the canteen, let those last few drops trickle down his throat. He started to dash the canteen away, but paused, hung the strap gravely over his shoulder. He turned, and went shuffling back as he had come, back past where he had entered the wash. He was too tired even to glance at his own trail where it entered.

Miles, miles, miles. Another day, but he might have been walking a million years. The wash was gradually growing smaller. And it had led into the very heart of the desert. Not a track in it, not a sign of anyone's having come this way. And a man could not possibly have gone this far without leaving at least another white scratch on a stone. He had guessed wrong; he would drop before he had got half way to the nearest water back that way.

That night he slept on a patch of sand in the wash; he was too tired to climb the foot or two out — the wash was very small now. It was far past midnight when he lay down, and he was up in the dawn. He had half a dry biscuit, and he ate it. Not that he was hungry any more, or even thirsty. The queer thing was how the desert about him seemed to heave in waves like the ocean; sometimes it waltzed half way around him and then slowly came back. He fell once, and lay laughing at how funny it was to fall down. But he got up. He shook his fist at a buzzard that was wheeling not fifty yards above his head, but he laughed at it at the same time.

"Hello, Tex! Won't be long now — you can eat me, Tex! You buzzard! Why, Tex, damn you, you —"

He started; Mona Fernel was listening, and here he was starting to swear! Finest woman God ever put on earth, Mona Fernel; he had not seen her in ages until now. He twisted his head to look at her, and the buzzard swooped by. Perhaps it was that evil bird's closeness that brought him to his senses. He wiped his hand across his eyes, shook his head jerkily, and went on. His feet were dragging.

"Won't be long now, Clint — old boy, old boy, old boy!" he told himself in a croak, but there was sanity in his voice, and a kind of grim humor.

He was leaving the head of the wash. And suddenly he gave a hoarse shout and ran a few steps weakly. There, under his feet, were the tracks of moccasins! That was why there were no scratches of boot heels; Tex had carried these moccasins for just such a trick; perhaps he had used them when he led Ranger Carmody to his death. Again Clint croaked.

"It won't be long now, Tex — old boy, old boy, old boy!"

And now he was almost walking fast, though sometimes he lurched to one side or the other. He did not notice that he had dropped his canteen. Noon, and still he was lurching on. A little pile of barren boulders lay ahead, thrusting themselves out of the sand. As he had done in all this mad, weary chase, he swung out wide around them, to pick up the trail at the far side; it was merely habit with him now, and did not call for thought.

He swung in on the far side of the boulders, far out from them. He swung farther. Why, the trail was not there! It was maddening, to lose Tex thus, after all that chase. He felt like sitting in the hot sand and crying. More and more slowly he went, until at last his own trail showed before him again. So that ended it; Tex had outwitted him. He would lie down there; he could not go another inch.

And then he raised his head slowly. Tex's trail still went on alone, toward that little pile of rocks. It took it a long time to come to him. Why, Tex was there! He had caught up with him! That thought made him sane again. He waved a hand toward those stones out there; he thought he shouted, but his voice could not have been heard fifty feet off. He saw a man stand up. And he could still hear as well as ever.

"Clint, you got me! If I walk up to you, will you shoot it out with me, even draw?"

Now, Clint's head had never been clearer in his life. He thought quickly. He could not make a siege of it; Tex would outlast him. He knew that his voice would not carry that far; he raised both hands to show them empty, and beckoned. He peered in astonishment at the scarecrow figure that came shambling toward him, staggering sometimes. Tex had always had water, plenty of it, but perhaps little food. No — it was that the man was physically softer, could not stand that eternal walking, walking, walking. Exhaustion had brought him down, not hunger or thirst.

313

Tex had crossed half the space now. And suddenly Clint remembered. Why, he could not shoot Tex! He had to take him in alive, and turn him over to Captain Donley. A few moments more, and he heard Tex speak again, close to him.

"Yancey, you poor fool! Don't you know I'm the fastest shot in Arizona?"

"Are you, Tex? Well, draw."

There was a grin on Tex's haggard face. He stood poised a moment; he did not try any trick. And then his hand flashed to his right thigh. A gun cracked — only one.

A queer, moaning sound came from Tex's lips. He raised his numb, empty right hand and stared at it. His dazed eyes turned to the man ten feet off. Clint had not only beaten him to the draw, but had picked the tiny, moving mark of the gun jerking out of the holster — and had hit it squarely; it lay shattered six feet off. With a despairing oath, Tex turned and started off in a shambling run. From behind him came a croaking cry.

"Stop, for the Arizona Rangers!"

Clint could get him in the back. Tex stopped; he turned slowly, his hands going up, although there was no need for that, since he had no gun. He saw the weird, emaciated figure before him fumbling with the left side of his shirt, and when Clint's hands came down there was a badge pinned to the pocket.

"Turn your back, Tex, and put your hands behind you."

Clint was coming on, his gun again drawn and pointed. There was a long wait; it is hard to tie a man

314

and keep a gun in the small of his back with the other hand. But at last it was done.

"Straight ahead, prisoner. Any — any water in those rocks?"

Tex did not answer, but when Clint got there he found only a canteen half full. He raised it to his lips, and sipped slowly, a few drops at a time. At last he lowered it by a mighty effort; the whole thing would not have begun to satisfy him.

"Clint, give me a drink too."

Clint surveyed him.

"You don't look in bad shape. You get a spoonful or two tomorrow about noon. Get going!"

"Which way?"

"You know better than I do. Only remember that if I don't get out of here alive, neither do you. Get going, I say!"

CHAPTER
TWENTY-NINE

Poison

Another sunset, and two scarecrow figures staggered up to a tiny seep under a baking ledge of rock; one had his wrists tied behind him. Tex had found water on each of the last two days, so Clint's lips had shrunk almost to normal size; but his dust-caked face was more haggard, his eyes red and sunken; he was blinking and peering near-sightedly. With a little water, his head had begun to clear; it was mostly hunger that weakened him now, and he realized it, although the very thought of food had become repulsive to him. This is the last stage of hunger, the stage that precedes death. This, too, he knew.

"Tomorrow," the one in front muttered thickly, "you'll have me there."

Clint squinted weakly out over the desert. He was thinking of how it had been feebly green when he crossed it with the cattle; it had not been so forbidding then. In frantic haste, before it was too late, the hardy, stunted weeds had shot up and tried to bear seed; the few blades of grass were struggling mightily to live.

Then, briefly, one could look out from the hills on a vast plain that seemed almost green, vaguely living. But since, the pitiless sun had swept up that little trace of moisture; the flowers had drooped, the grass had grown yellow as the sand. Here for another year lay the desert, bleak, parched, forbidding; its brief, dismal fecundity was over for another year.

In the furnace-white glare, Clint brushed his eyes with the back of his hand. For a moment, his eyes came to a focus, and he saw a low, reddish streak far ahead. It was sunset tinging the hills of the grass country! He thought he cried out in triumph. He croaked.

They staggered on again, the last few feet to the seep; their one canteen had been empty since morning. Tex got to the water first, and threw himself eagerly on his knees. He stooped, his bound hands sticking up behind him, and Clint knelt across from him. For a few moments both men were motionless, their lips in the water; then Clint, with a sigh, sat back on his heels and wiped his mouth with his hand. Tex had not yet raised his head.

And then Clint slowly stood up, his eyes fixed queerly on the other man. When Tex straightened, Clint stood looking at him a moment, a bitter, twisted grin on his swollen lips. He spoke, and his hoarse voice was very quiet.

"Tex, you didn't drink. You win!"

No answer, but a gloating look came to the dust-caked face of the other.

"Tex, you've poisoned me — this is poison water."

Now Tex threw back his head and croaked out a laugh.

"You'll be dead inside of half an hour, Clint. I am the desert man! I'll leave you kicking, and I can walk to water! I told you I'd never see the inside of a jail!"

Clint touched the butt of his gun; he seemed very calm.

"Tex, you're coming with me."

Again Tex laughed, weakly, hysterically.

"Think I care? You fool — you poor fool! — to think you could lock Tex Fletcher up alive!"

A queer, swimming daze surged into Clint's head, and he staggered. The first twinge. It passed off quickly. He went running, staggering, around the little seep.

"Lie down, Tex! Lie down!"

"Clint!"

"Lie down!"

Clint pushed him over; it was not hard. There was a short, weak struggle, but Clint got Tex's ankles tied together, and doubled back up and tied to his wrists. This was how he had always tied him when he slept; it was brutal, but he could not risk having his prisoner escape. Lying there on his side, Tex's eyes rolled wildly. There was an awful horror in them, a terrible fear. He was mumbling brokenly, thickly:

"*Clint!* My God, Clint! You wouldn't leave me this way — to thirst to death — and the sun, *the sun!*" He feebly screamed the last. "The coyotes, Clint! The buzzards! They'll pick my eyes out! You wouldn't — !"

"No — oh, no! No more than you'd poison me, Tex! Lie there, damn you, and watch me kick till I stop — and then keep on watching me."

The doubled figure was babbling now; Tex had broken at last.

"Shoot me, Clint! For God's sake, shoot me!"

Again Clint reeled; he almost fell. But he knew that when he did go down for the last time it had to be far enough away so that Tex could not hunch himself over and work the knife out of his pocket, to free himself. If Clint had been able to think more clearly, he would have thrown the knife away, or hidden it in the sand.

He went staggering off in a jerky zigzag; he had his hands out before him to break the fall he knew was coming. He crashed to his knees. The white, blistering desert was spinning around him, and something was clutching at his waist like great talons. On hands and knees, he stared dumbly into the stunted little bush before his face; his head was swinging queerly back and forth.

Why had he headed for this little bush. There had been a reason, but he could not remember it. That bush — that little bush — he had wanted to reach it. For some reason.

The thick stupor partly passed for the moment. He knew it would soon return now, and that it would not pass again. He'd fall over on his side — That bush! That bush!

He remembered! With a faint moan, he shot out a palsied hand and broke off a twig. A fairly long twig, with small, stiff leaves like feathers up its sides. He had to hurry — hurry! His head was going again! God, but he was sick!

He jerked the twig up, thrust its tip into his mouth, down his throat. It would not work; it was too late. Brutally, harshly, he pushed it farther down, twisted it.

And suddenly it had effect. His body twitched, and he fell out on his face, vomiting. He moaned, and lay closer to the sand. He retched wildly; now that it was started he tried to stop it, but could not. He flopped over on his side, his knees coming almost to his chin as he clutched at his tortured waistline. Without his will, his legs shot straight out in a quick convulsion, but in a moment he managed to bring them up again. The white desert was fading; his senses were slipping, slipping. Then they were gone.

A long time, he lay there stiff and still. Then he vaguely knew that he was looking up at swimming stars. Later, he found himself clenching his teeth until he almost broke them. He did not know how long he had been lying there, and he did not care; time had lost all meaning for him. Exhausted, he began to sleep in fitful, moaning snatches.

And when dawn came, he struggled to his feet and lurched across to that wild-eyed, staring figure lying tied in a knot by the poison spring. He even laughed — a wild, weak laugh.

"Are you glad to see me alive, Tex? Get up! Right ahead! Ahead, man!"

Often, as they staggered through the sand, Clint would stop and double his body, retching miserably; there was nothing left to vomit. He ached fiercely from scalp to toes; his whole system was rotten with the poison. The sun of the desert blazed down upon him, and sometimes he stood shivering in an icy chill, his teeth chattering. Once when he fell he got up and laughed crazily in the prisoner's face.

"I think you got me, Tex. But you'll be in jail when I cash in. I win, Tex; I win!"

That night, Captain Donley was sitting on the porch of the little hotel, talking sadly to Ranger Clayton. He shook his head at the tip of his cigar.

"Yes, the House has passed the bill, and it will go through the Senate tomorrow. The end of the Arizona Rangers. I was hoping we had a chance, with so many of the Silvermines gang in jail — but it was Tex they were howling for, the main one."

Clayton brushed the ashes from the cigarette in his fingers; he did it slowly, dismally.

"It's the devil, Captain! If they'd only given us a chance! But it's poor Yancey I'm thinking about — the best ranger of us all, and we —" Clayton sighed, shook his head.

"But all the evidence against him —" Donley turned in his chair and spoke sadly: "Clayton, it nearly kills me to think of poor Clint Yancey lying out there on the desert, his bones bleaching. If he could only have lived to know that we'd reinstated him when we found out!"

They sat a long time in silence. First one would sigh and then the other. Donley got up and tossed aside his half-smoked cigar; his thick shoulders sagged and his head was bent. Without a word, he started toward the door, to go to his room. He heard a sound down the street, and paused to glance toward it.

Two figures came staggering toward him up the dusty street; they were clinging to each other, it seemed. One fell, and the other, mumbling thickly, helped him up and shoved him on. They both fell in getting onto the board sidewalk, and again one helped the other up. They lurched against a wall, and came staggering on doggedly. Donley was a strict teetotaler; he swore disgustedly.

"Why doesn't the marshal keep them off the street?" And then, more loudly: "You fellows get home quick or I'll run you in, whether it's my business or not. Fine example for young people — you dirty drunks!"

They had now stopped opposite the porch, and from the darkness came a harsh croak — the voice started twice before it got going well:

"Cap-tain — Donley. Lieutenant Yancey reporting, sir — with a prisoner — with a — with a —"

Both were falling. With an incredulous grunt, Donley leaped off the porch to the sidewalk, and Clayton sprang after him. They were too late; the figures were sprawled in the dust, still. With shaking hand, Clayton struck a match and held it close to the face of the taller man lying there. A low cry came from his lips:

"Tex Fletcher! He brought him in — !"

A babble from the ground:

"Cap-tain — Don — Ranger — reports — poison water!" The voice rose feverishly, but still weak: "Ma'am, you *have* to eat — that biscuit! A biscuit — a biscuit — !"

"Rangers! Out!"

The cry woke the street up. Feet came running down the hotel stairs. Others than rangers were hurrying up too, to see what the excitement was about. There was a hoarse shout of incredulity:

"My Gawd! Yancey! And he brought Tex in!"

Donley's roar:

"Easy with him! Easy, damn it! Upstairs — the best room. Call a doctor! Get a doctor, damn it!" And he himself went running down the sidewalk, his spurs clanking.

Clint opened his eyes and looked around. It was very puzzling to find himself in white sheets — and it was broad daylight; he thought it was dark when he fell. He saw the grim, hard-bitten face of Ranger McNeil. Mac turned quickly in his chair, and his face was strangely softened.

"Awake at last, old-timer? How you feeling?"

"Uh — fine, Mac. Did — did I bring Tex in last night?"

McNeil gave him a sympathetic grin, and pulled the blanket over his shoulder.

"Well, not exactly — you brought him in a week ago Tuesday."

Somebody was lumbering around the bed from the other side, and the heavy face of Butch Tolleson came into view. It struck Clint as an odd sight to see rustler and ranger look happily at each other. He thought of the wolf and the lamb — but both of these were wolves.

"Hello, Butch. They — didn't lock you up?"

"Me?" Butch sounded astonished. "Why, heck, me an' the rangers is pals — ain't we, Mac? They let the whole kit an' caboodle of us out on our own — uh — somethin' or other, till our trials. I wrote the other boys to come in an' give up, an' it would be all right."

McNeil glanced toward the door and lowered his voice.

"It's not supposed to get out, but the Governor himself came down a couple of days ago. Those friends of yours are pretty nearly sure to be turned loose by any jury, after what they did — and giving up by themselves. If any of them are sentenced —" He glanced around again. "— I think we can arrange for immediate pardons." And he winked at Butch, who chuckled heavily and happily.

"Some of 'em," added Butch, "want to jine the rangers."

"Billy Armour?"

"Uh-huh — he does." He slapped his thick knee and grinned. "Funny, to think of my Sal married to a ranger! But," he added, "they can't be took in yet; things is kinda upset. Donley resigned, an' the new captain ain't got down here yet."

"New captain! Who is he?" asked Clint eagerly. That meant that the Arizona Rangers were not to be disbanded; the bill had failed of passage.

McNeil looked confused. He hesitated. Suddenly he made up his mind; he snapped to a stiff attention, saluted.

"Ranger McNeil reporting, Captain Yancey. Any orders, sir?"

"Huh!"

Clint lay staring at him; he felt that he was sinking down through the bed in his utter surprise. McNeil sat down and grinned at him.

You weren't supposed to know till you're up and well. That big wallapus of a Wilson made us all sign a petition to the Governor — said he'd take us all apart by hand if we didn't. He talked to the Governor a long time, and I wouldn't be a bit surprised if he threatened him too. But that's really why the Governor came down; to investigate your character and ability personally."

Clint lay staring at the two men, and presently McNeil went on soberly:

"When Wilson heard you were lost on the desert, he tried to start out to look for you, alone — it would have been suicide, of course, and Donley wouldn't let him. So all he did was to knock Donley clear over his desk, and then nearly kill three of us that tried to hold him. It took six of us to get handcuffs on him and lock him up — why, a bull is weak compared to him! Well, he's charged with everything from insubordination and attempted mayhem on up. Poor devil! He sat on the cot in his cell and cried like a baby, because we wouldn't let him go hunt his pardner."

Clint started to say something, but suddenly couldn't. He turned his head on the pillow and blinked a time or two — possibly it was only his weakness that caused it.

"But of course we let him out as soon as you got here. He stole Captain Donley's horse — the fastest in town — and lit out with all of us after him. He outran us and got away."

"Huh!" gasped Clint. "You mean — Wilson's gone broncho!"

"No. We found out that he was only rushing to get you a good nurse; we already had wired to Tucson for a specialist. But that big idiot has more sense than we thought; you began to pick up as soon as the nurse got here — it was touch and go before that. Here she comes now with your soup."

Clint could not understand why McNeil sounded so painfully innocent. There was a light step in the hall, and for some reason Butch and the ranger were hurrying out without even saying good-bye; Clint heard them whisper to her as they passed her.

He was getting drowsy, but it surprised him to see that the girl in the doorway was not in the usual white but in dark blue. He opened his closing eyes. They met another pair of eyes — great, brown ones.

"Mona!"

He jerked straight up, sitting in the bed. She hastily set down the tray and ran to him.

"Oh, you must lie down, Clint! You're sick!"

She helped him back, and arranged the pillows with swift, gentle hands. He had got control of himself by this time; he remembered.

"Thank you, Mrs. Fernel," he said politely and respectfully.

Her face flushed, and she bit her lip. She turned away quickly, but turned back again.

"Clint — you — you were talking a lot while you had fever."

"You — mean — ?"

She nodded, and the faint red crept up to Clint's pale face. She was placing an old letter in his hands; it had a Mexican stamp on it. She too spoke formally, almost coldly:

"Clint, I think you might like to see this — should see it. It will explain —"

He could read Spanish as quickly as English. The short letter dropped to the covers. He heard Mona speak again, in her quiet, grave tones — they went with her stately figure:

"I found it on Jim after he was killed. Jim and I had never — got along very well, but I thought he — When I saw this, I nearly went mad, to think that I'd been married to a man of that kind. That was why I — acted so queerly, and couldn't eat."

Clint lay in a daze; he did not know what to say. She smiled weakly, quickly, the smile vanishing before it had well come. Again she spoke gravely:

"And — you were the most perfect gentleman I ever met, even if you were an outlaw."

She blushed, and her eyes fell. They raised again, and a terrible fear was growing in them. Had she been mistaken all the time about how Clint felt? One never knows, and what a man says in delirium may not mean anything. Clint lay staring at her, openly for the first time. He could not believe that any one on earth could be so beautiful as this tall, grave, brown-eyed woman. He said nothing, but the pink crept into her face and her brown eyes began to glow. Somehow, she found one of her hands in both his.

They were sitting thus, in silence, when Wilson came stealing down the hall on tiptoe, making scarcely more noise than an elephant. He paused in the doorway; he tried to meet Clint's eyes and could not — the poor devil's red face looked pitiful in its shame.

"Clint — are you — uh — very sore at me, for bein' such a dam' fool? Uh — uh — I mean, Captain Yancey."

Clint grinned at him.

"Sure I'm sore at you, you big idiot. I'll beat your block off you when I get up."

A gasp of relief like the spouting of a whale. Three heavy strides brought Wilson to the bedside. He grabbed at the one free hand held up to him.

"Why, Clint! Why — pardner!"

Mona broke in gently.

"Uncle, you must not excite our patient. Would you mind running down to the postoffice to get the mail — or something?"

"Huh! Oh, you mean I'm in the way of — of —" For the first time he seemed to see where her right hand was.

Clint spoke softly, a wicked twinkle in his eyes:

"Yes, Uncle John. You can see me later — Uncle John."

"Uncle —"

Wilson scratched his head. And suddenly it dawned upon him.

"I got it! You mean — Lord, but I'm always buttin' into the wrong — Well — uh — congratulations, both of you."

And he tripped over one of his own spurs as he went hurrying through the door.

E

M.

BC.